If those weren't bedroom eyes, what were?

Nick stood in the doorway of the classroom, his hair rumpled and in need of someone—her perhaps—to run her fingers through it. He wasn't wearing a shirt, and the breadth of his smooth, bare chest was emphasized by his open jacket. He was magnificent! Her knees wobbled and she leaned on the desk. She glanced down at his hands hovering over the worn fly on his jeans. *Where are the twenty little chaperones we had the past two days?*

His hand moved.

He wouldn't!

He popped the button on his jeans below his navel.

We're in a classroom, for goodness' sake!

He inched the zipper downward.

She broke out in a cold sweat, reached out her hand...

And the bell rang. Her alarm bell. And suddenly there was her son waking her for school.

"Mom, you can stay home if you have a fever," the boy said sympathetically.

If only it was as simple as a fever. *That she could* cure. The only treatment drastic to even contempl

Dear Reader,

People are always asking me where I get my story ideas. Well, the inspiration for this book came right out of the newspapers. Truth *is* sometimes stranger than fiction. After reading a couple of articles on how judges are dealing with truant students and their parents in new, controversial ways, Nick and Hollie came to life. They, of course, are completely figments of my imagination and are patterned after no one in real life. I hope you enjoy their story.

Most of all, I hope you enjoy the wonderful holiday season!

Jenna McKnight

JENNA McKNIGHT

THREE WISE MEN & A BABY

Harlequin Books

TORONTO • NEW YORK • LONDON
AMSTERDAM • PARIS • SYDNEY • HAMBURG
STOCKHOLM • ATHENS • TOKYO • MILAN
MADRID • WARSAW • BUDAPEST • AUCKLAND

To Rich, who provides invaluable insight and then brags
on me every chance he gets. Thanks, honey.

ISBN 0-373-16660-5

THREE WISE MEN & A BABY

Chapter One

Son Truant, Mother Flogged

Hollie Landon had lots better to do than sit around in a stuffy courtroom and imagine front-page headlines. The Fagans' mansion had to be decorated for the Snowflake Ball. There were cookies to bake, cards to address and gifts to wrap—*if* she could afford to buy any after this little coffee break.

But most important, right this very minute, she had a baby to nurse. Unfortunately for her, he was at home with the neighbor. Of course, she'd left a convenient bottle with Terri, so Christopher, at least, wouldn't be uncomfortable. She, on the other hand, was full and aching. And plotting a very unhappy Christmas for the judge and anyone else who got in her path today. Trouble was, she'd been summoned to sit here in this blasted courtroom until the judge got around to her and Joey.

Sweet little Joey. Who would have thought he'd been cutting fourth grade? Not that Hollie hadn't ever done it herself, but then she'd been a little hellion at nine. Unlike Joey, who was just a normal kid with a single mother struggling to make it on her own.

Which is why she shouldn't be sitting in a courtroom waiting for the judge to take his sweet time getting around to her. Christmas was less than two weeks away.

Blond-haired, brown-eyed Joey tugged on Hollie's arm and stage-whispered, "Mom."

"Hush."

"But, Mom..."

She refused to look at him, sitting on the bench to her right. He was the spitting image of his father and always melted her heart—not something she needed just now. "You'd be better off not making me mad anytime in the next twenty years or so."

His sigh was louder than his whisper. So like his father...

When he scooted off the edge of the bench and wiggled around to get in her line of vision, she turned her head to the left, avoiding looking directly at the judge, as well. Better to occupy herself with the latest unfortunate soul to be summoned to court today.

Swaggering up the far side of the courtroom, a motorcycle helmet under one black-leather-jacketed arm, was a man who looked shaggy and disreputable enough to have been hauled in on a charge of disturbing the peace. His faded jeans, worn soft in strategic points, were certainly disturbing her peace of mind. As was the thick shock of black hair that fell irreverently over his forehead, like a beacon pointing to warm hazel eyes. Not to mention the friendly smile he flashed in her direction as he hesitated—not quite sitting, not quite standing—almost as if he were asking if she wanted him to sit by her instead of by himself. Of all the nerve!

So now she had nowhere to look. A hunk to the left trying to pick her up at high noon in a courtroom, the slow-asmolasses judge straight ahead, her wriggling son to the right.

"Mom."

"What?" She seldom snapped at Joey, but she refused to beat herself up over it this time.

"That's Mr. Nicholson."

She rubbed her temples. "He's a judge, sweetie. Judge Nicholson."

"Uh-uh. Mr. Nicholson's my teacher. The judge is his father."

She followed the direction of Joey's pointed finger—right back to Mr. Motorcycle himself. Now she understood why the first item on Joey's Christmas list was a black Harley T-shirt. He couldn't understand it wouldn't do for him what it did for his well-built teacher. Not for a few years and not without the help of a lot of testosterone.

"Swell. What's he here for? Reinforcements?"

She wished she could have afforded a lawyer for today's court appearance. Maybe if she hadn't cut so much school when she was a kid, she'd have gotten a better education, a better-paying job after she'd graduated, gone to a better college, and now she'd have been able to afford a lawyer who would blast father and son to hell and back. It was a sure bet if they'd made schoolteachers that had looked like that when she was a little girl, she'd have spent more time in class. Instead, they'd all been females, who had covered themselves from head to toe in black, and worn rosaries.

"I thought Mr. Sherman taught fourth grade."

Joey gave her his long-suffering look, as if he wondered if all moms lost their memories when they approached thirty. "Don't you remember the snow, Mom?"

Did she ever! She'd been marooned with two kids and intermittent electricity, and had fallen three days behind in her work. She'd been luckier, though, than Mr. Sherman and the car pool of teachers who'd collided with a tree and were all still recuperating.

"Joey Landon," the judge intoned.

"Finally," Hollie muttered. She hoped this was the beginning of a quick end. She glanced at her watch to see if there was just the slimmest possibility Christopher hadn't had his bottle yet. Maybe she could get through this in record time, rush home and nurse him until this increasing ache in her breasts was relieved. Quarter after twelve; no such luck.

Joey stood by her knee, jabbing at her seasonal green knit pants with his finger, looking as if he didn't know what to do next. He obviously thought *she* should get up and do something. He tugged at her hand and glanced over at his teacher with a smile that showed he was in awe of the man, not in the least angry that he'd turned him in for cutting school.

"Sometime today, Mrs. Landon, if you don't mind."

"Now he's in a hurry," she muttered, pleased and vexed at the same time. She grabbed Joey by the hand and headed toward the judge's bench as he shuffled through a sheaf of papers.

"I see this isn't the first time Joey's been truant."

She scowled at her son. "It's the first I heard of it."

He graced her with a quelling glare. "More's the pity, Mrs. Landon, when a mother doesn't know what her child is up to."

She bit her tongue about the school system's lack of supervision and notification. She stifled the urge to glance at her watch. Joey yanked his hand out of hers and shook it until he got some blood back into it.

Judge Nicholson peered over the rim of his half-glasses. He wasn't a small man to begin with and, up on his raised bench, he was an imposing figure. She might not have the legal know-how to spar with him, but she could give his son a tongue-lashing he wasn't likely to forget—as soon as she got the opportunity. He was bigger than his father, broader, probably more dangerous, but none of that mattered. She had one son to get back in school, another to nurse and a business to run, none of which was happening today, no thanks to him.

"Well, young man," the judge addressed Joey. "Has your mother told you that it was wrong for you to cut school?"

"Yes, sir."

Hollie didn't know whether to be pleased that Joey stood there looking like a poised little gentleman, or disappointed that he wasn't screwing the toe of his shoe into the floor in embarrassment.

"And did she explain how serious this is that she had to come to court with you today?"

"Yes, sir."

"Did you tell her where you'd gone?"

Joey's gaze faltered then. He looked down at the floor and said, "No, sir," in a small voice.

"Why not?"

Joey shrugged.

Hollie nudged him in the shoulder. "Tell him."

Joey glanced up at Hollie, just long enough for her to see that the normal light in his eyes had been replaced with a stubborn determination. Then he resumed his study of the floor. "Just around."

Hollie nudged him again, trying to prod him into finally divulging where he'd gone and what he'd been up to.

He tacked on, "Sir."

Judge Nicholson watched him and waited for more than that. His pause unnerved Hollie enough to think that, if she'd been nine years old, she'd have come clean right then and there. But she'd been on Joey's case for days and hadn't had any luck getting an answer out of him.

When the judge turned his attention back to her, Hollie didn't know what to say, so she remained quiet. She'd never been in court before, and she never wanted to be again. She just wanted to get it over with and get home.

"It's been my unhappy experience in dealing with truants, Mrs. Landon, that very little can be accomplished by dealing with the child alone. Nor have I been able to garner any worthwhile results by simply fining the parents responsible for allowing this to continue."

Thank God, no fine. Her budget didn't include items like that.

"So I'm going to try something new."

No more walking to school. I'll drop him off myself every morning at eight o'clock sharp.

"I'm sentencing you, Mrs. Landon, to attend school with your son, Joey, every day until Christmas break. Starting Monday morning."

She opened her mouth; nothing came out. Her hand fluttered in the air, but whether to ward off evil or fan herself, she wasn't sure.

"What the hell?"

She was barely aware that the motorcycle hunk had surged to his feet and landed beside her. His deep voice registered in her brain—it was too deep and angry not to—but she was still unable to move. The scent of leather and fresh pine insinuated itself into her brain when she struggled to think of some objection—*anything*—that might sway the judge's decision.

The gavel pounded.

"You can't do that!"

The judge graced his son with a cursory frown at his attire. "I can and I did. Your lunch break is over. Get back to school."

"No, wait!" Hollie refused to back down, even when they both glared at her as if she'd lost her mind. After all, this was *her* life. People occasionally tried to tell her how to live it, but that was as far as they got. "Please, Judge—Your Honor—" It sounded like groveling to her, but she'd stoop so low as to call him "Your Majesty" if it got her out of this. "I have to work. I can't go to school with Joey."

Judge Nicholson did not turn a tender ear toward her. "Work something out, Mrs. Landon. If you don't show up every morning and stay all day, and make sure Joey stays, too, I'll have you up on contempt charges. Then we'll meet back here on your account."

The gavel pounded again, the final sound going right to a doozy of a new headache and reminding her she'd only *thought* the morning had gotten off to a bad start.

She was a one-woman business; she couldn't afford to take off. She was a single mother; she couldn't afford not to.

She hadn't budgeted extra money to pay a sitter, either. Even if she had, it wouldn't help. She wasn't ready to wean her four-month-old infant off a bottle just because some circuit court judge thought he was Scrooge reincarnated.

Her in-laws were coming to town on December 26, too late to help.

All in all, Hollie thought she'd rather be flogged.

UH-OH.

Joey stared out the courtroom window at the falling snow. Most kids would be craning to go make a snowman. Or throw snowballs at the little girls to hear them squeal and watch them run and hide in spite of the smiles they flashed in return. He just wanted his shovel, a couple of undisturbed hours and Old Lady Simmonds's driveway and sidewalk.

At nine, he was too young to understand everything that went on in the adult world. In a world gone crazy, however, he was still the son of a single mother who'd given birth to his baby brother two years after his father had died, and he understood a lot more than most kids his age.

But *this*—this sounded bad. Really, really bad. Worse than losing his allowance, his cartoons and his video games all in the same week. His mom in school with him? Every day? What would he tell his friends? Who would play with him ever again? Who would *talk* to him?

He wouldn't have a minute to himself. Jeez, he hoped his mom didn't follow him into the boys' room. How would he find time to sneak away and collect the money Old Lady Simmonds already owed him?

He wanted his life back to normal. Well, normal for him. He wouldn't give up his baby brother for anything.

The older boys had warned him about Friday the thirteenth, but those eye-dripping, missing-body-parts, monster stories were nothing compared to this.

NICK SLUMPED into the nearest seat in the courtroom.

Judge Nicholson shuffled court documents to one side of his bench. "I thought you wanted my help."

"Yeah, with Joey, but—"

"Well, you got it. This is the best thing for him."

Him, maybe. But what about me?

If his father thought having Hollie Landon spend every day in his classroom was a good idea, he was certifiable. A Rome, Wisconsin, wanna-be who had forgotten what temptation was all about. Nick would be staring straight at her all day. At about five foot five, she wasn't exactly petite, but she didn't have the frame to carry such full breasts.

It'd be tough to keep his eyes above her neck, but with twenty-five nine- and ten-year-old chaperons, he figured he'd better.

He resolved right then and there to concentrate on her eyes. They'd flashed green sparks of indignation when he'd sat down and tossed a smile to Joey. Okay, so maybe he'd noticed too much about her eyes.

He'd concentrate on her hair. That should keep him out of trouble. It was dark. Brunette, actually. Past her shoulders. Thick, with a come-hither wave begging to be touched and a ribbon he wanted to untie.

No two ways about it, he was in deep trouble unless she sat in the coat closet.

His dad called the next victim as Nick strode out through the double doors. He rounded the first corner, right into a scene that involved a lecture, a wagging finger and flashing green eyes. Joey slumped against the hall wall and had enough wits about him not to roll his eyes or look bored. In fact, he paid rapt attention to his mother's quiet words, confirming Nick's suspicion that the judge had gone overboard. Big time.

Nick cleared his throat softly. He got one of those if-looks-could-kill glares from the lady in question, and a silent save-me-please appeal from Joey.

"I'm sorry."

Hollie grabbed Joey's hand and whirled toward the exit. "If you're not yet, I'm sure you will be on Monday morning," floated back to Nick.

Joey had no choice but to follow his mother as, red scarf flying and coattails flapping, she barreled down the hall toward the front doors of the courthouse.

Monday morning was going to be very interesting.

"SO USE A BREAST PUMP," Terri Farrel advised over a cup of coffee at Hollie's kitchen table. She was Hollie's neighbor, best friend and the source of her free legal advice.

Hollie gagged on her juice. "That's your best advice as a lawyer?"

"Lawyer... friend, what's the diff?"

"According to your fee schedule, more than I earn."

"You know I'd represent you for free if I could, but—"

Hollie held up a hand to stop her. She wouldn't endanger Terri's job for all the world. "I'm just grateful you could take Christopher today."

Terri's laugh was short and ironic, a wry mixture of joy to have some time off before Christmas and displeasure that she was stuck with a bad sprain. Another victim of the early December snowstorm, she kicked her crutch with her good foot and listened with a satisfied smirk as it banged onto the tile floor. "Yeah, like I've got so much else to do right now. I can give you some free advice, though."

"I'm not getting a breast pump. I'd feel like a dairy cow."

"Women do it all the time."

"You're missing the point. I don't *want* to do it. My right to make this decision is being taken away from me, and I don't like it one bit."

Terri gave her a second to simmer down, so she'd only have to give the advice once. "Ready?"

"Can't I fight this?"

Terri's sigh spoke volumes. "Save your money, Hollie. Do the time. I can take Christopher during school hours."

"No!" She noticed Terri's raised eyebrows and feared she'd hurt her friend's feelings with her quick rejection. "I mean, nothing personal, Terri, but I didn't have Christopher so I could farm him out to a sitter every day."

"I know that, but, Hollie—"

"I'd rather take him with me before I do that." *That* presented the beginnings of a wonderful picture. If she took Christopher to school *with* her . . .

Terri made another attempt at reason. "How about your in-laws, then? I'm sure they'd like to spend time with Christopher, and maybe you could get over this 'sitter' hang-up. It'd be healthy for you, you know."

Hollie's mind was elsewhere as she murmured, "They just retired. They deserve some time to themselves."

"You know, I haven't seen that look on your face before. It makes me feel a little like Ethel Mertz, and I should be trying to talk you out of something, 'Lucy.'"

A broad smile lit up Hollie's whole face. "I can make his life a living hell."

"Oh, now, Hollie, you can't be thinking—"

Hollie turned a hopeful look on her friend. "I wouldn't be breaking any laws, would I?"

"If what?"

"If I take Christopher to school with me?"

Terri grabbed a handful of her own hair and pretended to tear it out by the roots. Hollie took that as a no and smiled as a picture of Monday morning unfolded.

"Good. The teacher got me into this mess, he can get me out of it. When he gets sick of seeing the two of us for hours on end, he can go get his dad to reverse his decision, or whatever it's called."

"You can't be serious!" One look at Hollie's face and Terri knew she was dead serious. "You can't play fast and loose with a judge's order like that. He'll have you up on contempt charges so fast you won't know what hit you."

Hollie chewed the inside of her lip. "How do I avoid that?"

"Leave Christopher with me."

"Work with me, Terri. Give me some free advice I can live with."

Terri sighed dramatically. "You have to go along with the spirit of the order. You can't be obnoxious or rude or set a bad example in front of the kids."

"You mean, be pleasant?"

"Yes!"

"I can do pleasant."

"Not with that look on your face, you can't."

Monday, December 16

MONDAY MORNING'S CHILL followed Nick into the building. He loved his Harley, but, at twenty-nine, he was beginning to consider getting an old junker car just for the winter months. He didn't even care if the heater worked; he just wanted something with windows to roll up against the wind.

He checked his mail slot, found a request to visit the principal's office ASAP and left his motorcycle helmet on top of the file cabinet.

He entered the inner sanctum without knocking. "You wanted to see me, Ed?" he asked the stout man sitting behind his cluttered desk.

Ed Nelson, long-standing principal of East Bay's only elementary school, had been in the same office when Nick had been a student. Nick had never been in much of a hurry to get into the principal's office then, but he'd been just as brazen.

"Mr. Nicholson, if I've told you once, I've told you a hundred times, you must set a good example for the children and address me as Mr. Nelson."

Nick sprawled in the wooden chair in front of Ed's desk, one jeaned knee hooked over the armrest. "There aren't any kids here now, Ed. I called you Mr. Nelson yesterday in the cafeteria, remember? Just like you wanted.''

"Yes, I noticed.''

"So, what can I do for you?''

"I'm following up on the sex-education class you're teaching. How's it going? What feedback have you gotten from the parents?''

"Uh, none.''

"Not one comment?''

"Nope.''

"Well, how are the kids handling it?''

"Uh, Ed . . .''

"You *are* teaching it.'' It carried all the implications of a question that better not need an answer.

"Not too much.''

"How much is 'not too much'?''

Nick picked at the seam on his jeans. "None.''

The principal, a man whose overweight status should have slowed him down but didn't, jumped to his feet, rounded the desk and towered over Nick. "What do you mean, none?'' His face was red, nearly purple in spots, and Nick felt a moment of serious concern for the man's health.

"I wasn't comfortable with the topic.''

"Hell, man, none of us are comfortable discussing sex with a roomful of nine- and ten-year-olds, but it's part of the curriculum. You have to do it.''

"But—''

"And you have to make up for lost time. I want you to bring those kids up-to-date by Christmas, or else.''

Or else? Nick knew Ed couldn't fire him. They were short of warm bodies as it was, and he'd been put in charge of the annual Christmas play. Nobody else would want to take it over at this late date, especially since he'd been making changes.

Not that he had a burning desire to teach fourth grade and be in charge of their play. He really wanted to teach high school drama, but in small, close-knit East Bay, Illinois, the town's former bad boy didn't just waltz back in after eleven years and get what he wanted. Not without passing their idea of a "test" first. Even if he was the best man for the job.

Many of the board members had known him personally in high school. They had kids in East Bay High now. If Nick couldn't handle fourth grade, if he screwed up a traditional play, they wouldn't give him the time of day, much less consideration for a position on their staff. Not exactly the criteria he'd use for judging someone, but then, this was East Bay, Illinois, not New York City.

The principal studied him shrewdly. "If you need more time to catch up, I can cancel play practice."

Nick grinned. "Oh, those kids need practice."

"Not if I cancel the play."

Nick's grin faded abruptly. "Cancel the play? But...it's tradition."

Ed's grin grew in inverse proportion to Nick's. "Since when are you big on tradition?"

He took Nick by the arm, tugged him up out of the chair and directed him, sputtering like a fool, out the door. He clapped him heartily on the back, propelling him out into the office where the secretary sat at her desk and two other teachers were going through their mail.

"Don't worry, Nick," he said. "Sex gets easier with practice."

THE CHILDREN ENTERED the school with a burst of cold Christmas-is-coming energy, squealing, laughing, pushing and shoving. Nick, who should have been reviewing the sex-education booklets and figuring out where to start, instead stood staring out his second-story classroom windows. Waiting. For her.

Would she come? He wanted her to—for her son's welfare, of course. Joey obviously needed more guidance than what he was getting at home. If he cut a couple hours of school here and there at age nine, what was he going to do when he got to high school?

Nick should know; he'd been there, done that. What was different now was the attitude adjustment he'd gone through while living in New York City and Los Angeles. As he approached thirty, tradition didn't sound like such a dirty word anymore, and East Bay didn't come off quite as rigid as he remembered. Strange, yes—thank God he hadn't changed that much—but they made up for it with the way they protected their children and kept them safe.

He'd never heard of men having biological clocks, but three and a half months ago, when he'd found himself directing the worst bunch of theater brats he'd ever encountered, he suddenly realized he wanted to live in a place with continuity and values. A place to raise good kids with solid backgrounds, parental support, the works. So he'd come home and applied at the high school, where he'd be able to put his stage talents and worldly wisdom to good use.

Only he'd ended up in charge of fourth grade because they were desperate for a substitute. And because he cared, he'd taken a special interest in the fatherless Joey Landon.

He expected Hollie, as a single mother, to arrive—if she came at all—in an older car. Maybe with a dented fender or a loose bumper or an engine knock—something that needed a man's attention. Instead she pulled into the parking lot in a two-year-old station wagon. It looked practical, efficient, in perfect shape. He raised the sash and listened for an engine about to blow a hole through the hood, but heard nothing out of the ordinary. So, she managed her car better than she managed her own son.

Joey bounded out of the passenger side, slid into his purple backpack, then ran around to the driver's side to help his mom. The makings of a little gentleman. Nick grudgingly gave her points for that, then took them away again as he watched her hand her son a huge purse. No, not a purse exactly. More like a . . .

She got out of the car, opened the back door, reached in and came out with a baby.

"A diaper bag!" he roared.

The children lapsed into momentary silence, then ran to the windows to see what had caused their normally cool teacher to start sputtering like a cartoon character.

"She's bringing Christopher," nine-year-old Linda announced.

"He can't come to fourth grade," Timmy said.

"Why not? My mom says Joey's mom has to come to school until Christmas."

"She does?"

"Why?"

Nick tuned them out. He stared in horror at the scene unfolding in the parking lot, Joey carrying a diaper bag over his shoulder, Hollie wrapping the infant up against the cold and cradling it against her chest.

He groaned as he remembered what she'd said about him being sorry come Monday morning.

"What's wrong, Mr. Nicholson?" Linda asked.

"Does she have to learn what we do?" Timmy asked.

With a baby in class, Nick was afraid nobody would be learning anything—at least not anything in the curriculum. Except maybe sex education.

Chapter Two

Nick charged out of the second-floor classroom. He didn't pause to tell the children to put their coats and lunches away and take their seats. He didn't make a mad grab for his leather jacket. He just barreled for the nearest set of stairs that would get him outside to the parking lot in time to stop Hollie Landon from moving baby and baggage into his classroom.

In spite of his mad dash, he was passed on the stairs by three of Joey's cohorts, who had no regard for speed or gravity. He made a vindictive mental note to tell the high school track coach to be on the lookout to recruit those three in a few years. By the time he reached Hollie and the station wagon, she was handing them things to carry...and some of them didn't look like baby things.

"What are you doing?" From the puzzled look on her face, he suspected that some of his words had gotten lost between gasps for oxygen. He took a deep breath and grabbed the shirt collar of the nearest boy, Timmy, who was carrying a plastic infant seat. "Put that back."

Hollie smiled up at him sweetly. He had to take another deep breath.

"Christopher likes to sit in that. It helps keep him quiet."
She bent at the waist and ducked her head back into the
station wagon.

Nick was afraid to see what she was going to come out
with next. He hung on to Timmy's collar, in spite of the
boy's tugging. "He can sit in it at home."

Her arms full of Christopher and his blanket, she
straightened up with the most beautiful, hopeful smile he'd
ever hoped to see. "You mean the judge changed his
mind?"

"Uh, I didn't say that."

She reached down with a mother's no-nonsense ap-
proach and pried his fingers off Timmy's collar. The feelings rushing through Nick when her skin came in contact
with his, however, carried no mother-son connotations. He
forgot why he was trying to stop her. He forgot he was in a
short-sleeved T-shirt and there was a windchill of five below. Another minute and he would have forgotten his own
name, except that she continued to direct his students. If he
wasn't careful, she'd soon be running his entire classroom,
and his chances of getting on the high school staff would fly
right out the window.

"You can go on up with that, Timmy," she said. "And
thank you."

"No, wait!" Nick ordered.

Timmy hesitated, clearly as surprised by Nick's raised
voice as Nick was himself and unsure whether to move until Hollie waved him on. Nick watched the youngster run
into the school without looking back again, and he knew
he'd lost the battle. If he wasn't careful, he'd lose the war,
too.

"What's that T.J. was carrying?"

Hollie pulled the blanket closer over Christopher's face
to protect him from the frigid breeze.

"Hollie?" He shouldn't have said it. He should have stuck with Mrs. Landon. Her first name sounded like Christmas on his lips, complete with a white blanket of snow, twinkling lights and presents under a real tree.

She seemed very interested in seeing to Christopher's comfort, even though Nick suspected the baby was asleep. "Hm?"

"Ooh, look!" Linda squealed.

"Can I see him?" Mary Margaret begged.

They were suddenly surrounded by all thirteen girls from his class, none of whom had donned their coats or hats. They quickly circled Hollie, elbowing and shouldering Nick out of their way. They stood on tiptoe to peek at the baby, cooed appropriately and hopped up and down in their excitement to see Christopher come to school.

"Everybody back inside!" Nick roared.

He could have saved his breath. Maybe one little girl peeked sideways at him to see if he was really serious, but he couldn't be sure. All he could see was that it was going to be a long haul until Christmas break.

He had to regain control. He followed Hollie and the children through the front doors of the school, up the wide staircase and along the tiled hallway. He felt as if he were the lone tree left standing after the storm. The children were the wind. Hollie was the driving force behind it.

THE BELL SHOULD HAVE indicated the beginning of class. It always had before. All it did this morning was accentuate the fact that Nick hadn't any idea how to battle Hollie and Christopher's influence without coming off like a grumpy, scowling Scrooge.

"Boys! Girls!" He didn't like having to raise his voice.

The boys scurried into their seats. The girls glanced at him, but maintained their close circle around the newcomers, plying Hollie with questions about Christopher's age, if he could sit up yet and if they could take turns feeding him his bottle.

He refused to yell again. They probably got enough of that at home. He grabbed the nearest hardback book and slammed it down with a resounding smack on his wood desktop.

Everyone jumped. There was momentary silence as twelve boys, thirteen girls and one woman stared at him. The silence was broken by a high-pitched wail. Christopher.

The stares changed to outraged glares as the girls quickly passed sentence on Nick without a trial. Their puckered eyebrows and pouty lips made him feel like the meanest of villains, far lower than a simple Scrooge. Worse, they were right. But it didn't stop him from snapping at Hollie.

"Can't you give him a bottle to shut him up?"

The girls' faces were transformed with delight as they laughed loudly, very unladylike, as if they knew something he should know, but didn't. Hollie jiggled the baby, trying to soothe him. She planted a kiss on his forehead.

Nick's libido outrageously wished he were the recipient of that kiss. Her lips would be soft on his skin, he knew. Warm. Womanly. Nothing motherly about them.

"I didn't bring any bottles," she answered.

"You didn't? But..." He found himself pointing at all the baby paraphernalia on the floor around her feet. Didn't mothers carry bottles in diaper bags? *Please, God, let her have a bottle in there.* "Maybe you should look."

Her smile lit up the room, except for the spot where he was standing. He felt as if he were about to pass through the floor into the bowels of hell. She'd been right; Monday morning was here, and he was definitely sorry.

"I don't need to look."

"Surely you don't intend..." God, he *hoped* she didn't intend what he thought she intended!

The little girls were all giggling now and whispering to the little boys. They smirked.

"Yes—" she smiled "—I do."

Jeez, how often did babies nurse? He wasn't going to be hungry soon, was he? Nick didn't even bother to wonder whether Hollie was teasing him about the bottles, or lack thereof. He doubted the kid had ever had a synthetic nipple pass between his lips.

Perhaps he should step up the sex education. Then, when it came time for Hollie to whip up her fuzzy red sweater and plunk a breast into the kid's mouth, he'd be ready and in control. He'd use it as a learning experience. A teaching tool.

Though from the expectant looks on their less-than-angelic little faces, he had a feeling they thought he was the one who was going to be getting the learning experience. Well, they'd just see about that.

He turned his back on all of them, took a deep breath and swallowed any reservations he might have. He knew better than to let the children see that something so natural as a nursing mother would throw him off base.

He was in complete control when he turned around to face his class. "Mrs. Landon." He prided himself on the fact that he remembered not to use her first name again. Too personal. "Could I see you out in the hall?" His voice was moderated, calm, natural.

The boys saw right through him. The girls jumped up, each one offering to hold the baby until Hollie returned.

Nick was a patient man—with children who wanted to be in the Christmas play, the way *he* was directing it. Waiting for Hollie to appoint a baby-sitter before he could get her out into the hall, however, strained his patience to the breaking point.

"Well, I guess we could do this alphabetically," she mused.

"Forward or backward?" the girls wanted to know.

"Mary Margaret Abernathy," Nick snapped.

Twelve disappointed girls groaned as Mary Margaret proudly sat sideways in a desk and accepted the bundle known as Christopher. He filled her lap and arms, stared at her face and reached for her red curls as he quit fussing. Joey hovered beside them as if he questioned a girl's ability to hold his little brother.

Nick, to get this show on the road, latched on to Hollie's arm. If he didn't, it'd be lunchtime before he got anything done. He hadn't counted on what touching her arm would feel like. A man didn't think those kind of thoughts in a fourth-grade classroom, but his hand sent all sorts of messages to his brain about how soft, yet firm, her arm felt beneath her sleeve. When he inhaled something that smelled distinctly of vanilla and reminded him of home-baked cookies, he refused to debate whether it was her shampoo or soap.

"*Now*, Mrs. Landon," he urged as he tugged her toward the door, then released her arm suddenly before his thoughts strayed further.

She followed him into the hall. He made sure the door was closed firmly behind them. He never appointed anyone in the class as monitor; he'd always hated it when teachers did that.

"I think I should tell you this is the one and only time I'm coming out into the hall with you," Hollie began before Nick could organize what he wanted to say.

"What?"

"I spoke with my lawyer over the weekend—"

"You have a lawyer?"

"—and she advised me to carry out Judge Nicholson's instructions to the letter."

He felt his jaw move, but nothing came out to stop her from continuing.

"He ordered me to sit in class with Joey, and that's what I intend to do. Sit in class. All day, every day."

"But—"

"I'm sure he didn't want me to spend time in the hall."

"But—"

"Unless, of course—" she smiled sweetly "—you can get him to change his mind."

"Ah." He understood now that she had a plan to make his life hell. "I suppose you'd like me to talk to him tonight?"

"Would you?"

He knew he'd been alone too long when she made the simple, expected question sound as if the idea had been his in the first place.

"Of course."

Her hand landed on his forearm, a light presence that burned all the way through his skin and down to his bones. As she leaned toward him, he forgot what he'd brought her into the hall to tell her in the first place. Instead, he had visions of a prolonged, grateful kiss to thank him in advance for talking some sense into his father.

She brushed his cheek with the lightest of pecks and retreated back into his classroom, the moment having come and gone a full thirty seconds before he could recover and summon up enough strength to propel himself behind her.

He'd thought Joey was the student whose father had died two years ago. He'd thought he was a young boy who needed a man's influence, a guiding hand on the confusing road to maturity and responsibility. But there was a four-month-old baby that obviously said otherwise.

What *had* the judge been thinking?

"WHO HAS THE ANSWER to problem three?" Nick asked as he strolled the aisles between the children's junior-size desks.

After the first half hour, they had settled right into their morning routine. Now they were working on their arithmetic without any more distraction than usual. He assumed most of them had siblings at home and were used to tuning them out. Nick, however, was having real problems with Christopher's increasing fussiness. Hollie wasn't ignoring the baby, but she wasn't in any hurry to quiet him, either.

Christopher had spent part of the morning in his infant seat in the back of the classroom. Hollie had alternately played with him and then allowed him to amuse himself. Now he was squirming around on his tummy on a blue blanket spread out on the floor, arms and legs moving as if he were trying to swim. Hollie was squeezed into an under-size desk, one leg stretched out so that her red-and-green Christmas-socked foot rested in front of Christopher's nose. She even had a little jingle bell sewn onto the ankle. She wiggled her toes and bounced her foot from time to time, which just thrilled the baby to no end.

And if Nick knew all that, then he'd been paying far too much attention to the two of them.

Hollie finished whatever she'd been working on, then bent down and picked up Christopher. She cooed at him and nuzzled him playfully with her nose. He rammed his little fist into his mouth in anticipation, then whimpered his displeasure with that. Hollie had one hand under her sweater before Nick could stop her.

"Uh, Mrs. Landon?"

"Yes?"

He watched the movement of her fingers beneath the fuzzy red top. "Maybe the hall would be a more appropriate place for that."

She smiled sweetly. "Oh, I couldn't do that. I have to stay in here."

He forced himself to look away. He prayed the little girls weren't learning womanly wiles at too young an age. He thought all the children would be peeking at her curiously, especially the boys, but they were staring at him to see what he'd do next.

He matched her smile with one of his own. One that used to get women to give him whatever he desired. One that had made audiences swoon when he was on stage. "Then I suggest you face the back wall."

"You mean like I'm being punished?"

If he were casting a regular play instead of the annual fourth-grade Christmas one, he'd hire her in a flash. Not many actresses could pull off such innocence.

"No, I mean like you set a good example of modesty to the children, and, in turn, they will be polite and keep their eyes on their work or toward the front of the room."

"I can be modest without hiding, Mr. Nicholson."

Joey raised his hand. "I have the answer to problem three, Mr. Nicholson."

Nick knew from the smirk on Joey's face that not only was the boy not dismayed by his mother's spunky streak, he was delighted by it. Took his cue from it.

"So do I," Timmy chimed in.

"Me, too," Mary Margaret added, with an especially warm smile for Joey.

"I'll do my thing. You do yours," Hollie suggested to Nick, with a nod in the children's direction.

With months of practice behind her, she quickly and discreetly settled Christopher at her breast. For Nick's benefit, she draped a receiving blanket lightly over her chest, even though she was quite well covered. He had nothing to complain about, but he looked as though he wanted to.

She suspected he was seldom at a loss for words, just as she suspected he was seldom out of control of his class. Well, he had his father to thank for that, not her.

HOLLIE HAD PLANNED on getting what she wanted—her freedom—by being difficult. She'd seen the anticipation in Nick's eyes when she'd kissed his cheek in the hall, though. She hadn't been with a man in a long time, but she knew heat when she saw it. And confusion. The poor man hadn't a clue what to do with her and Christopher. Perhaps she could do just as well by being cooperative?

Nah. She'd stick with difficult and keep a lid on her attraction to him.

She didn't follow Joey to recess, lunch or the boys' room. She was used to living with two little people. She was used to working throughout the day with Christopher nearby. Her spare bedroom was a full-time studio between feedings, diaperings and playtime.

She was, however, not used to twenty-four unrelated children distracting her, nor a man who could make big bucks as a model for a Harley ad. All he needed was a pair of leather chaps. He'd gone to lunch with the children, but even without him in the room with her, she had a perfect picture in her mind of how he would look in chaps. Jeans hugging his hips, black leather hugging his sturdy thighs...

Thoughts in that direction could lead to nothing but trouble. She forced her mind back to the Snowflake Ball design work on the desktop in front of her. Trying to cram her normal free-drawing style onto a pitted, scarred surface the size of a cereal box was impossible. Envisioning ideas of how to get even with someone for this fiasco was simple. Of course, Nick was her best bet for that someone. She was midway between the idea of sketching his chalkboards full of caricatures of him, then hiding his erasers and stocking up on spitballs in the pencil tray, when the door to the classroom opened.

"Oh, you're still here." The hunk in question paused at the door, a solid wood chair gripped easily in one hand as if it weighed no more than a notebook.

She glanced guiltily at the pencil tray, just to be sure she hadn't really started on the spitballs.

"Of course you're here. Where else would you be?"

It was a rhetorical question, and she didn't deign to try to answer it. She was afraid once she got started, she wouldn't quit. Or she'd just blubber something—hopefully incoherent—about leather chaps.

He set the full-size, straight-back chair next to her little desk. "I thought this might be more comfortable."

She knew she'd been living alone with children too long when the first words that flowed reflexively out of her mouth were, "Oh, how sweet."

His grin was crooked and warm and made her forget the kinks she'd acquired in the undersize rack she'd been sitting in all morning. She shamed herself for having thought of how to torture him, mentally erasing the caricatures from his chalkboards and returning his erasers.

"I mean...that's so thoughtful of you, Mr. Nicholson."

His hazel eyes twinkled merrily. "I liked your first thought better." His hand landed on the back of the chair in invitation. "Come on, try it out."

She contorted her body out of the small desk, then looked longingly at the chair. "This isn't a bribe, is it?"

"No." He urged her toward it with a gentlemanly gesture, so very at odds with his shaggy hair, worn jeans and her picture of him in black leather chaps. "Would it work if it were?"

"No."

"There, see, I didn't think so."

She was conscious of his watchful eyes as she eased herself down onto the spacious seat. Never had crossing her legs felt so good. "How did you know?"

"There's barely enough room for you in that desk, let alone the baby when you're trying to, you know, nurse."

He craned his neck to peek at her drawings, but not before she noticed a very slight pink flush to his cheeks. She vaulted out of her new chair and patted her papers into a neat pile before they both found out whether she'd actually sketched him in his chaps or just imagined it.

"You're an artist?"

"Interior designer."

"That's very good," he commented on the Christmas scene on top of the stack. "Reminds me of a roaring fire and marshmallows on Christmas eve."

"Chestnuts," she corrected.

Again that grin. "Tell that to my mother. We did marshmallows. What ones we didn't string on the tree."

"That's supposed to be popcorn."

He shrugged, not in the least embarrassed that his family had taken liberties with tradition. "Do you and Joey do everything like everyone else?"

She snorted in a very unladylike fashion, covering it as best she could with a laugh. "Uh, no. Not exactly."

"I didn't think so. As a matter of fact—"

The bell rang long and loud, sounding as if it would never end, giving her time to remember that she was going to have to be very careful or she'd find herself liking this man. And she had no plans on that. She needed to annoy him until he begged his father to let her off the hook. The door burst open as the children poured into the room.

"I need to talk to you about Joey. Can you stay after school?" he asked.

"I don't think so."

"Just a few minutes before play practice? It's really important."

"Depends on Christopher's mood."

PLEASE, GOD, it's two-forty. Just twenty more minutes.

Today had gone all right, actually, Joey thought. So far, so good. His friends had eaten lunch with him. They'd played with him at recess. His mother hadn't followed him to the boys' room.

The girls all thought his baby brother was neat. He did, too, but he couldn't imagine thinking someone else's baby brother was anything special. He'd heard on TV sitcoms that babies were "chick magnets." If it started this early, he was going to make sure he wasn't the one left holding Christopher next time his mom had to go out into the hall with his teacher. He didn't need Mary Margaret, Linda or any of the other girls drooling all over him.

FIFTEEN MINUTES BEFORE the three-o'clock dismissal bell, Hollie started packing up. The judge expected her to be in class all day, and Nick wanted her to stay after school, too? Nerve must run in his family.

Snowflake Ball designs went into her portfolio. The portacrib and the large blanket on the floor could stay until the judge let her off the hook. If it got in the janitor's way, then he could complain to the judge, too. Everything else of Christopher's went into the diaper bag.

"Mrs. Landon?"

She spared a glance at Nick as she knelt on the blanket beside Christopher and got ready to bundle arms and legs into his little navy blue snowsuit.

"Mrs. Landon, are you going to stay a few minutes after school?"

"Nope."

"Class dismissed," he announced loud and clear.

Hollie was sure the children's delighted screams could be heard throughout the building. They startled Christopher, but instead of crying, he waved his arms and legs as if he wanted to run to the coat closet with them. She gave up on trying to capture his limbs in the snowsuit until after the children ran out the door.

"Now we can talk."

"I have to be getting home."

"You have to stay until the bell rings."

She had Christopher zipped up in his snowsuit in record time, then stood and cradled him against her chest. "No, I have to be here with Joey. If he gets to leave early, so do I."

"He's what I wanted to talk to you about."

Hollie held Christopher in one arm, slung the diaper bag over her shoulder and found it impossible to grasp the portfolio, too.

"I'd counted on the boys to help me with this stuff," she informed Nick pointedly, "but they're all gone." No thanks to him.

"I'll give you a hand as soon as we talk."

She dropped the diaper bag onto the chair and glanced at the clock. Four minutes to three. She'd give him until the bell. "Okay. Talk."

"I'll admit my dad went a little overboard—"

Her eyebrows arched. "A little?"

"—but we have no choice except to make the best of this situation for the next week."

"Meaning?"

"Meaning you've got to quit undermining my authority in the classroom, embarrassing your son and—"

"Earth to Nick," she interrupted by waving her hand in front of his face.

"What?"

"Can you stand there and tell me you honestly believe my son was embarrassed?" If she expected him to break down and admit he was grasping at straws, she discovered she had a long wait. Even under her most wilting stare, the one that always worked on Joey and had even worked on his father before him, Nick stood firm.

"I'm sure he was."

"I'm sure he wasn't. In case you haven't noticed, Joey's very mature for his age."

"Yes, I'd noticed. I'd prefer he be a little less mature sometimes."

"Less mature?" She pressed the tip of her index finger against her chin and asked sassily, "Oh, does cutting school count?"

"Mrs. Landon, please."

"No, Mr. Nicholson, you please. I may have to sit here every day, but I don't have to listen to any lectures you feel like giving me. Joey is a very loving, very responsible little boy who made one mistake."

"Four."

"Excuse me?"

"He cut four times."

She sighed. "Four times! What were you saving that information for? His transcript?"

"I only have Joey's best interests in mind."

"Then get me off the hook so I can earn a living, or we'll be out on the streets."

He glanced at Christopher. "There's no Mr. Landon?"

"No." She felt no compunction to share her private life with him. All he had to do was go stand in the grocery store for fifteen minutes and keep his ears open.

"I see."

She doubted that. No one else in East Bay did. Except Joey. And Terri.

"So Joey does need, shall we say, a man's influence?"

She preferred not to get into a down-and-dirty argument whereby she'd call him narrow-minded and he'd refuse to sway his father.

"Joey's doing just fine, Mr. Nicholson. He's well ahead of his age."

"At the rate you're going, he'll be ready for college next year."

She sugarcoated her smile. "Then I certainly hope he learns enough from you to get a scholarship."

The bell rang. Hollie wasn't at all sure whether she'd won round one.

"DAD, BE REASONABLE."

Nick's father was cozily ensconced in his leather recliner, his socked feet arrowed toward the flames dancing in the fireplace, the newspaper spread out on his lap, his half-glasses perched low on his nose. He sat quietly while Nick, who immediately after letting himself into the house, set about pacing the length of the cherry-paneled study.

He knew his father took pleasure in having him home again after an absence of so many years. By home, he meant in the same town, not the same house. Nick had hitchhiked east instead of going to his high school graduation, determined to make his mark on the world of the stage. He was less of a stranger now than three months ago, but it was still a case of a man trying to get to know another man when neither of them was comfortable enough to expose his feelings to the other. The fact that Nick had roared back into his father's life on a powerful Harley and wearing black leather hadn't softened the transition any.

"Hello, Nick. So nice of you to drop by this evening."

Nick refused to be distracted with social amenities. He'd left town as an angry teenager and returned as a man with his emotions under control, but not *that* much control. The high school had taken one look at him and found they didn't need him, his teaching degree or his drama experience. He'd been cool about their rejection, but he wasn't calm now.

"I'm serious, Dad. You've got to let Hollie go back to work."

"Hollie?" The judge mused thoughtfully, as if he were sorting through myriad confusing cases. "Would that be Mrs. Landon?"

"You know damn well it is."

"Watch your mouth."

"We're not in court, Dad. You can't throw me into jail for contempt in your study."

The judge's lips twitched, but didn't quite reach a grin. "You'd be surprised what I can do."

Nick's laugh was short and enlightened. "Not after today, I wouldn't."

"Good."

"That's why I know you can reverse your decision and let Hollie off."

His father removed his glasses and set them carefully on the table beside his chair. "And what would that accomplish?"

Nick's pacing picked up. "She could go to work. She has to earn a living to support herself and her two sons."

"And Joey?" When Nick stopped and stared at him, his father steepled his fingers and continued. "What about his truancy?"

"I can watch him closer."

"You mean you weren't watching him close enough?"

"That's not what I said. I try to teach my students to be responsible for themselves."

The judge nodded. "You're only one man, Nick. You can't be in twenty-five different places at one time. What do you think would happen to Joey if his truancy were to resume?"

"Couldn't we do school arrest or something? No recess. No lunchtime out of my sight."

"And you'd station a guard outside the bathroom? No, son, that won't work at all. If I let Mrs. Landon go back to doing things the way she's always done them, then Joey will cut school again, and I'll have no alternative but to take drastic measures."

Nick raked his hand through his hair, tempted to yank it—hard—to make sure he wasn't having a nightmare. "You don't call this drastic?"

His father grinned, the first clue Nick had since Friday that the old man might be human, that he actually realized how controversial his ruling had been. That he was *enjoying* it.

"You don't understand, Dad. She won't leave the classroom."

"That's a bad thing? I wish more people would follow my orders to the letter."

"She has a baby."

"Yes, I know."

"She brought it to school today."

"So I heard."

"She intends to bring it every day."

"I would imagine so."

"Dad, she nurses it. You know, no bottle? The...natural way."

"I see. Well, that could pose a problem."

Nick smiled. Finally, he was getting through to the old guy, making him see the light. He perched on the edge of the matching recliner, prepared to hear that this warranted some welcome news.

"Well, then, I guess she needs special arrangements."

Nick jumped to his feet and threw his arms up in the air. "That's what I've been trying to tell you." He pictured the warm reception he'd get from Hollie when she heard she wouldn't have to come to school in the morning. He'd ride over to her house tonight when he left here. She wouldn't care how late it was when he got there; good news like that would be welcome anytime.

"You may tell her she has my permission to go out to the hall to nurse the baby."

Chapter Three

Tuesday, December 17

Hollie packed Christopher's diaper bag with a vengeance on Tuesday morning. He'd had a restless night, no doubt due to all the extra stimulation and confusion of spending all day Monday in a room full of active, older children and devoid of his crib. He wasn't handling the change in his routine much better than she was handling the change in hers.

Bibs, receiving blankets, changes of clothes, toys—she threw them all into the bag with enough force to put them through the bottom if it hadn't been sitting on the top of the dresser.

"I'm ready," Joey announced ten minutes early. And he was. Coat, hat, gloves, backpack—the works.

She handed him the diaper bag wordlessly. He didn't need her snapping at him. After all, it was Nick's head she wanted on a platter.

She drove to school lost in thoughts of how to step up the conflict with Nick. This had to end. Soon. She couldn't go through many more restless nights, or days where she fell behind in her work, hour by hour.

His motorcycle was already in the parking lot. She wondered how anybody could tolerate such a cold ride—the meteorologists were predicting record lows this week—but her perverse side wished for the wind to step up on his way home that afternoon. Joey flung his seat belt aside and bounced out of the car, so eager to get upstairs that she had to remind him to carry the diaper bag while she lugged in the portfolio and Christopher.

One look at Nick was her reward. Her encouragement. He was rumpled. She refused to think of it as "sexily rumpled," even though it was, with his black hair looking as though he'd forgotten to comb it this morning. Or maybe he'd been raking his fingers through it again, overcome with feelings of guilt and remorse over what his father had done, no thanks to his interference.

"You're here early." He sounded relieved.

She kept herself busy so as not to study him further, finding an out-of-harm's-way place for her portfolio, unbundling Christopher and hanging their coats in the closet that spanned the whole back wall of the classroom. She'd noticed too much about his hair already. And his eyes. A warm, hazel brown with golden flecks. Eyes that smiled in spite of the grim expression on his lips.

Her inner voice stepped up in his defense, reminding her he'd gone out of his way to bring her an adult-size chair yesterday.

She stepped on her inner voice. Thinking such positive thoughts about him was no way to make his life difficult and get out of his classroom.

"You look like you didn't get much sleep," she said, finally acknowledging him.

He ran his fingers through his hair, then absently tried to smooth it down. "I had a lot of phone calls from parents last night."

Hope surged through her, erasing the lingering effects of her bad night. "They called to complain about my being forced to stay here every day?'' Now, if she could only get them to call the judge.

"I wish." He didn't continue. Even though she knew his reticence was psychologically designed to get her attention, it worked; she looked at him. "They called to complain about the sex education yesterday."

Her eyebrows puckered as she thought back to the day before. "I must have dozed off there somewhere. I don't remember you teaching sex ed yesterday."

"That's because I didn't. *You* did. Breast-feeding 101."

"Oh, that." She dismissed his complaint with a wave of her hand. "They wouldn't have even noticed if you hadn't made a big deal out of it."

"Me? You should have heard their parents."

"Tell it to the judge."

"Ah, the judge. We had a little talk last night."

"Since no one called me with good news, I'll assume there isn't any."

"As a matter of fact, there is. He says you can go out to the hall to nurse Christopher."

From the glow on his face, she assumed he thought he'd made progress. She couldn't have that. "Where's my note?"

He looked as though he thought he should know what she was talking about, but, due to sleep deprivation, hadn't the slightest idea what she meant. "What note?"

"Didn't the judge send a note?"

"Why would he do that?"

"You wouldn't let a student out of class without a note, would you?"

"Of course not—"

"Well, then, since I have to sit in your classroom like a student, I have to have a note, too."

"That's ridiculous!"

"Oh, sure, you say that now. But what if I go out to the hall to nurse, and then the judge hears that I left your classroom and hauls me back into court?"

"He's the one that said it was all right."

"That's what you say. I want it in writing."

Nick threw his hands up in the air. His lips moved, but she couldn't tell whether he was cursing or praying. No matter; she'd gotten him rattled, and that's what she'd wanted.

When he finally managed to find his voice, all he said was, "Unbelievable!"

Nick couldn't believe what he was hearing. She doubted his word? In order to prove himself to the board, he was willing to substitute teach the fourth grade temporarily—just until Mr. Sherman recuperated. He wasn't so sure he was willing to take this kind of abuse, though.

One hand massaged the back of his neck. He rammed the other one into his jeans pocket. He kicked open the door to the hall.

"Where are you going?"

There was a musical quality to her voice, as though she thought she could fool him into thinking it an innocent query. He knew better.

"To find the nearest phone."

He knew where it was—on the secretary's desk. He strode right past it, slammed the door to the principal's office behind him, hard enough to rattle the glass, and jerked the telephone receiver off Mr. Nelson's desk. It took five minutes of ranting and raving and swearing he really was the judge's son, not some lunatic, before the woman on the courthouse phone would interrupt Judge Nicholson in chambers.

"Nick? Is that you?"

"Yeah, Dad—"

"Didn't she show up this morning?"

"Yes!"

"Then what are you calling me for?"

"You're not going to believe me when I tell you." Even he didn't believe it, and he'd been standing there when she said it.

"She came without Joey?"

"No, Dad, listen. She won't go out to the hall to breast-feed without a note from you."

He was rewarded with silence on the other end. It wasn't often he found his father speechless.

"Do you think she'd take my word for it over the phone?"

"Are you laughing?" Nick hadn't heard his father laugh since he'd come back to East Bay.

"No, son, I'm not laughing."

"Snickering, then. I'm stuck here with this madwoman, and you're snickering about it."

"Let me talk to her."

"Hold on." Nick wasn't too gentle about setting the receiver down on the wood desk. Perversely, he made sure it wasn't cushioned on the blotter, but banged on the wood soundly.

He waded through the halls of children, ignored the teachers who tried to get his attention and charged back up the stairs and into his classroom. "He wants to talk to you."

Hollie was kneeling on the blanket on the floor beside Christopher, laughing at his antics with every fourth-grade girl circled around her and the baby. She was still smiling from ear to ear as she glanced up and asked, "Who?"

"The judge."

"Now?"

"Yes, now."

"But I need to change Christopher."

Five girls shot their hands up in front of her face, vying for the privilege of showing off their maternal skills. That was all Nick needed, for the kids to go home and tell their parents they were studying the male anatomy in his class— in the flesh.

"I don't know," he argued, not too sure about the wisdom of such a move.

"Where did we leave off in the alphabet yesterday?" Hollie asked the girls.

Her smile was open and soft, and Nick wished it were for him. Not likely anytime in this century.

"Linda Magreggor." He grabbed Hollie by the hand and tugged her to her feet. He pinned little Linda with a no-nonsense glare. "You may watch him, but absolutely no diaper changing until Mrs. Landon returns."

"But, Nick—" Hollie said as she had no choice but to follow him out the door.

"He'll live. This won't take but five minutes."

He strode through the hallways with her in tow. He glanced back once, noting with some satisfaction that she had to jog to keep up with him. Unfortunately, he was also quick to zero in on how her full breasts bounced beneath her blue shirt.

He careened off the wall and nearly tripped her in the process.

"Watch it, Nicholson."

I was.

"I'd like to get there in one piece, if you don't mind."

He muttered, "Damned walls," and kept his eyes forward after that. He adjusted his pace to be more comfortable—telling himself it definitely was not for her, but so she couldn't claim later that it had affected her milk supply or something. He entered the principal's office without acknowledging anyone else's presence.

"What the hell?" he roared when he found the phone in its cradle.

"Good morning, Mr. Nicholson." The principal rose when he saw Hollie. "Mrs. Landon."

She stuck out her hand for the formalities, while Nick frantically punched in the number of the courthouse. When she looked as though she was going to leave the office and go back to Christopher, he grabbed her, circling her wrist with his long fingers and holding tight.

He was aware he probably came off sounding like a maniac this time, solely because he had Hollie's wrist in his hand. It wasn't tiny or delicate or fragile, and yet he was suddenly aware of the differences between them. Not just that he was bigger and stronger, but primitive man-woman stuff that boiled down to her being a new mother and how he should be protecting her, not imprisoning her. He was intrigued by such a cavemanlike attitude and wondered where it came from, but still he didn't let go.

She flexed her arm once to test his grasp—nothing she couldn't have gotten out of if she'd wanted to—and it didn't escape his notice that she didn't want her freedom very badly. Wondering why was enough to fluster him until he heard his father's voice.

"Here she is," he snapped into the phone, then shoved it toward her.

"This is Hollie Landon," she said in a tone that he knew was supposed to sound businesslike, but carried a slight tremor.

He didn't know whether it had to do with her having similar thoughts to those running through his mind, or because she was talking to a man who had the legal power to do any number of things to make her life miserable.

"I see." She glanced at Nick. "Yes, he told me, but I don't think it's really necessary." She listened a moment. "Well, thank you. No, your word's good enough for me."

He didn't ask what wasn't necessary. He knew she thought he was making a big deal about nothing, but he couldn't stand another day staring at her with Christopher at her breast, knowing she was exposed even if he couldn't see anything. Today she was wearing a chambray shirt, appliquéd with a red-and-green Christmas motif—trees, ornaments, garland and such. Thank God he was getting this taken care of now, before he was forced to watch her unbutton it one hole at a time. He concentrated on safer territory—her matching hair ribbon.

She handed him the phone and smiled up at him. "Now, wouldn't a note have been easier?"

He stared at her back as she left the office. The principal cleared his throat to hint that Nick should get out of there, too.

"Hey, Ed, can I ask you something?"

Ed sighed, but didn't remind him to address him as Mr. Nelson. "Yeah, sure."

"What do you think my chances are of getting hired on at the high school?"

Ed recited, "Cut your hair, sell your motorcycle, buy some slacks..." His voice trailed off.

"And?"

Ed glanced at the door through which Hollie had exited. "And remember she's the mother of one of your students."

Like I could forget. He'd give anything if he could.

Teaching high school had to be easier than this. Besides adding sex ed to his schedule, now he had to figure out how to win Hollie over and put an end to this war. Mostly because he was constantly losing.

His mother had always said he was too charming for his own good. He hoped she was right.

HOLLIE WAS USED to having an entire room of her small house at her disposal as an interior design studio. She'd covered the walls with light-colored cork for hanging sketches and swatches. She'd salvaged a huge, antique library table where she could illustrate with free-association. The only thing Nick's classroom had going for it was the bright light bouncing off the snow and streaming through the long wall of windows.

She had a few minutes before Nick returned to the classroom, and she used her time well. It wasn't something her teachers or her parents used to praise her for—just the opposite as a matter of fact. Too often she'd used her time to display some new, independent streak that had scandalized her family and set the nuns to saying extra rosaries.

Now, however, she excelled. Before Nick returned, she repapered his Christmas bulletin board with Snowflake Ball sketches, with the help of Mary Margaret, who handed her color-coded pushpins. Hollie was very careful to remember Terri's legal advice; she maintained an air of complete innocence in front of the children.

"Joey, Timmy, would you clear off Mr. Nicholson's desk for me?" They didn't ask what to do with his desk tray or pencil cup, and she didn't ask what happened to them. She spread out her ribbon and bow samples in an artistic arrangement, then stepped back to study them with a practiced eye.

Nick strode into the classroom. Twenty-five children rushed for their seats, leaving her alone in front of the room as Nick silently surveyed his newly decorated bulletin board. Hollie acknowledged his presence with what she hoped passed for a friendly smile, then pretended to resume working while she waited for him to blow his cork.

He circled his desk wordlessly. He glanced from the samples there to the sketches on the bulletin board and back again. He studied them. Hollie was as curious as the children as to his behavior and nearly broke down and asked him if it was all right if she used his desk. Fortunately, he turned abruptly toward the supply closet before she could weaken past the breaking point.

"Well, children, since today's lesson seems to have been misplaced, we're going to start a new subject," he announced. "I have some booklets here I've been saving."

As curious as the children, she watched as he pulled a cardboard box off the top shelf and plunged his hand inside. He counted out and handed five booklets to the first child in each row with instructions to pass them back. Little-boy snickers and whispers rippled progressively through the rows and alerted her that Nick was up to something.

When he strode toward her with an indecipherable gleam in his eyes, she stood her ground, her back to the chalkboard. The cardboard box was tucked in the crook of his arm, exactly the same way he toted his motorcycle helmet around. His free hand reached toward her, then raised upward. His arm extended past her ear, so close that she could smell fresh pine on his sleeve. The scent distracted her with pictures of Christmases past when she and her sisters used to gather by a fire and string their freshly cut tree with lights and popcorn. She struggled for control of her thoughts; better to concentrate on the present year's Snowflake Ball and how the heck she was going to get it done if she was stuck here in a room with him and twenty-six children, counting both her own.

As his arm lowered near her shoulder, so did the poster he unrolled on its bracket. "Today we're going to start sex education."

The children laughed and pointed. Hollie whirled around to see a large diagram of a male figure standing next to a female figure, much as she was standing next to Nick, but reversed.

Nick picked up his pointer. "We're going to start with the female."

In one swift glance, Hollie took in the chart, the pointer and Nick's devilish grin. The children called out suggestions and waved their arms like little traffic cops, trying to get Hollie and Nick to change places so they'd be lined up with the proper anatomical picture. She fled between two rows of desks to the relative safety of the back of the room.

Nick's pointer landed on the chart on his intended target's foot. "This is the female."

He can't be serious!

In her day, the nuns had taken the girls into one room while the priest talked to the boys in another. They'd shown a film. A gynecologist had come in and discussed monthly hygiene. And they'd been in sixth grade, not fourth!

"Mr. Nicholson." Hollie's voice sounded weak even to her own ears, and Nick didn't give any indication he'd heard her. She took a deep breath and repeated, more firmly, "Mr. Nicholson."

"We'll have questions after the lesson, Mrs. Landon."

Her hands balled into fists. Her teeth gritted. "I don't have a question."

Twenty-four pairs of eyes flitted back and forth between them. The other pair belonged to Joey, who sat between two girls. She'd seen that look on his face before. He was bored.

Another deep breath as she counted to ten. "I have a suggestion. I think you should—"

"Class has started, Mrs. Landon. Please take your seat."

"But—"

"Maybe she has to use the ladies' room," a little girl piped up. "You're supposed to raise your hand and hold up two fingers so Mr. Nicholson knows where you're going."

"Thank you, Kathleen, but I don't think Mrs. Landon has to follow that rule while she's here."

"Why not?"

Hollie tuned out Nick's answer, easier that than the twinkle in his eyes. She was much more concerned right now with Joey's behavior. While the two dozen other fourth-graders were intent on this adult exchange, Joey was bored?

Well, she knew he knew a lot about the birds and bees already. She'd very carefully explained what he'd needed to know about Christopher's conception and birth. After all, there was no man in her life, and she didn't want Joey to grow up believing in Christopher's immaculate conception. But he should at least be a nice shade of pink, sitting between two pretty little girls for such a delicate topic.

"You should separate the boys from the girls for this subject," she blurted out.

The children's heads whipped back and forth as if they were at a tennis match. Joey yawned and didn't even try to hide it.

"You think?" Nick asked with what sounded like naïveté about his near catastrophic mistake.

She was relieved that he was finally seeing the light. Good thing she was there; if he thought he had a lot of parents calling him last night, it would have been nothing compared to the mistake he'd almost made.

"Okay. All the girls move to the desks by the windows. Boys, take the other side."

Not only the children stared at him with horrified looks, but Hollie, too.

"Come on, move." He wandered among them, urging them along as they crept out of their desks.

The children's expressions changed from horror and shock to confusion at this unheard-of arrangement, then to frowns of displeasure. They poked. They groaned. They dragged their feet and dropped their books and tripped one another on purpose. And through it all, Nick just stood there with a stupid grin on his face, aimed right at Hollie.

Joey's bored yawns gave way to pouting as he pushed out his lower lip and left it there. He kicked his new desk. He slumped in it. He opened the lid, looked inside, then slammed it.

Hollie was strong and firm at parenting when she had to be, but was this one of those times? She was, after all, on Joey's turf. He would have to spend every day here after the judge let her return to her normal routine. Should she just give up and give in? Go with the flow? Maybe she was making a big deal out of nothing, as Nick had yesterday with breast-feeding.

Nah. It wasn't nothing, but it was just one battle in the war for her freedom. She could forge ahead and risk Joey's discomfort, or she could give up, give in and "do her time."

Giving up now would set a bad example for Joey. He needed to learn about principles in action, especially since *her* presence in his class was a consequence of *his* actions. But retreating gracefully from one skirmish didn't mean she was giving up. Otherwise, if she pursued this, maybe all the other parents would be mad and calling *her* tonight, and she had precious little time to work as it was.

She took her seat.

"Thank you, Mrs. Landon. Now children..."

She wasn't giving up, though. The judge's order was unfair. She had to show him—and Nick—the error of his ways before the school was full of parents just like her.

IT WAS THE LONGEST morning Nick could remember. Longer than his first day as a teacher solely in charge of nine- and ten-year-olds, when his real love was high school and drama. Give him a stage and a script, not a small class-room and a sketchy curriculum. Especially not one that in-cluded the birds and the bees. Apparently that analogy had gone out of style since he'd been a kid. *That* he could have handled. Maybe.

He got through fifteen minutes of sex education without looking once in Hollie's direction, then decided he couldn't take any more pressure and changed subjects. If the princi-pal asked if he'd tackled the topic yet, he could honestly say he had. He'd wait to do more until he could see what kind of phone calls he was going to get from the parents tonight. He hoped none, because he really needed to get some new scenery painted for the Christmas play. Normally, the art teacher took care of that, but she'd been in Sherman's car at the time of the accident.

The morning was nearly over. The children were quietly absorbed in their work, in spite of Christopher's fussiness, when Nick noticed Hollie settling him on her lap. When she reached for an ornament-shaped button on her shirt, Nick cleared his throat quietly and cocked his head toward the door.

She sighed. He squelched a grin. No need to tell her she reminded him of Joey at such a time, but he wondered if Joey had learned "the sigh" from her, or vice versa.

With a huff, she stood and carried Christopher out into the hall. Nick figuratively patted himself on the back for his strong but silent handling of the situation.

It didn't last long.

Within a minute, she was back. "Sorry," she mouthed as she tiptoed in. She cradled Christopher against her chest as she crossed the back of the room, grasped the top of her straight chair and dragged it behind her toward the door.

As the chair legs scraped across the floor, the children turned in their seats, their concentration broken. As the door banged shut behind her, they squirmed and glanced at the clock.

"Okay," Nick said softly, "back to work."

The children were just settling down when the door opened again. Hollie tiptoed in and mouthed, "Sorry," with an apologetic smile that he knew would earn her an Oscar if she ever took up acting as a profession. She retrieved the diaper bag and left the classroom without another word or sound—except for the bang of the door shutting behind her.

She opened it again and poked her head in. "Sorry," she stage-whispered, then disappeared.

Timmy dropped his pencil. Mary Margaret twisted her red hair around her fingers. Joey sighed. Linda raised her hand in the air, two fingers up. Nick didn't know from what century Mr. Sherman had gotten that code. He glanced at the clock.

"Just a few more minutes, Linda. Wait for the bell."

The bell! The entire school would be in the hall in three minutes, headed for the cafeteria. Not only the parents of his students would be calling him tonight, but the entire school body would go home and tell their mothers and fathers there'd been a woman sitting in the hall with her breasts exposed. His only hope was to insist Hollie come back into the classroom to nurse.

And therein lay his dilemma. If he did that, he'd be stuck with watching her nurse Christopher on a daily basis until December 23. If he didn't, he might as well get back on his motorcycle and leave town because every member of the high school board would just nod their head and say, "I could tell by the way he was dressed that he was too radical for us.''

Two minutes to the bell. He really had no choice. He had to hurry or he'd be trapped in the hall with her, and then the story the children would tell their parents would be that there had been a woman in the hall with her breasts exposed . . . in front of Mr. Nicholson.

Chapter Four

Hollie patted Christopher on the back. She hummed to him softly, swaying soothingly as she walked the halls.

He'd have none of it. If he could have talked, he would have blubbered, "I want my bed and I want it *now!*"

It occurred to her that maybe she was going about this all wrong. Maybe she should pop in at the judge's house each evening to show him how crabby a baby got when his routine was interrupted—like going to fourth grade about nine years too early. She'd ring his doorbell, burst inside when he opened the door, then sit in his living room until Christopher dropped off to sleep. That should be about midnight, if she had to guess. See how the high-and-mighty Judge Nicholson liked having *his* routine interrupted.

But then he could summon the police to drag her off, so that wasn't too good an idea. She could do the same thing at Nick's place. His only recourse would be to call up his father and beg him to reconsider.

Though the thought of sitting in a room—in Nick's house, his personal territory—with him all evening, without a lot of children to act as a buffer, was disturbing. What would they talk about?

It didn't matter; she wouldn't be there to talk. But if she didn't talk to him, she'd be staring at him and thinking about him. And that would definitely get her into trouble. She'd wonder where his bedroom was. Then she'd wonder what a macho, motorcycle guy such as he wore to bed. Probably nothing.

Hollie's mouth went dry.

She'd have to use his bathroom at some point in the evening. His shaving cream would be there. His razor. An image leapt into focus of him standing in front of the sink, a towel slung loosely around his hips while he looked in the mirror and shaved.

Christopher squirmed, and Hollie realized she'd tensed up. She relaxed as much as possible, which wasn't much, and sat down in the chair she'd dragged out to the hall. For the first time ever, she disliked owning such a vivid imagination. She was far safer thinking about harassing the judge and then talking her way out of him having her carted off.

She was weighing the merits of that idea when Nick came tearing around the doorjamb of his classroom. As the lunch bell rang, he raised his jacket up with both hands as if he were going to throw it over her. As if she had no sense.

She bit her lip trying not to burst out laughing at the comical look of relief on his face. She twisted in the chair and turned her back on him. It was obvious he thought she was out here doing some kind of breast-feeding striptease to get even with him. Not that he didn't deserve it, and not that she wouldn't have fleetingly considered it back when she was younger. But Joey had to go to school here for several more years and he didn't deserve it. Funny how having a kid tended to mellow her; it put a definite crimp in how far she could go to get what she wanted. What she deserved.

"Uh, Holl...Mrs. Landon..."

She could barely hear him over the hoards of kids swarming through doors and roughhousing on the way to the cafeteria. When she composed herself enough to turn and face him, she noticed he now wore his jacket and the remnants of a slowly receding red face. She'd succeeded in making his day difficult. She bit her lip, harder this time, to keep from smiling in triumph.

"Mr. Nicholson, just the person I need. Can you hold Christopher while I use the rest room?" Without waiting for an answer, she stood and leaned toward him to shift her son to a new set of hands, a new chest, with as little disruption as possible.

And such a broad chest it was, framed by the zippered edges of his black leather jacket, which lent him a rebel aura. Something she could identify with, if she wanted. Which she didn't, because that would only complicate matters. Better to stick to the business at hand.

"Here, you have to support his bottom."

She left Nick little choice about taking Christopher from her. She'd intended to force her son on him for a few minutes; she needed some time to take care of herself and there wasn't a baby-sitter in sight that she'd trust just then. She hadn't intended to get so close or make him so uneasy that his large hands would, in an effort not to drop the baby, brush against her breast. Her shirt actually, as her placket was securely buttoned again, but she felt the contact as strongly as if his fingers had touched bare skin.

She jumped. Slightly, to be sure, but it was so obvious to her that she felt her face flame. "Got him?" she squeaked.

"Yeah. What do I do with him?"

When she saw his attention was riveted on Christopher and not on how close they were standing or how close they had come, she was able to recover her poise. "Hold him. I'll only be gone a couple minutes."

The children had all disappeared into the cafeteria, and Hollie walked down the empty hall, extremely conscious of Nick's gaze following her. Was he watching the sway of her hips? Or was he staring daggers at her back for leaving him unexpectedly in charge of four-month-old Christopher, wondering what the heck to do until she returned? She didn't turn around to see.

Nick stared at the infant cradled in his hands. He was small and warm and soft. He smelled of baby powder.

Christopher scowled and whimpered.

"Hey there, fella," Nick crooned softly in a voice he'd never heard himself use before.

Christopher screwed up his face and wailed.

"Oh, great. You start that, and I'll really be in the dog-house." Nick tried to remember what Hollie did when the baby got fussy.

Nope, can't do that.

He'd been around babies before. He couldn't remember when exactly, but he'd seen women rock them, jiggle them, pat them on their backs. He tried it, only to find it was as awkward as when he'd been in junior high and someone had asked if he could rub his stomach and pat his head at the same time. It took practice.

He started with the rocking and swaying. At the same time, he paced the hall, looking for one of his students who might have decided not to eat lunch today. Mary Margaret was particularly good with Christopher. For the past day and a half, though, she'd been following Joey around with a moonstruck look; she was probably with him at this very minute.

Nick added a light, rhythmic patting motion on the baby's back. His cheek rubbed against the soft hair in a soothing embrace as old as time. Christopher quit wailing, but he still fussed.

Nick reevaluated his position. Dumping the baby on one of the girls in his class wouldn't set a very good example. It would show them men were useless around babies. It would show the boys there was an acceptable inequality between the sexes. It would show Hollie he couldn't handle absolutely anything she threw his way.

On the other hand, if he could quiet the baby and impress the heck out of Hollie, it would help him get on her good side. She'd warm up to him. She'd already kissed his cheek once. He'd been caught totally off guard that time. He'd be ready in the future.

"BETH-LE-HEM," Nick gently corrected Timmy. "Not Beth'lhamburger." He repeated it slowly and had all the children say it out loud for the twentieth time since play practice had started an hour ago at the stage end of the gymnasium.

He reminded himself they were only nine and ten years old. This wasn't Broadway. It wasn't even off-off-Broadway. But he was too aware that Hollie had parked herself in the third row to watch. In the two days they'd been thrown together, she'd proven what Nick had guessed just from knowing Joey; she was as near a perfect mother as a woman could get. If he were the single parent trying to work out of his home and support two children, and a judge came along and did to him what his father had done to her, he didn't know how he would handle it. His past history was to stick out his thumb and leave town, but he certainly hoped he'd outgrown that.

Now that he'd seen what she did best, he felt an urge to show her what he did best. It wasn't teaching fourth grade. It wasn't comforting her baby while she went to the rest room—which had earned him a polite thank-you and nothing more.

Nick was at his best teaching drama. He knew it. Acting students knew it. The colleges that had offered him teaching positions knew it—and they hadn't cared that he was a little overdue at the barber, that his jeans were faded nearly to oblivion or that he wore a black leather jacket and rode a motorcycle. But the rebel inside had wanted to return in glory to teach at his old alma mater, in a town that still held the same values and traditions that had driven him nuts years ago. And now he wanted to impress a woman he'd known only a couple of days.

What better way to do that than run herd on twenty-five kids, whip the play into shape the likes of which this town had never seen before *and* put a new coat of paint on Baby Jesus at the same time?

Joey's attention was diverted by his little brother's fussiness and he hopped off the stage—whether to complain or console, Nick didn't know.

"What's the matter with him?" Joey asked as he hovered over Christopher in his infant seat. "Is he hungry again?"

"No, honey—"

"Does he need changing again?"

"No, I checked."

"But he's always so good. Why's he crabby now?"

Hollie smiled at Joey. "Sometimes babies just need to know they're loved and safe." She reached down and gave the baby a loving pat under Joey's curious eye. Christopher gurgled his gratitude. "See?"

Nick's view of Hollie and her family was blocked as Linda ran over to him, blubbering. "Mr. Nicholson?"

"Yes, Linda?"

"Timmy says I have to be the donkey's ass."

Nick shot a dark look in Timmy's direction, who was suddenly very occupied with practicing his pronunciation of Bethlehem. Out of the corner of his eye, he watched a grin spread across Hollie's lips. So much for impressing the heck out of her.

"Of course you don't have to play the donkey's...
behind, Linda. Okay, kids, that's enough for today. Say
your lines for your parents at home tonight, and I'll see you
in the morning."

Nick laid his thin paintbrush down and took a close look
at what little touch-up work he'd gotten done in the past
hour. He blew on the last little dab to dry it.

"His finger's broken," Joey noted.

"Yeah, I know. It was broken twenty years ago when I
was in this play, too."

"Really?"

"Did Mr. Nelson give your class that this-nativity-is-
thirty-years-old-so-take-good-care-of-it speech before I
started substituting?"

"Uh-huh. Only he said it was fifty."

"I guess it is, now."

Nick wanted to say that Mr. Nelson should get a life and
realize this was only a statue, but he knew Ed—and many
others in East Bay just like him—would never change. Joey,
the truant, didn't need Nick, the rebel, putting ideas in his
head. He and his mom were in enough trouble already. And
truth be told, Nick had come back here because he wanted
to teach kids whose parents instilled values in them. It
seemed values and tradition went hand in hand in East Bay.

"Are you gonna fix His finger?"

Nick sighed. "I wish I had the time, but I don't think
anybody that doesn't already know will notice." He smelled
baby powder and vanilla, and looked up to see Hollie hovering near his shoulder. "Unless, of course, you'd let me put
Christopher in the manger?"

"You already have your hands full," she said.

"Yeah, it was just a thought."

"Isn't there someone to help?"

"Yeah, normally two people, but one's got a fractured pelvis and the other's too sore to do anything but answer a few questions over the phone—like where the key to the prop room was."

"Well, the parents or the room mothers should be helping you."

"I don't mind doing a little painting."

"But you have more important things to do."

This was one of the few opportunities he had to be around her without worrying about what two dozen kids would go home and report to their parents. "Hey, Joey, would you put Baby Jesus away for me? You know where He goes, don't you?"

"Sure, Mr. Nicholson." Joey took the statue and carefully carried it toward the prop room, where it had its very own blanket-lined drawer.

"I'll meet you at the car," Hollie called after him. "Two minutes, no more." She turned to Nick. "I won't keep you. I just wanted to remind you to talk to your dad tonight about changing his mind."

As if I could forget. He just wasn't sure anymore what he wanted to say to his dad.

"I'll be happy to call him." It wasn't exactly a lie. He'd call him, all right, but he knew, what with all the publicity his dad had been getting over Friday's controversial ruling, that his dad's phone would be off. He waved his arm toward the stage with its shabby stable and manger props. "*If I get time.*"

"Well, I'm sure having me in your classroom is cramping your style. You'll have much more time when you convince your father I shouldn't be here."

If her business relied on sales pitches like that, he knew she'd be a whopping success. He watched her walk across the gymnasium floor and out the door, Christopher's cherubic face peering back at him over her shoulder. The room suddenly felt empty. Who would've thought that adding two more people to his classroom during the day would make him feel lonely later?

His father?

No way. He was sure his father wouldn't have done anything so rash. True, Nick had complained he didn't know what to do about Joey's truancy. It had been over dinner at the judge's house one Sunday evening. Nick certainly hadn't been seeking a legal remedy; he'd just wanted a little advice—for two reasons. One, he needed the advice. And two, he thought approaching his father on common ground would give the two of them something to talk about. They'd worn out reminiscing over the time he'd been playing Tarzan in the orchard and broken his arm, the beagle he'd grown up with and his high school football career.

Nick strolled closer to the window and watched Hollie buckle Christopher in, in spite of the snowball Joey targeted right smack in the middle of her back. She playfully scooped up a handful of her own, but the little monster laughed and ducked in the passenger side.

He tried to envision tomorrow if the judge rescinded his order. Hollie wouldn't come to class with Joey. He'd be all alone in a classroom full of nine- and ten-year-olds, who'd been taught the correct way to request a bathroom pass was to raise their hand with two fingers up. Nick shuddered and said a quick prayer he would be offered a position on the high school staff the day after the Christmas play.

As it stood now, she'd continue to come every day. He could get to know her a little better in their hours together and see if maybe, sometime after Christmas, he might want to ask her out. If the judge rescinded his order, Nick would lose that opportunity to get to know her beforehand when there was less pressure. Not good; almost depressing. And if he rescinded the order and Joey cut again, there was no telling what his dad would do next. If he'd threatened contempt charges before, he might find some way to lock Hollie up to make a point, send a message or whatever the hell the old man was trying to do.

All in all, the status quo was looking pretty good from where he stood.

JOEY LAUGHED as he buckled his seat belt. "Gotcha, Mom."

She backed out of the parking space, then tossed him an evil grin. "You're not safe in the house yet, buddy."

"Uh, I have to go right in and do my homework."

Her eyebrows arched.

He lifted his backpack off the floor and hugged it in his lap. "See?"

It bulged at the seams. "I didn't hear Mr. Nicholson assign *that* much."

"Well, uh, there's no sense putting it off."

She felt his forehead with the back of her hand. "Who are you and what did you do with my son?"

He laughed and pushed her hand away. "Well, you know, Santa's watching."

"I thought we discussed Santa last year."

Joey held his finger up to his lips dramatically and glanced at Christopher in the back seat. No wonder he'd been picked for the lead in the play.

"Oh, pu-lease," Hollie said. "He's four months old."

"Gotta get in practice, Mom."

Hollie gave up. If the kid said he was going to study, who was she to complain? She could make good use of the extra time that would give her to finish the elves for the Snowflake Ball. They should have been done days ago.

WHEW! THAT WAS close.

Joey knew he'd have to be more careful if he didn't want to be found out. Stuffing Baby Jesus into his backpack had seemed like a good idea fifteen minutes ago. His teacher wanted Christopher to be in the Christmas play; his mom didn't. But if there was no Baby Jesus statue, she'd have to give in.

He always *tried* to be good. Sometimes he had to make choices, though. His mom said part of growing up was learning to make decisions. She promised it would get easier as he got older, but he was almost ten and it wasn't getting any easier yet.

In fact, sometimes it seemed downright impossible.

"HEY, POPS, let me in," Nick called to the night custodian through the glass door of the high school.

Ernest Dobbs, as stooped over as he'd been when Nick had been the hellion of East Bay High, shuffled a straight line to the door. He studied Nick through the glass before turning the lock and stepping back so he could enter. "You're a bit late for graduation, Nicholson." His chuckle wasn't lost in his constant wheeze.

Nick stuffed his hands into his jeans pockets as he gazed around the commons. He'd seldom seen it so empty. "Mind if I check out the auditorium?"

"I heard you wanted to be an actor. No market for that in East Bay."

Nick grinned. Of all the people in town who'd wanted to say that to him, only Dobbs had the spine to do it. "I was wrong. I want to be a teacher—a high school teacher. In drama, of course."

"Of course. Well, break a leg, kid." Dobbs turned and wheezed his way down the hall. "But not on my shift."

Nick let himself into the dark auditorium. He flipped the lights on one by one, slowly bringing it to life. Nothing in this life happened instantly, he'd found. One step at a time. One light at a time. And when the large room with its sloped floor and padded seats was fully illuminated, Nick strolled down the achingly familiar aisle.

Someday. Someday I'll teach students here.

He'd have students who could pronounce Bethlehem without murdering it. Students who could take direction and knew their right from their left a hundred percent of the time. Students who could remember their lines, who could catch a ride with friends instead of relying on their mothers to fit them into predetermined carpool schedules, and who wanted to be on stage as much as he wanted to direct them.

"Find what you're looking for?"

Nick jumped, so absorbed that he hadn't even heard Dobbs's wheezing behind him. He turned and clapped his hand on the older man's shoulder. "At least now I *know* what I'm looking for."

"Well, I guess it's true, then."

"What's that?"

"Me'n the other custodians sometimes wonder whether high school kids ever grow up." He studied Nick carefully. "If you did, I guess there's hope for the rest of 'em."

Nick grinned. "As usual, Dobbs, you're the first one in town to know what the heck's going on."

Wednesday, December 18

HOLLIE THOUGHT the classroom was empty when she arrived, until she saw Nick standing at the doorway of the supply closet. His hair was rumpled and badly in need of someone—her, perhaps?—to run their fingers through it and smooth it. That boyish lock still dipped over his forehead, pointing southward to warm hazel eyes that had no place in a classroom. If those weren't bedroom eyes, she didn't know what were.

"I guess I'm early."

Her voice sounded far away as she noticed he wasn't wearing a shirt. The breadth of his smooth, bare chest was emphasized by his open jacket, his maleness accentuated by the dark leather and prominent zippers. The incongruity of the setting—they were in the dead of winter and he was running around bare chested—didn't occur to her. How could it? He was magnificent. She couldn't breathe. Her knees wobbled, and she leaned on the wooden chair he'd brought in for her comfort on Monday. He'd carried it into the room with one hand. She glanced at his hands, expecting to see they were large and powerful, instead finding them hovering over the worn fly on his jeans. Dangerous territory. Where the heck were all those little chaperons they'd had the past two days?

His hand moved.

He wouldn't.

He popped the button below his navel.

We're in an elementary classroom, for chrissakes.

He inched the zipper downward.

She remembered him tearing around the corner of the doorjamb at the sound of the lunch bell, jacket in hand to throw over her. *And he'd thought I didn't have enough modesty?*

She saw no sign of briefs. Her mouth went dry. The rest of her broke out in a sweat. To touch or not to touch; the invitation was there.

The bell rang. She plopped into the chair before she threw herself in his arms and twenty-five children poured into the room to witness it.

The bell continued to ring. Only one child showed up, and he was shaking her shoulder.

"Mo-om. Get up or we'll be late."

She pushed her hair back out of her face, not surprised to find it clung to her sweaty skin.

"Are you sick? You look funny."

She glanced at the alarm clock, then, feeling as if she were moving in slow motion, found the right button to turn it off. "I'm fine," she lied. She forced her traitorous body to throw off the covers and sit up.

Joey peered at her more closely. "You can stay home if you have a temperature."

Too close. She reached out and rumpled his hair, wishing she had something so simple as a temperature. *That* she could cure. *That* would go away. The only treatment for what ailed her was too drastic to even contemplate.

How could she look at Nick all day now? She'd never wondered about a man's underwear before. Now she'd wonder, not about his choice between briefs and boxers, but whether he preferred to be au naturel beneath his jeans. He looked just rebellious enough to do it.

She distracted herself with the thought that he chose really low briefs. Ugly white ones with holes worn in them.

"Mom?"

"You'd better go get dressed. I'll take a quick shower."

"But you showered before you went to bed."

"What's your point?"

"You *must* be sick."

For the first time ever, Hollie took a cold shower. In a chilly bathroom with an outside wall in the middle of December, it worked. She forgot all about her erotic dream and had to rush to school because she was fifteen minutes behind schedule.

"Do you have all your books?" she asked Joey as she drove.

"Yeah."

"Your bag doesn't look as full as last night."

He wrapped his arms possessively around the backpack sitting on his lap. "Uh, I took my extra shoes out."

"Extra shoes?"

"Yeah, I, uh, took a pair for Timmy to see."

She pulled into the parking lot, saw Nick's motorcycle and forgot her resolution to not think of him. He had no right to be in her dream in the first place. Just because he was a nice guy who went out of his way once to get her a chair was no reason to lose it over him. Well, okay, he also was concerned about Joey's welfare, in a misguided, confused, interfering sort of way, but that was no reason for her subconscious to set the man up on a striptease.

Joey helped her lug her stuff upstairs. She paused outside the classroom door, set down her portfolio and smoothed a hand over her hair. It wouldn't do at all if he thought she was late because she'd lost any sleep over him.

She caught a reflection of herself in the glass in the door, her hand busy trying to rearrange the mess the cold wind had made of her hair.

"This is ridiculous," she muttered. She yanked the portfolio off the floor.

This will never do! She had to make this her last day, no matter what it took. And if she needed her secret weapon, it was already loaded in her station wagon.

THE RECESS BELL RANG, and the children rushed to the coat closet. In their hurry to get outside, they left behind mittens and hats and didn't zip their coats. Nothing earth shattering. But Hollie dreaded being alone with Nick, and she would have liked nothing better than to go to each one and do up their outerwear for them. Then again, she needed to ask how he'd done with the judge last night, even though she hadn't gotten a phone call and she really already knew the answer.

Nick saw the last child out the door, then turned and strolled toward her. She paced the floor by the windows.

"I was worried when you weren't here on time," he said.

"I was late."

He smiled. "I figured that out all by myself."

She could have slapped herself for such an inane comment. "Sorry, I didn't sleep too well." If she kept *this* up, they'd be toting her away in a white jacket by noon. "How'd you do with the judge?"

Nick shoved his hands into the front pockets of his worn jeans, drawing her eyes downward to where she didn't want them to be as she watched his fingers inch down against his pelvis. She turned abruptly and stared out the window.

"No luck." When she didn't reply, he stepped closer, peeking around her shoulder for a closer look. "You okay?"

She whirled on him, her jaw clenched. "Stop being nice to me!"

He backed off one step and studied her.

She folded her arms across her chest. "And stop staring at me," she snapped.

He smiled sympathetically. "Christopher keep you up all night?"

"No, trying to figure out how to get out of this stupid sentence did."

He shrugged. "I'm afraid chances of that are pretty slim."

"It doesn't help matters when your father refuses to answer his phone all evening."

"He can be very stubborn."

"So can I." She threw open the nearest window and yelled down to the playground, "Joey, I need you to help me get something out of the car."

NICK STOOD AT THE BOARD, chalk in hand, his back to the children as he demonstrated how to solve an arithmetic problem they were having difficulty with. "And four from nine is..."

Instead of an answer, he heard a whir. An electrical whir. He spun on his heel and zeroed in on Hollie. She sat in her straight chair, facing the front edge of a child-size desk, her head bent over her task.

"Mrs. Landon," he said so sharply that the children jumped. He strode to the back of the room. The children pivoted in their desks so as not to miss anything. "Mrs. Landon!"

She glanced up from her sewing machine. "Oh, don't mind me, Mr. Nicholson."

"I have to make a living, you know."

She lifted the foot, adjusted the fabric of the tree skirt she was piecing, then lowered the foot and set the machine to whirring again. "So do I."

He felt his hands ball into fists. He recognized the old urge to punch and run, the one from his high school days when he'd taken on any boy who hadn't the sense to stay out of his way. He looked down on thick brunette waves cascading over a very independent set of feminine shoulders, and he squelched that urge. They were just two people, butting their heads against a brick wall, trying to do what they loved in order to earn a living. His wall was the high school board. Hers was the legal system.

Hollie paused in her sewing and looked up at him. "Tomorrow's Thursday."

He nodded, wondering what that had to do with anything except that, by tomorrow morning, she'd have three days of her sentence out of the way. He didn't need any more time to know he wanted to see more of her—when this was all over and definitely outside of the classroom.

"I do volunteer work on Thursdays. If you can't convince the judge by tonight, I'll have to do it here."

She bent her head over her work and set the machine to whirring again. Nick glanced at his class, wondering how much time he could spend trying to drag the information about the nature of her volunteer work out of her, knowing she wasn't going to tell him. He had to try.

"What kind of volunteer work do you do?"

"You'll see."

He strode back to the front of the room, muttering, "That's what I'm afraid of." He'd ask Joey later.

SEX EDUCATION wasn't as tough as Nick had feared. He knew all the answers to the boys' questions and any they were likely to come up with, unless, of course, they asked him how to figure out women. As to the girls' questions, so far he'd known all the answers. Kids weren't too technical at this age. And not too shy, either, he noticed as Linda's hand went up again.

"Yes, Linda?"

"How come Mary's a virgin?"

"Mary who?" slipped out before he realized, as a teacher, he shouldn't be answering *that* question with another question.

"The Virgin Mary."

He breathed a sigh of relief to hear they weren't discussing someone's sister. "Oh."

"My brother says if a woman has a baby and a husband, she can't be a virgin."

If he'd thought he would dread sex ed, it was nothing compared to the horror of mixing it with religion. "Mary was an exception to the rule." He hoped that would handle it and gladly turned to another hand when it shot up. "Yes, Mary Margaret?"

"Is Joey's mom a 'ception to the rule, too?"

"Joey's mom?" He glanced at Hollie, wondering why Mary Margaret would ask such a question. Hollie was quietly sketching, totally absorbed in her work and unconcerned about how he would answer.

"She had a baby without a husband, so does that make her a virgin?"

"Mr. Landon died recently," Nick said as tactfully as he could muster. A bit of quick math in his head confirmed the man had to have been alive at least thirteen months ago to have sired Christopher. That was recent enough to qualify in his explanation. "She had a husband when she got pregnant."

"No, she didn't," Joey said, seemingly surprised that anyone would think so.

Nick had barely a second to wonder why Hollie wasn't on his case about the way this discussion was headed.

Joey volunteered, "He died two years ago."

Nick saw Hollie's reputation shred to pieces before his eyes, knowing every child in class would repeat this discussion at home tonight, and not knowing how to stop it. Other than to give her a chance to redeem herself, of course.

"Maybe Mrs. Landon would like to respond to that?"

Chapter Five

"Mrs. Landon?"

Hollie's hand hovered over Nick's navel. He was bare chested beneath her pencil, showing off the same broad, smooth, hard chest as he'd done in her dream last night, gracing her sketch pad with far too much masculinity to be contained by mere paper. The same naughty-little-boy lock of dark hair tumbled down over his forehead, drawing her eyes unwillingly, unerringly to a gaze hot enough to sizzle a weaker woman's blood. Hers was close to boiling just remembering how his long fingers had eased down his zipper and how he'd teased her with a view of firm, flat stomach and no briefs.

He wasn't wearing jeans in her sketch. He wasn't *not* wearing them, either; she just hadn't filled in any below-the-belt details that she would be embarrassed for one of the children to see. Or to question her about as only a relentless fourth-grader could do with an odd mixture of naiveté and going-on-thirty wisdom.

She'd intended to make several working sketches for the Snowflake Ball decorations, but there was Nick, black leather jacket and all, standing in front of the multipaned bay window where the fifteen-foot Christmas tree was supposed to go. And Nick leaning against the balustrade where the pine roping was supposed to swag its way, complete with large, red velvet bows, up the curved staircase to the second story. And Nick beside the wide oak mantel where the candles were supposed to flicker and glow above a crackling fire. And there was nothing *saint*ly about the way she was viewing this particular Nick.

If she couldn't keep her mind on her work, he was at least *supposed* to wear jeans on the long legs that materialized beneath her fingers on the paper. She gripped her pencil with a firm hand, determined to cover with denim and boots the set of well-defined legs, the same ones that straddled a Harley and roared through town on a daily basis.

With a mother's well-seasoned ear, she grew increasingly aware that the classroom had gotten too quiet. Her head still bent over the page, she glanced up through lowered lashes, as if any sudden movement on her part might draw attention to herself and the body she shouldn't be sketching. The children were all turned in their desks, staring at her, waiting for... what? An answer?

Had Nick or one of the children asked her a question? Was she supposed to come up with some sort of a response here? Momentary panic set in, reminiscent of being back in school and having the teacher call on her when she'd been doodling instead of paying attention. The judge never said she had to pay attention.

She was more than a little surprised to find Nick hovering a mere foot away from her chair. When had he gotten so close? She ever so casually draped her arm over the page and hoped he hadn't seen anything except the Christmas tree, the balustrade and the mantel.

"Sorry. Did—" she cleared her throat to banish the huskiness from her voice "—did you ask me something?"

His eyes were hooded—whether to hide amusement or confusion, she wasn't certain.

"A question came up regarding virgins that I can't answer."

A grin spread slowly across her face as she wondered if he didn't know the answer or was just too embarrassed to share. "I *told* you to segregate the boys from the girls."

He indicated the class with an encompassing sweep of his arm, a white piece of chalk clutched between his fingers and thumb. "You want me to split them up again?"

"No!" She couldn't bear that again. She didn't have to help him teach his class, but if the kids needed to know something he couldn't tell them, what the heck? "Maybe I can help. What was the question?"

"They want to know, since you had a baby without benefit of a husband, if that makes you a virgin?"

Her eyebrows arched in delight. "And you don't know the answer to that?"

"I think they want a few more details."

She wanted to wipe the grin off his face and the amused twinkle from his warm hazel eyes. And she knew just how to do it.

"Well, Mr. Nicholson, it's your class. If you think they're ready to learn about freezing sperm and artificial insemination..." Her explanation tapered off as she let him absorb the implications.

Murmurs and whispers rustled among the children as they wiggled in their seats. Nick's grin faded abruptly; the twinkle dimmed slightly. He raked a hand through his hair. He glanced at the clock.

Hollie didn't feel the least little bit guilty. She let him stew while she closed her pad. She was more concerned about whether he'd seen what she was sketching than how he was going to explain artificial birds and bees to the children. If he hadn't seen himself taking form on the paper—and what form!—she considered herself lucky. This time. She put the pencil away; she obviously couldn't be trusted with one in her hand. She looked up to find Joey facing the blackboard, chalk in hand, drawing.

"This is an egg." The circle was large enough for everyone to see. "And this is a sperm." He drew a tiny circle and aimed it for the larger one by sticking on a wiggly tail.

"Uh, Joey—"

"Just a minute, Mom," he said with dismissal and continued to address an all-ears roomful of children.

Joey was now teaching sex education for Nick? Hollie wasn't sure whether to interrupt again; it was Nick's class, after all. She'd wanted to wipe the grin off his face, and Joey had managed to do it for her. She'd let him continue unless he went too far.

"The doctor takes the egg and mixes it with sperm in a little dish, and then puts that in the mom's uterus. And that's how it's done."

Hollie studied the basic diagram Joey had drawn on the chalkboard. The egg to sperm ratio was accurate enough, and at least he was no longer bored. He'd kept everything straight and hadn't fed his classmates any erroneous information that would come back to haunt her—unless she'd missed something when she was trying to hide her sketches from Nick.

"How's he put it in the uterus?" Mary Margaret asked.

Nick's tan—what little he had left by midwinter—blanched to white.

"JOEY, I'D LIKE to talk to you for a minute."

Hollie had stepped out of the classroom a short while ago with Christopher, and Nick wasn't about to let this golden opportunity slip by. He needed to find out what kind of volunteer work Hollie was threatening to bring to class tomorrow. Joey, his coat unzipped and flapping, was on his way to recess, elbowing and squeezing his way out the door with his friends. Nick stopped him with a gentle hand on his shoulder.

"Sure, Mr. Nicholson." Joey swaggered away from the door. Instead of being embarrassed that he'd been singled out from the others, he wore a grin—slight, to be sure, but amused.

Nick thought he was entirely too self-confident for a nine-year-old kid.

"You want me to explain it to you, Mr. Nicholson?"

Nick sighed with relief that he wouldn't have to tap-dance his way around the subject. He wished he and his father had been so quick to communicate with each other. "Yeah, if you don't mind."

Joey picked up a piece of white chalk. He drew a tadpolelike figure on the board again. "This is a sperm." He turned and faced Nick again, seemingly prepared to explain everything in very simple terms so there would be no misunderstanding. "It's not really this big, but—"

"Not that!" He'd ended the sex questions earlier by copping out with, "That's in a later lesson." He wasn't about to let the boy get started again.

He noticed the puzzled look on the little fella's face, then his shrug, as if to say, "What, then?"

"I hear your mom does volunteer work on Thursdays."

"Yeah . . ." Joey glanced out the window at his friends' impromptu snowball fight.

"What kind?"

"What kind of what?"

Nick moved between Joey and the window and captured the little boy's attention.

"What kind of volunteer work does your mother do?"

He thought Joey was entirely too young to have that devilish glitter in his eyes.

"She teaches."

"Teaches?" If he'd known that, he'd have let her handle the sex education class from the very beginning. The parents could hardly complain about that, could they? Not like they were going to when they heard Mr. Nicholson was letting Joey explain the answers to questions about virgins. And God knows what else he told them while Nick was preoccupied with Hollie.

"Teaches what?"

Joey grinned and shrugged. He craned his entire body in an effort to look around Nick and see out the window again.

"Stuff." As if that covered it all.

Nick was nothing if not persistent. He took a deep breath and maintained his cool when what he wanted to do was growl at the kid until the information came spilling out. "Sewing? Child care? Interior design at the junior college? What?"

"No, not those things. Like you, Mr. Nicholson. Everything. Can I go out now?"

Everything? Well, that covered a lot of nothing.

"Yeah, sure."

And Nick had thought they were going to *communicate?* Joey was a lot like the judge; both were enigmatic and tricky, each with their own hidden agenda. He'd like to see the two of them go one-on-one sometime without Hollie in the middle as a buffer.

As Nick saw it, he had two options tonight. He could go home, take his phone off the hook, leave all the lights off and hope there were no repercussions from today's class. Or he could stay at school until very late, work on the set for the Christmas play and fantasize for hours about someday teaching drama to students old enough to be as passionate about it as he was.

Either one would be a lot safer than fantasizing about Hollie. She was one sexy, single lady, successfully raising two boys on her own—one of which was way too bright and very well-adjusted. She ran her own business, kept a roof over their heads and food on the table. Every kid in his class adored her—they'd all forgiven her for getting them temporarily "segregated" the other day. She fit volunteer work into her busy schedule. She was artistic.

Was there anything the woman couldn't do? And why, with his rebel background, would he want to fantasize about someone so perfect?

He nearly gave up on the spot—perfect was way too much for him to handle—until he remembered her standing in the courtroom in front of his father, fussing and fuming and getting nowhere. Nick grinned as he relived the picture of her trying to talk her way out of his father's decision. She was no more successful than Nick had ever been.

So, they had some common ground, after all.

OH, MA-A-AN.

It was a silent moan on Joey's part as he ran down the stairs to get outside with his friends. Only ten minutes left to play.

Having his mom sit in the back of class hadn't been nearly as bad as he'd feared. Until now.

He didn't mind the fact that his mom and Mr. Nicholson were making dopey eyes at each other when they each thought the other one wasn't looking. He didn't mind that class got interrupted several times a day while they argued—though his mom called it "verbally sparring," whatever that was.

But he didn't like it when her being there caused his teacher to interfere in his playtime.

AFTER TWO LONG, restless nights with Christopher and then reinforced by Terri's "you look like hell" earlier that morning, Hollie gave up. She decided that when Christopher got fussy and announced he was hungry, that it was in his best interests to nurse somewhere other than Nick's classroom or the hall.

She found the teachers' lounge. It was outfitted with the requisite Formica table, plastic chairs, hissing coffeepot and an ancient, yellowed refrigerator. Through an open doorway, in an adjoining room labeled overhead as "the annex," an orange, cracked vinyl couch kept company with matching chairs. She sat with her feet up, Christopher warm and content at her breast.

Terri would be pleased. She'd been adamant about Hollie taking better care of herself.

"I'm telling you," she'd offered for the millionth time over her cup of coffee at Hollie's kitchen table that morning, "you can leave him with me. I'll put him down for his nap in his own bed. You'll be able to sleep at night again."

Hollie hadn't wanted to tell her that not all of her sleep had been lost on Christopher's account.

"You're on crutches," she declined around a sleepy yawn.

"I can get by with one."

Hollie had set the diaper bag on the table and, with fingers still numb from her ice-cold shower, she'd thumbed through the contents to be sure she'd have everything Christopher would need that day. Diapers, wipes, change of clothes, toys, blanket.

"You're not listening to me," Terri complained.

Hollie hummed absently.

"Hollie!"

She jumped, then glared at her good friend. "What?"

"You can't keep this pace up."

Hollie felt as if a light bulb went on. She lit up. "You're a professional person."

Terri took on a guarded look.

"You're a lawyer."

"I've known that for quite some time." She looked as if she didn't want to hear whatever was going to follow.

"You know Judge Nicholson. Personally."

"Yeah? So?"

She gathered Christopher in one arm, as much paraphernalia as possible in her other. When she looked sufficiently loaded down—the picture of a pack mule is what she strove for—she called Joey in and instructed him to carry their lunches, as she hadn't enough hands to go around. Then she fixed a steady, sleepy look on Terri.

"So...you call Judge Nicholson. You give him your professional opinion that I can't keep up this pace."

"Hollie—"

"Until then, I'll keep doing what I have to do."

For hours now, Hollie had hoped—irrationally, she knew—that Terri would be able to get through to Judge Nicholson sometime during the day. That a phone call would magically come into the school office. That the principal would rush down the hall to Nick's classroom and send her home, putting her out of her misery.

With visions of freedom dancing in her head, Hollie slouched farther down on the orange vinyl cushion. Her arms safely around Christopher, she relaxed into an altered state, not quite awake, not quite asleep. Until she overheard two teachers come into the lounge for coffee.

"Did I hear right? Has the Christmas play been canceled this year?"

Hollie's eyes popped open. Around the corner from her, the two women continued to chat as they helped themselves to coffee. They obviously thought they were alone.

"Not yet. I think Mr. Nelson's waiting to see if Nick can toe the line before he does something that drastic. Can you imagine this town if they don't get their annual three-wise-men-and-a-baby fix?"

Gentle laughter filtered toward Hollie.

"I heard Nick was revamping the play. Can you imagine if it flops? They'll run him out of town."

"And he had such high hopes for getting hired on at the high school."

"You don't think he will?"

Again the laugh. "Honey, he didn't have a chance when he moved back here and he hasn't changed anybody's mind yet. Imagine them putting him in charge of teenagers! The girls'd be strutting through the halls like cats in heat and the boys'd be doing wheelies down Main Street."

"Well, I think he's kind of cute."

"Mm-hm."

"And he's not that bad. He's just . . . his own man."

"If he doesn't keep the kids in order and get the play on track, he'll be his own *unemployed* man. My money says he won't make it until Christmas."

The two teachers left the lounge without ever knowing Hollie had been in the annex. It was just as well. She couldn't have found her voice to carry on a conversation with them.

All she could think about was Nick. The work he put in with the children. The patience he bestowed on them. The any-question-goes environment he encouraged to keep them curious and informed. The way he had to corral the kids, practice their lines with them and paint a broken-fingered Baby Jesus at the same time, because he didn't have the help he needed or deserved.

She'd been amused before. She was worried now. And not just for Nick. If he got fired before Christmas, she'd end up sitting in someone else's classroom with Joey. She'd be no better off. While Nick's influence with the judge so far seemed to be about nil, at least there was still hope. She could keep badgering him day in and day out, and he could keep trying to reason with his stubborn old goat of a father. No other teacher would have that advantage.

The idea of starting over with another teacher was too awful to contemplate. Would someone else have noticed her crammed in a small desk and brought her a chair? Would they have designed this week's spelling words around babies? Would they turn a blind eye to her Snowflake Ball samples filling their bulletin board?

No two ways about it, she had to get the judge's decision reversed *before* Nick got fired. Before he got run out of town. Or, she supposed, she could help him out.

She contemplated that for all of five seconds.

Nah. There was still a principle involved here. She didn't belong in Nick's, or anyone else's, classroom in the first place. If she made herself useful, the judge might make a habit of sending parents to school against their will.

"OKAY NOW, Joseph and Mary, you look adoringly at the baby in the manger. Timmy, you stand behind Joseph. And don't stick your finger down your throat and gag yourself this time," Nick directed.

Less than a week to go.

"But there's no baby," Mary Margaret complained.

"What's adoringly look like?" Joey asked.

Nick was jealous. Hollie got to sit in the folding chairs a few rows behind him in the gymnasium-turned-theater and sketch her little heart out. He was stuck with one kid who couldn't pretend and another whose vocabulary had suddenly vanished. High school as his goal was beginning to take on all the connotations of heaven.

He raked his hand through his hair, hoping he wouldn't
pull it all out by Christmas. "Linda, would you please go get
Baby Jesus out of the prop room and put Him in the manger? Joey, however you look at whatever you want most for
Christmas, that's adoringly."

"It is?"

"Close enough."

Joey gave that a scant moment of thought. "But I want
a T-shirt."

A T-shirt?

"That's all?"

"A black Harley one, like yours."

Nick knew just how the kid felt. Of course, Nick had
graduated to the real thing long ago, but when the mercury
rose above forty, he still looked at his bike pretty adoringly.

"And some other stuff," Joey added urgently, making
Nick wonder if the kid knew the truth about Santa.

Joey rattled off what he wanted. A water bottle for his
bike. Candy. A video game. Candy. A new hockey stick and
skates. Candy. A puppy. None of it sounded nearly as sin-
cere as the Harley T-shirt. Except maybe the candy.

Nick took the opportunity to stretch his legs as Joey rattled on. He strolled silently up the center aisle toward Hollie. Three seats into the row, she sat in deep concentration
with her head bent over the pad of paper on her lap. Her
dark hair fell like a curtain around her work, obscuring it
from his line of vision. Her hand moved in short, furious
strokes beneath the waves. She didn't even seem to be aware
that she was in the middle of a gymnasium, perched on the
edge of a folding chair, while the fourth-grade class mur-
dered the ancient names of Bethlehem and Balthazar.

She'd hidden her sketches from him in the classroom,
making Nick wonder what an interior designer would draw
that was so private. Curious, he stepped carefully, so as not

to give her warning by thunking the heel of his boot on the hardwood floor. It wasn't as if he was going to steal her ideas or anything. And he certainly didn't think she had a shy bone in her body.

Limited by the row of chairs in front of him, Nick craned his neck to peek over her shoulder and around her hair. Shiny, thick brunette waves caught what was left of the sunlight coming in the windows and glowed with a vitality that begged to be touched. He jammed his hands into his pockets.

She glanced up, surprised to see him so close. Her arms immediately covered the page with as much guilt as a kid caught writing a note.

"What's that?" he asked softly as Timmy, up on stage, took his turn competing with Joey's Christmas list.

"Nothing."

He grinned. "You're working awfully hard on nothing."

"It's just something I do."

"So I've noticed."

She chewed the inside of her lip.

So, she does have a shy streak.

"I see things as they could be," she explained. "And I draw them."

"Kind of like an addiction?" He reached for the pad of paper.

"No, more like a habit." Her elbows stuck to it like glue, and she shielded it with her body. "Shouldn't you be teaching something?"

He grinned. "We're in a gymnasium. It's play practice."

She smiled, turning the artificial sweetness factor up as high as it would go. "Of course it is. So go practice."

"I want to see what you drew."

"No, you don't."

"Yes, I do."

His hand tunneled through her dark tresses to get to the sketch pad. He couldn't see what he was doing, but he was very careful to grab somewhere near her knees and not higher up. No need to get slapped for an accident.

She grabbed the pad with both hands and stood, but there was little room with him on one side of her and Christopher in his infant seat on the floor on the other side.

"Maybe I shouldn't stay for play practice. I should go start dinner. I'll come back for Joey later." She reached for her purse and the diaper bag. With three items to keep track of, she fumbled them all.

Nick's fingers closed over the spiral edge of her sketch pad and he tugged at it gently. Her hands were too small to grasp the pad and hide the drawing, too. Even upside down, he could tell it was a nativity scene.

"Wow."

Not only that, it was *his* nativity scene, not the same old props the school had been using forever. It was fresh. It was detailed—so detailed that he thought the baby in the manger looked a little like Christopher, when he used to think all babies looked alike. It was—

A shrill, little-girl shriek ripped through the gymnasium. "Mr. Nicholson!"

Nick shoved the pad back at Hollie, who took it even as she zeroed in on Linda's whereabouts.

"Mr. Nicholson!" Linda, blond hair flying behind her, came running from the direction of the prop room with all the urgency only a little girl can muster.

"What is it?" He was out of the row and on his way down the aisle, Hollie hot on his heels. "Who's hurt?"

Linda raced up to them, a wave of classmates in tow. "Mr. Nicholson—" she danced nervously back and forth from one foot to the other "—somebody kidnapped Baby Jesus!"

Nick quickly ran an assessing eye over the boys crowded around him, Hollie and Linda. He expected to see a couple of them exchange smirks, elbow each other in the ribs or, at the very least, look too innocent to be true. It only took a second to ascertain that none of them had taken the statue—none of them were good enough actors to carry off such innocence. In fact, he'd only seen one person in East Bay Elementary capable of it. He whirled on Hollie, the bane of his existence since last Friday.

"You!"

Chapter Six

Hollie had difficulty changing gears so quickly. One second her adrenaline was rushing and she was prepared to practice any first aid necessary until the paramedics arrived. The next, she had visions of interrogating every child there until she and Nick could determine who had the audacity to play a prank with Baby Jesus.

And finally, she was the target of hazel eyes that were no longer warm and golden, but heated with suspicion and anger.

"Me?" she croaked in response to Nick's accusation. She thought he'd been spending far too much time with overly imaginative nine- and ten-year-olds.

"You've made my life hell ever since Friday."

All of the fourth-graders pointed and snickered and cajoled him for his language, but Nick paid them no attention.

"*I* made *your* life miserable?" She couldn't believe his audacity. If it weren't for the roomful of students, she'd show him what hell was like.

"You waltz in here on Monday morning like you own the place, with a baby, his da . . . arn portacrib—"

"Please, Nick, the children." Not to mention her heart was breaking.

"The children have been practicing hard to get this play ready." He leaned closer, snapping off each word with irritation as his breath mingled with hers. "They have no motivation for sabotaging it."

"And I suppose I do?" She balled one hand into a fist and rested it on her hip. She thought of using the other to whack some sense into him with her sketch pad.

"If you're thinking of holding Him for ransom, you'd better think again."

Her eyebrows arched. "Ransom?"

"You heard me."

"You think I'd use a statue to blackmail you into—what? Going to your father and saying—" she lowered her voice in a cheap imitation of his "—Gee, Dad, you'd better let her off the hook so we can get Baby Jesus back in the manger."

She saw the hesitation in his eyes as he wavered in his conviction that she was the culprit, but he snapped, "Yes!" anyway.

"Get real, Nicholson." Making no attempt to be gentle, she grasped several pages of her sketch pad and tore out the illustrations for the stage set she'd been working on during rehearsal. She ripped them in half and shoved them at his chest, giving him no option but to grasp them.

"What's this?"

"I had considered helping you, but you can forget *that*." If the play flopped and they ran him out of town, she vowed she wouldn't care. She spun on her heel and snapped, "Joey, get your things. It's time to go home."

She stormed up the aisle to her seat and gathered up Christopher in his infant seat, the diaper bag, her purse and her coat. She pushed half of her stuff at a dazed and silent Joey, her urgency forcing him to shoulder the diaper bag with no more than a worried, backward glance at his teacher.

"Hollie, wait," Nick said.

She didn't even break stride as she stomped up the aisle and burst through the double doors. One slammed open against the wall with a satisfying smack.

"Please wait."

He sounded sorry, maybe even apologetic, but she didn't look back. Joey did, though. His friends were wide-eyed. His teacher was red in the face. Joey spotted the sketch pad he'd dropped halfway up the aisle the same time Nick saw it.

Nick strode forward. Joey started to go back for it.

"Joey!" ripped back into the gymnasium from down the hall.

"Coming, Mom." Joey didn't budge.

Nick gave him a reassuring smile. "You'd better go, champ. See you in the morning."

Joey glanced at the sketch pad on the floor midway between them.

"Joey!"

"Go on," Nick said softly. "I'll save it for her."

The door banged shut behind Joey. The gymnasium was silent—eerily so, Nick thought, considering there were still thirteen girls and eleven boys still in it. They gaped at the half sheets of paper Hollie had shoved into his grasp.

He remembered how good the one nativity sketch he'd seen had been. He thumbed through the rest. It was a pretty tough task through the damage. He smoothed them out against his chest, ironing the wrinkles out with his hands, then crouched in front of the first row of folding chairs and matched right and left halves on the metal seats. The children inched closer until they were crowded around him.

Looking at the drawings, it was easy for Nick to see Hollie had a way of bringing the stage to life much as he'd imagined it when he'd rejected the old props. Hoping she hadn't torn up all her drawings, he picked up the sketch pad and started flipping through the pages.

He was brought up short by a naked image of himself. "What the—"

He slammed the pad close to his chest and glanced over his shoulder to see if the children had seen. They were still looking at the sketches on the chair seats.

Thank you, God. He held the pad as close to his chest as if he'd glued it there. He also grinned, knowing Hollie had never seen him without his shirt on, wondering if he thumbed through the pages if he'd find himself without pants on, too.

He rose to his feet slowly, hoping not to distract the kids from their discussion of the nativity scenes. He wanted a few minutes to himself. He wandered up the aisle. He flipped through the pages one by one, slowly at first, then more quickly.

No such luck.

She didn't appear to Nick to be the type of person who did anything halfway, though. He'd bet, from the well-muscled physique she'd put on the pages so far, that she'd at least imagined what the rest of him must look like.

He closed the pad with a snap and glanced at the clock. They had fifteen minutes left before the car pools started leaving. He faced the children. "Let's get back to work."

They stared at him, some still confused by the heated exchange, others openly excited by Hollie's view of their set. One thing they did agree on, though. They blocked his path with two dozen pairs of censorious eyes—all aimed at him.

"Okay, so I lost it," he admitted.

"You made her mad," Linda accused, looking near tears.

Mary Margaret stamped her foot and folded her arms across her little chest. "You made her take Joey home."

"What are we going to do without Baby Jesus?" Timmy demanded.

If he hadn't made Hollie mad enough to leave, Nick figured they could have borrowed Christopher for practice. He'd be a really cute addition to the play.

"And Joey," Mary Margaret added. "Don't forget about Joey. We need him, too."

"I'll apologize." It didn't sound like such a bad prospect to Nick. Surely not as bad as seeing that hurt look in Hollie's eyes every day for the next week.

"When?"

"Yeah, when?"

Nick sighed. They were going to be as tough on him as his father. "First thing in the morning."

"You made her mad," Linda said again.

"All right, already. Help me look for Baby Jesus until your car pools leave, and I'll go apologize tonight. Okay?"

"What if she slams the door in your face?" Timmy asked.

Nick knew it was a distinct possibility. "Then, in the morning, you'll understand if I haven't been able to talk to her."

"Nu-uh!" Mary Margaret and Linda warned.

Nick sighed and raked his fingers through his hair again. "Look, I'll do my best, okay?"

They stared up at him as if measuring his mettle.

"You two take the prop room," Nick ordered John and David before any one of the stubborn little monsters could point out that he might be lacking in tenacity. "Timmy, look backstage."

Nick continued to give orders like a general, even though waving around Hollie's notebook as he gave directions only pointed out one thing—he had proof that she was intensely interested in him. As a man, not as her son's teacher.

He hoped.

OH, MA-A-AN.

Joey sat quietly on his side of the car, listening to his mom sniffle as she drove. She clutched the steering wheel like he'd gripped his hockey stick when Jerry, a husky sixth-grader, had tried to take it from him.

"Mom—"

"Not now."

"But, Mom—"

"Not now, Joey. I'm serious."

"When, then?"

"Better count to a thousand."

He took a deep breath, prepared to let out a sigh that was as long and drawn out as he could manage. Then, when he remembered how much she hated that, he stifled it prematurely. This time she didn't even shoot him that Don't-sigh-at-me-young-man look—undeniable evidence that she was really, really upset at his teacher.

"I can cook a pizza tonight," he offered quickly, saying no more than he dared.

Her eyes darted between him and the road ahead. "Huh?"

"If you don't want to cook, I remember how to turn on the oven and put in a pizza."

A strangled sound burst from deep inside her.

"Oh, no, Mom, don't cry." He didn't mean to make her cry. This wasn't working out at all as he'd planned. "Don't be sad."

"I'm not sad." She brushed tears off her cheek, then rumpled his hair with her damp hand.

Confused, he watched her warily. "Uh-huh. Where're we going?"

"To pick up a pizza."

NICK BIDED HIS TIME in the grocery store checkout, pining for the detachment of the big cities he'd traveled through and lived in. Cities where he could go into the supermarket and know he'd get through the checkout line just as fast or slow as anyone else because, chances were, the checker and the person in line in front of him didn't know each other and wouldn't have anything to talk about other than paper or plastic, and coupons.

Not so in East Bay.

The checker was in her fifties, with tightly permed salt-and-pepper hair and a uniform that consisted of a green apron over her baggy sweater and jeans. It irritated Nick that she wasn't able to talk and scan groceries at the same time.

"Did you see her?" she asked the lady in front of Nick.

"Who?"

"That Landon woman. She was just in here. She'd obviously been crying. Her baby was bawling his eyes out, and her older boy was whining about something or other."

The lady in line tsk-tsked.

"I knew she couldn't handle it. She had to buy a frozen pizza for supper. Now I ask you, what kind of nutrition is that for a growing boy?"

Nick cleared his throat, hoping to spur her into at least looking as if she was going to scan something sometime in this century.

The checker barely spared him a glance. "A woman isn't meant to have babies after her husband dies."

That perked up his attention.

"You'd think she'd just get married again," the neighboring checker contributed. *She,* at least, could scan and talk at the same time. "She's pretty enough."

"Pretty's got nothin' to do with it. She's too independent for her own good. No man'll have a woman with that much of a mind of her own." The checker's laugh sounded like a cackle to Nick. "Scares 'em, she does."

Nick cleared his throat louder this time, earning him an apologetic glance from the customer in front of him. She shoved some groceries along the motorized belt in a half-hearted attempt to get the checker moving, though she was plainly more interested in hearing the latest gossip than getting home.

"You're a man."

Nick glanced around, then noticed the checker had zeroed her beady gaze in on him. He glanced over at the next line to see if it was moving any faster. He debated switching regardless.

"What do you think of a woman so darned independent that she has her husband's baby after he's been gone two years?"

"Uh, I really hadn't given it much thought. Do you think maybe you could...you know...ring up some groceries while we chat?"

The lady in front of him glanced at him nervously. "Yes, Mabel, I really have to get home and bathe the children before bedtime."

"Just as I thought," Mabel said with a satisfied smirk as she started the belt moving. She pinned Nick with a glare. "That Landon woman scares you just as much as the next man."

"She ought to," the neighboring checker said with a smile. "She sits in his class every day."

Mabel's mouth dropped open. "Oh, so you're the one! That'd explain it, then."

He couldn't help it; he was suckered in whether he wanted to be or not. "Explain what?"

"Why you're afraid to say what you think, of course." Having said all she wanted on the subject, she scanned a loaf of bread and turned her attention back to the lady in front of him. "So, Mrs. Johnson, how old are those boys of yours now?"

By the time he got out of the store, he knew Mrs. Johnson had two boys, aged five and seven. And no, she wasn't having any more; she'd sent her husband to the doctor to take care of that. It was far more than he thought he had a right to know, but typical for East Bay.

Nick looked forward to going to Hollie's house tonight. She wasn't nearly as scary as Mabel.

Though, if she was still in tears as Mabel had indicated, with a cranky baby and a sullen son, he might have his work cut out for him. He needed a plan of action.

"WHERE'RE WE GOING now, Mom?"

Hollie drove home the long way. It was out of her way, of course, but she needed to see the mansion again. Sitting in a room full of children and Nick all day had drained some of her Christmas spirit. It was hard to be all cheery and nice when she knew she was falling further behind in her decorations—her livelihood—and in her own enjoyment of Christmas.

She'd rather be shopping and wrapping gifts for the boys and baking cookies. She and Joey had had such fun getting their Christmas cards out earlier in the month. A simple thing, to be sure, but they'd done it *together*. It was a memory she'd cherish forever. A tradition they'd continue. In a few years, Christopher would help, too.

"I, uh, need to see something." Hollie pulled into the long, winding driveway. The owners were in Florida. They'd left the key and their beautiful, white-brick mansion at her disposal. They'd be home shortly before the Snowflake Ball was to take place. It was an annual big deal—and the first year they'd turned the decorations over to someone outside their family. They'd trusted her. And, no thanks to Nick's father, she was in danger of letting them down.

Joey unbuckled his seat belt.

"I'll just be a minute, honey. You stay with Christopher, okay?"

He didn't seem to mind. Hollie thought he was probably still in shock that she'd not only given in to having pizza for supper, but that she was actually going to let him cook it by himself.

She hurried up the wide, ivy-lined flagstone walk and let herself in through the front door. The foyer was bigger than she remembered from her earlier visits, the ones she'd made repeatedly in order to get this job in the first place. It nearly doubled her own living room. Not that she was jealous; she loved her little house. It was just right for her and her little family.

She closed her eyes, took a deep breath and remembered the sketches that had won her the job. She could smell the fresh pine boughs and the hickory wood smoke. She could hear the crackling fires in three different fireplaces and Christmas carols on the CD player. She could see the gaily dressed people, who had been invited weeks ago, and taste the hors d'oeuvres that were legendary in East Bay.

The Christmas spirit flooded back to her, filling her. The trees were scheduled for delivery. She'd hang thousands of glittering glass ornaments and red velvet bows. She'd drape fragrant pine garland in every room, tape rolls and rolls of bright red and green and gold Christmas wrapping paper around hundreds of boxes, frost the windows to simulate snowdrifts, and cover the trees with tiny white pinpoints of light. More ideas came to her every day.

At least they had before she got sentenced to sit in Nick's classroom with Joey. Now she wondered where she was going to find the time to do it all. She wanted to make wall hangings. She needed to finish the tree skirts. She prayed she could finish the ceramic village and get the trains set up.

The horn tooted. Joey probably wanted her to know he was hungry and Christopher was fussing. She took one quick, last look at the magnificent house, pictured the Snowflake Ball one more time, then locked the door behind her. Renewed, refreshed, she was ready to spend the evening—after her quality time with Joey and Christopher, of course—putting some final touches on the ceramic village still laid out in her studio.

NICK FOUND Hollie's house situated on a small lot on a quiet, tree-lined street. Every yard had Christmas lights glowing somewhere—some along the roof lines, some on the traditional, pyramid-shaped evergreen trees, some twinkling from leafless branches of maples and ashes, making wonderful, shapeless forms against the night sky. Wooden sleds and orange plastic toboggans dotted the snow-covered lawns, as if waiting, hoping for the children to come back and play with them again.

Nick left his small bag of groceries on the back of his motorcycle. He parked his helmet on the seat. He patted his jacket where he kept his peace offering warm inside, nestled against his chest.

The porch light came on after only one ring of the doorbell. When Hollie pulled the window curtain back and peeked out, then hesitated, he offered a small, hopefully friendly smile. She chewed the inside of her lower lip as if debating the wisdom of answering. She looked soft, rumpled, vulnerable.

She pulled the door open, but she didn't move aside in a silent offer to let him step in out of the cold. He thought she looked far more inviting in her purple, polar fleece robe and fuzzy slippers than she ever had at school. Her hair was freshly shampooed and looked nearly dry. There was a warm glow about her, as if she'd been sitting in front of a toasty fire and roasting marshmallows, but there was no telltale, crackling-flame sounds coming from the living room just off the foyer, no white goop clinging to her lips.

Her eyebrows arched expressively in sudden anticipation, drawing Nick's gaze upward. Away from her mouth, but not away from temptation.

"You talked to your dad?"

The hope in her voice tugged at his heart. He didn't think she'd been about to say the first word at all, except that the right news from his dad would be too good to wait for. He couldn't say yes and get her hopes up for no reason. And if he said no, she'd be disappointed, maybe angry enough to close him out before he could get another word in.

He glanced over her shoulder. Joey wasn't anywhere in sight. Christopher was also absent and blessedly silent. No telling when either would interrupt.

He unzipped his jacket slowly, carefully, not wanting to ruin his gift. Her eyes widened, as if she thought he had some ulterior motive and was just waiting to see how far he'd go before she had to throw cold water on him and leave him out in the freezing weather.

"I came to apologize," he said, getting it out of the way before she remembered she was mad and slammed the door in his face.

She uncrossed her arms. Her chin came down a notch.

He dipped his hand in near his heart and came out with the ruby red rose—the most perfect one in the shop, the florist had assured him. It was still in perfect condition, just beginning to open, fragrant enough to blend with the vanilla scent of her shampoo. Or had she been baking Christmas cookies? If he apologized nicely enough, maybe she'd invite him in and he'd find out which it was.

"I was a complete jerk."

"And?"

"And I made a donkey of myself."

She laughed then, a light sound, like a small, brass wind chime on a breeze. Apparently she agreed with him.

"A donkey?"

He shrugged and smiled. "I'm trying to clean up my language since I've been teaching fourth grade."

Besides not holding a grudge, she had the good grace not to remind him how his language had slipped in the gymnasium.

"Forgive me?" He held the rose just beneath her nose, offering it to her to sniff.

She softened, bending forward just slightly. Her eyes fluttered closed in silent appreciation as she got a sweet whiff. Her hand landed lightly on his.

It was his undoing.

Yes, he'd planned on her establishing a truce with him. Probably inviting him in. Maybe even smiling at him. But voluntarily touching him this way? Burning a path up his arm on its way to deeper regions he'd be better off not thinking about right then? Not without incentive, he knew.

Thus the rose.

But never in his wildest imagination had he thought she'd lay her hand on his in such an intimate way. Not tonight. Not after what he'd accused her of. Not without a lot of groveling on his part. He hadn't even begun to grovel.

Perhaps he could skip it.

He withdrew his hand slowly, noting that her hand followed his, tilting her body even more toward him. He lifted the rose safely out of harm's way as he pulled her into the circle of his arms.

He gave her no warning. He didn't want to give her a chance to resist. She came to him softly, her lips warm beneath his, her body pliant, her heartbeat matching the rhythm of his own.

One kiss was all it took. One kiss to know if he didn't put some space between them, he'd be lost. One kiss to make him want to protect her from his father for reasons other than the fact that she was making his days miserable.

A couple inches—that's all the space he was willing to give.

Later.

He stepped into the foyer, sweeping her along with him as his thighs pressed firmly against hers. His hand caressed its way up her back, into her hair, finding it damp, as he'd known it would be. He kicked the door shut behind him, not wanting her to catch a chill. Though if she was as hot as he was, there was no way.

He held her tenderly, even as he gave them a minimum of breathing space, as he held the ruby red flower between them. Ever so lightly, he traced the silhouette of her forehead and nose and lips and chin with the soft, fragrant petals, skimming it downward ever so slowly. He dragged it down her throat to the V of her robe.

In the blink of an eye, her hand was on his, her fingers molding themselves to the backs of his, stilling them from their sensuous travels.

"Why are you doing this?" she whispered unevenly.

"Doing what?"

"Haunting me at home."

It was a breathless answer that set his heart to racing faster.

He grinned, trying to lighten the moment, knowing it could go no further tonight. Not with two children on the premises. Not if he was going to be able to stand in front of the class tomorrow and keep his wits about him.

"Because you haunt me at school."

"What?"

"Turnabout's fair play, Hollie."

"But, I don't—"

The basement door slammed. "Mom!" Joey called from the kitchen. "Can I have a..." His voice trailed off when he found his mom standing at the open front door, a single rose in her hand, staring out into the cold night.

Nick's motorcycle roared to life.

"Hey, it's Mr. Nicholson. Hey, Mr. Nicholson!" Joey tossed Nick a wave, then turned back to his mom. "Did he bring you a flower?"

"It's, uh, an early present from Santa."

"Don't you like it?"

"Yes. Why?"

"'Cause you look all funny. Like you're gonna be sick or something."

Hollie closed the door silently, firmly, wishing she could lock up her reactions to Nick as easily as she locked the door. She helped Joey get his bedtime snack without hearing a word he said. All she could think about was Nick. And his kiss.

Wow! What would have happened if they'd been alone together for a little while longer? Or worse yet, a long while longer?

For the millionth time, she thought it was too bad the judge had thrown them together against their wishes, though now she had a different reason for thinking it was so terrible. No thanks to the legal system, starting last Monday morning, she had to work twice as hard right up until the Christmas break to get her design job done. Now, suddenly, it wasn't just her picturing a naked Nick in her Christmas sketches that was going to slow her down. It was knowing Nick was looking back at her. Knowing he'd been affected by their kiss. Knowing he'd remember it, too, and he wasn't going to let her forget it.

"Ouch."

She looked down where a thorn had pricked her thumb. A crimson drop of blood beaded up on her skin. A pertinent reminder she didn't have time for romantic games with the town's bad boy, especially when his reputation all but said he'd be leaving town if he didn't land a job at the high school.

But she could dream, couldn't she?

NICK TOOK THE LONG WAY to his dad's house, then rode around the block three times before parking his motorcycle at the curb and storming the front door. He had to wade through half a dozen persistent reporters on the porch, all eager for a quote from him about his father's controversial ruling since they hadn't been able to get one from the judge himself.

These people weren't from East Bay. They had big city written all over them with their nice suits, wool overcoats and fancy haircuts, each competing against the others in their dog-eat-dog profession.

"Why don't you call the police on them?" Nick asked when he found his father sitting in his cherry-paneled study, lit only by the Christmas lights twinkling on a tree outside the window.

"Are they trampling the bushes?"

"No."

"Littering the lawn?"

Nick shrugged. "A few cigarette butts, maybe."

His dad grinned devilishly. "Then let them freeze their rear ends off all night."

Nick sat in the leather recliner on the opposite side of the cold fireplace, then slid down until he found a spot that was comfortable for him and would annoy his father no end. Body language was an important thing for an actor to learn, and Nick had learned from some of the best. He studied the older man's rigid posture, the fingers tapping on the burgundy armrest, the erratic breathing and tightly compressed lips.

"I suppose you've come here tonight to tell me I'm wrong, too."

Nick perked up. Someone had told the almighty Judge Nicholson he'd been wrong? Made a rash ruling? And he was listening? Nick needed to study their technique.

"Some people think I should reconsider," his dad continued.

"Oh?"

"They think I should fine Mrs. Landon instead."

"Oh."

"I know how you feel about it."

"Well, Dad—"

"I know you never wanted her in your classroom in the first place."

"Yeah, well, that was before—"

"I suppose it doesn't occur to them any more than it did to you what kind of message that would send to the other children and their parents."

Nick's hackles rose. He had nothing but his students' best interests in mind. That's why he'd asked his dad for advice in the first place. Advice that had somehow, strangely, gone awry.

"It occurred to me," he stated out through clenched teeth.

"Five hundred dollars sounds good to me."

"Five hundred dollars because her little boy skipped school?"

"It's a nice round number. It's big enough to send a message."

"Well, let's not be hasty."

His dad's sharp, shrewd eyes zeroed in on him.

Nick cleared his throat. "I mean, she's a single mother, and all. Working to support herself and two kids. I've seen her house. It's not all that large. Probably mortgaged to the hilt."

The judge's eyebrows rose.

"I mean, just the entry hall, of course. I, uh, had to drop off something this evening. Anyway, it's not like she's got expensive stuff sitting around."

"Oh?"

Nick thought his father was reading far too much into this conversation and missing the whole point entirely.

"I don't think she could afford five hundred dollars. She's self-employed, works out of her house. No employees. No baby-sitter."

"You've certainly learned a great deal about her in three days."

"Uh, kids talk, you know. I think a fine like that might really hurt her. She could lose her business, her house, have to go on welfare..." Nick let that train of thought hang in the air between them.

His dad's nod indicated he'd pretend to accept that story. For now. He stood. "Well, I've got all night to think about it. Lock up when you leave. Wouldn't want those reporters in my bedroom in the middle of the night."

Nick rode home with a lot on his mind. He didn't want Hollie to get hit with a five-hundred-dollar fine. He didn't want her to get a small fine, either, because she could maybe afford that, and then he wouldn't get to see her every day.

What kind of monster was he? He should be wishing she'd get off scot-free. Joey was a good kid. Hollie was a good mother. Even if his dad let her off, he'd still get to see her. Wouldn't he?

Why, then, did he hope his dad's ruling would stand?

Chapter Seven

"What's PMS?" Timmy asked during sex-education class.

For the first time, Nick had second thoughts about his any-question-anytime policy. Now he knew why some of his college professors told students to hold all questions until the end of class, then lectured nonstop right up until the bell rang. Survival.

"My big brother says it's picky mother syndrome," Kevin blurted out.

Mary Margaret rolled her eyes. "Nu-uh."

Nick opened his mouth to restore order, but instead of hearing himself speak, he heard a very distinctive ringing noise.

"What's that?" T.J. asked.

"Someone's beeper."

"Who's got a beeper?"

"My big brother has a beeper."

Nick let them have their say as he stormed down the aisle toward the nearest cellular phone—the one in Hollie's hand. The one pressed up against her ear, nestled in among those generous waves. For this he'd asked his dad to reconsider a five-hundred-dollar fine? This . . . aggravation!

He held out his hand, no differently than he would to one of the children had they been guilty of such a stunt. His body language alone was enough of an order, but he barked, "Give it to me," anyway. Just in case she wanted to pretend not to get the message.

She held up one finger, indicating she needed just another minute. She glanced up at him from beneath her long lashes, aiming her sweet smile right where it would do her the most good. And him the most harm.

He took a deep breath and regathered his forces. "Now!"

"By Valentine's Day? How many did you have in mind?" she asked in a businesslike, yet sweet, voice. "Sure, that will be no problem."

She turned her back on him as she continued her phone conversation. Nick felt twenty-five pairs of eyes studying the situation, waiting to see how their authority figure was going to handle this. He couldn't back down now. He'd never get control back in his room again. He'd never get the teaching position he wanted at the high school. Hell, he probably wouldn't even get another job in the county once people learned what a soft touch he was.

Hollie broke the tip of her pencil and reached for another, her shoulder bumping into Nick's hip as she did so. He closed his eyes and took a deep breath. He willed his body not to react, not to remember how she'd felt in his arms last night.

It was no use.

She smiled a sweet apology, then jotted down business notes. Nick gritted his teeth and reached for the phone.

She twisted away, but he had a hold of it. And her soft, silky hair. And her warm, smooth hand. He nearly dropped his catch, but seeing his future flash before his eyes—him on the road looking for another job, alone, without Hollie in his life—gave him the fortitude to hang on tightly.

"Ow, you're pulling my hair."

He made sure he was only hanging on, not pulling, with one hand while he reached down and flipped the phone shut with his other.

"Hey!" she objected.

He worked to extract her hair from the phone and his hand from her hair. It wasn't easy with fingers gone suddenly clumsy.

"That was a business call," she informed him.

He forced down a pang of guilty conscience, knowing she, as adept as any of the children, had learned just which of his buttons to push to get the desired response. Well, he wasn't going to give it to her.

"This is a classroom, in case you hadn't noticed lately."

He finally got loose from her hair and tugged the phone out of her hand.

She grabbed for it. "I have to call them back."

He raised the phone over his head out of her reach and matched her quick grasp with a side step of his own. He nearly knocked over the bud vase she'd set up on the little desktop—the one that held the single red rose he'd given her last night.

"What's that doing here?" he demanded, surprised by how hoarse his whisper sounded.

She would have had to have taken great pains to get the rose to school without it freezing, and—even more difficult—up to his classroom without crushing it among baby and artsy things.

The corners of her eyes crinkled delightfully, devilishly. "I couldn't bear to leave it home all day."

"Why the he—" he lowered his voice "—heck not?"

"Because there's no one there to enjoy it. Now, if I were there instead of here . . ."

His imagination filled in the rest, as he was sure she'd intended.

"Can I catch PMS?" Timmy asked. When neither of the adults responded, he persisted. "Hey, Mr. Nicholson."

The girls giggled. Hollie's smile lit up the flashes in her eyes, making Nick think of twinkling green Christmas lights.

"Better answer the question before they get restless."

All Nick could do was stare at the rose and remember last night's kiss. How her lips had been as soft as the petals he'd traced over her skin.

He'd never known he had as much strength as he did then, in front of all the children. He resisted the temptation to drag her up against his chest again, to crush her lips beneath his, to let her feel how much he wanted her. The most he allowed himself was to inhale her vanilla scent, knowing now that it was her shampoo and not Christmas cookies.

He'd been crazy to take her that flower, but he'd promised the kids he'd make up with her.

Well, hell, he hadn't known she was going to bring it to school with her, for chrissakes. If he'd known that, he'd have tried to get by with a simple apology.

"Mr. Nicholson!"

"Huh? What?"

"Can I catch it?" Timmy asked again. He'd been told the answer by nearly every kid so far, but he wasn't convinced.

"Catch what?" Nick could barely remember what subject they were on.

"Men's troll syndrome."

Nick took one look at Timmy's worried face and pictured him as a typical spiky-orange-haired troll.

"Premenstrual," he corrected, fighting back a grin, thankful for the vivid diversion.

"That's what I said."

"No, you can't catch it, Timmy."

"But your sister can," Michael added with a laugh.

Nick sighed. He had to handle this one very delicately if he didn't want every kid's mother calling him on it. "You want to explain it?" he asked Hollie.

"Why, no. You're the teacher."

"Yeah, that's what I heard about you, too. Maybe you can tell me about it later."

He turned back to his class then, but as he did so, he thought he heard her say, "Yeah. Maybe." And it sounded more like a threat than a promise.

Hollie watched Nick stroll forward toward his desk, her phone clutched tightly in his hand. If his white knuckles were any indication, she could safely say she'd gotten him perturbed with the cellular phone. She glanced at her rose and smiled. Bringing that had been a nice touch, too. She wanted to laugh at the fact that he'd given it to her, and now its presence was bothering him.

Except that it had been awfully sweet on his part. She only wanted to needle him into swaying his father, not make fun of him.

She watched as he got the kids back in order, answered their questions and prompted more. And, for once, Joey wasn't bored. Worse, he seemed upset.

Had he seen her kissing Nick in the foyer last night? For three days he'd been supportive of her little antics to get out of the classroom. Now, however, his little shoulders were tensed up. When they changed subjects, he slammed his books around harder than necessary and let his desktop fall with a resounding bang.

It was time for Hollie to have another talk with him, to reexplain the principles behind her drive to get out of the classroom. It would be wrong for her to give up and give in and just sit there every day like a good little mommy while the judge figuratively slapped her hand. She had to make Joey understand that. She'd talk to him at the end of recess. She was going to use the break itself to make another bid for her freedom—and to thank Nick for the rose.

HOLLIE ENJOYED every minute until recess. She would have been mad at Nick for cutting her business call short, but she knew the woman she was dealing with, and the woman knew exactly where Hollie was spending her days and why.

But watching Nick trying not to look at the rose was too enjoyable to miss. It was difficult for her to keep her mind on her work; she was afraid she'd miss him tug at the neck of his T-shirt, rake his hand through his hair one more time or forget how to explain a simple arithmetic problem.

She played with Christopher, then, shortly before the break, settled him on the floor on a blanket to amuse himself and let her do what she had to do.

The bell rang. The children pulled on their coats and tumbled out the door. As Hollie strolled up the rows of little desks, she noticed Nick watched her with hooded eyes and a wary expression. He set his book aside and held his ground as she stopped and stood directly in front of him.

"I wanted to thank you for the rose."

He didn't answer right away. She could tell he was thinking back to last night. She wondered what parts he was remembering.

"Just for the rose?" he teased. "Nothing else?"

Obviously he remembered the same thing that had kept her awake half the night, and it wasn't Christopher.

"The thank-you is for the flower. This," she said as she rose up on her toes, "is for the kiss."

She leaned into him slightly, slowly easing herself closer until their lips touched.

She'd meant it to be quick, but not too quick. Bold, but not too bold. A lip-to-lip, hands-on-his-chest-for-balance-only kind of kiss. Just to drive him nuts. Not herself.

Instead, on a scale of cold to hot, she blazed all the way to inferno. Her lips molded themselves to his as if they'd been welded there. Her hands slipped up over his broad shoulders on their way to thread themselves through the hair at the back of his neck. Hair that curled over the collar of his leather jacket—when he wore it. She almost wished he were wearing it now. Then she wouldn't be able to feel the heat radiating off his skin, through his T-shirt and into her body.

Then she wouldn't be thinking she'd made a mistake by getting so close.

Last night had been one thing; he'd initiated it and they'd been in her house. This was something else entirely.

It took several moments for her to realize that Nick had put some space between them. Not enough, but some. Any adult who happened to walk into the room at that moment wouldn't be fooled. He held her hands in his.

"Not here," he said.

She was pleased to hear the catch in his voice, the hoarseness that told her she wasn't alone in her feelings. Otherwise she'd have been mortified.

"What time does Joey go to bed?"

Joey who?

Oh, yeah.

Did she really want him at her house again? She needed to keep him off balance, make him crazy, drive him nuts, not seduce him!

"Uh, eight-thirty or nine."

He dipped his head in what she knew was going to be another kiss. She turned her head away, then cursed reality for gypping her out of one last kiss to remember him by.

"Tonight's no good," she said, mentally kicking herself for being so strong on the outside when she really wanted to indulge this inner weakness she'd never encountered before.

"Why not?"

She dragged her hands from his, and his fingers held hers until the last possible second. His gaze never released her, but her green eyes slid from his darker ones, afraid he'd see too much.

"I have to wash my hair." It sounded as stupid as it had in high school. And it conjured up the memory of his hands in her damp hair last night. She stared at the T-shirt stretched across his chest.

"When, then?"

Was that a chuckle she heard in his voice?

She shrugged. "I don't know. Later."

"You'll let me know when?"

She couldn't say yes. Nor did she want to say no.

He took in a deep breath and eased away from her. "I guess that's just as well. There's some props I need to get painted. And I still haven't found Baby Jesus."

As Nick increased the gap between them, Hollie felt a new emotion. What was it? It seemed vaguely familiar, something from long ago.

"And if I don't go over the lesson plan, tomorrow will be wasted," Nick continued. He turned away.

I'm being dumped!

It was as effective as the old I-have-to-wash-my-hair routine. Maybe more so. And she didn't like being dumped any more now than she had as a teenager. Even if she did know it was for the best. Even if she had refused to let him come over first.

She was here to fluster *him,* not vice versa.

She marched back to her space in the rear of Nick's classroom, knowing his eyes followed her. She bent down and sniffed the fragrant rose as a reminder of what he had done. The bell rang, startling Christopher at first, then sending him into joyous, wave-riding, swimming motions with his arms and legs.

Hollie glanced at the clock, then at Nick. "Oh, I wanted to talk to Joey before recess was over. Think I can have him for a few minutes?" she asked as the children filed in noisily and hung up their coats in the closet.

Nick looked worried.

"Don't look so scared," she assured him with a laugh. "I'm not planning on absconding with him."

"That's not what worries me." He studied her over the heads of the children who were noisily laughing and pushing and slowly taking their seats.

"Afraid I'll enlist him in some new, devious plan?"

"Timmy, is Joey in the boys' room?" Nick asked.

Hollie's head swiveled around. Joey's desk was vacant.

"I dunno, Mr. Nicholson."

"Michael?"

Michael shrugged eloquently.

Hollie, being closer to the closet than Nick, glanced inside. No one was in there.

Nick was beside her in a flash. "Just like before." He smacked the palm of his hand against his forehead.

Hollie felt as if she was on very unfamiliar, very shaky ground. "What?" she asked, even as she dreaded the answer.

"He's cut school again."

THEY'LL NEVER KNOW I'm gone.

Of course, that's what Joey always thought. And Mr. Nicholson always missed him. But after seeing how his teacher and his mom had been eye-locked today, he hoped they'd be too distracted to notice his absence.

They were acting kind of goofy, even for grown-ups. His mom had been so careful getting that flower to school—she'd covered it up as warmly as she did Christopher. She carried it as carefully as she did Christopher. She even talked to it like she did Christopher.

As for that early-present-from-Santa story… Who did she think she was fooling?

And as for Mr. Nicholson, he'd had that same look in his eyes that male movie stars got before they kissed a woman. *Yuck!*

So he was pretty sure they wouldn't miss him. The judge didn't need to know, either.

Chapter Eight

"What do you mean 'Joey's cut school again'?" Hollie demanded in a whisper. She was afraid to say the words any louder for fear the judge would somehow hear them. Irrational, she knew, but she wasn't willing to take that chance. She had too much at stake here. "He wouldn't do that!"

Even as she said the words, she was afraid they might be true, though Joey knew how important it was that he stay in school. He knew the judge was angry. He understood the man's power. He really wasn't any happier about her being in class with him than she was.

She should have let him believe in Santa Claus a couple more years. That would have curtailed these pre-Christmas pranks, if that's what cutting school was to him.

Desperate, she grasped at the most likely straw. "He's probably in the boys' room, like you said."

"Yeah, right."

She didn't need an interpreter to tell her Nick wouldn't bet any money on it. Neither would she.

"I'm going to go look, anyway."

She turned to collect Christopher and found he'd fallen asleep on his tummy on the blanket. It would be a shame to wake him for a mad dash around the school to find his naughty brother. As a picture of herself back in court flashed before her eyes, she glanced at the girls in the class, trying to remember whose turn it was to baby-sit, but she was too frantic to think straight.

Nick, being more astute than she'd given him credit for, offered softly, "You can leave him here."

She hesitated, surprised by his offer. She wanted to give him a chance to think about what he was saying even as she wanted to rush out the door. "Are you sure?"

She prayed he was. She needed to get Joey back into class. She tamped down an image of Judge Nicholson levying a hefty fine on her.

She didn't even want to think about how she couldn't afford that. Her parents would say she'd chosen her own path when she'd elected to have another child without a husband. They'd warned her. Then they'd closed the door on her and Joey as soon as she'd received the wonderful news she was pregnant again. Her in-laws lived out of town and, though they were emotionally supportive of her "giving" them another grandchild, they were on a fixed income and wouldn't be able to help.

Nick rolled his eyes and waved her toward the door. "I think I have enough willing baby-sitters if Christopher should happen to wake up."

Hollie dashed out the door without looking back.

"Just hurry back!"

As if he needed to tell her that! She was sure he really meant "don't let the judge see you running around when you're supposed to be in here."

The boys' room was empty, except for one kid with a soggy hall pass. Not that she asked to see the pass, but he volunteered—probably because she scared the poor kid at the urinal when she yanked open the door and tore into the rest room like a madwoman.

The nurse's office had a little girl napping on a cot while she waited for someone to come pick her up. The nurse took one look at Hollie's strained face, didn't recognize her and moved protectively toward the little girl. Hollie fled without explanation and outran the nurse, who pursued her down the hall.

Her escapade through the nurse's office prompted another fear. Could Joey have fallen off the jungle gym and knocked himself out without anyone noticing? Maybe everyone had already been on their way in from recess. Maybe he'd been afraid he'd be late, so he'd hurried and hadn't been careful and slipped.

Hollie, coatless and hair flying, raced out the door and down the concrete steps without feeling the December cold. The jungle gym was empty. She looked behind the utility shed and found a couple dozen short cigarette butts, but no Joey. She went into the gym and checked the playground equipment storage locker, hoping he had gone to return something and accidentally locked himself in. Surely the judge couldn't fault him for an innocent mistake like that.

No such luck; the door swung open easily.

At this point, Hollie thought Joey would be better off if she did find him hurt somewhere, say, lying under the bleachers with a twisted ankle. Otherwise, she was going to ground him until he was twenty-one.

She wandered around the playground and checked beneath the bleachers. She jammed her ice-cold fingers into her pockets. Her car keys were there, beckoning her. Christopher would be well looked after. She'd be gone only a short while, she hoped. She glanced up at the windows to Nick's classroom. She could see the top of his head as he moved around inside, doing his thing. She got into her car and did hers.

Frantically, she drove home and back several times, taking different routes, circling around, passing by all the spots Joey might be likely to go—the pet store, the hobby shop, the sporting goods store, the park playground.

She finally had to admit that a nine-year-old boy, on the lookout for his mom in her car, would be able to elude her easily. She just hoped he eluded anyone who might recognize him and report back to the authorities.

She drove back to school, turned into the parking lot and discovered her worst nightmare had just begun. There, in front of the door, was a police car.

NICK WATCHED OUT one of his classroom's windows as the scene below him unfolded. Hollie pulled into the parking lot and braked suddenly. She sat there in her car, in the middle of the entrance, as if debating what to do. He figured she'd want to throw the car in reverse, back out, drive away and keep looking until she found Joey on her own. But he knew she wouldn't leave again with Christopher inside the school.

He shifted the baby to his other shoulder, bouncing him lightly as he'd seen Hollie do. He put a cloth diaper over his shirt because Hollie had told him that detergent residue in clothing irritated Christopher's skin. If anyone had asked, he'd have said it was because the last thing he needed was a fussy baby, but he really did it because he liked the little guy. And his mother. Even though they both were a pain in his classroom.

He watched as she slowly pulled her car into the space she'd left a half hour ago. The wind whipped her hair as she got out, folded her arms across her chest in an effort to stay warm and headed for the front door of the school. She only covered a few steps when she remembered she'd forgotten to close the car door and had to turn back.

Nick had known she'd left without her coat, but the fact that she would be freezing hadn't really hit him until he saw her hunched over against the wind. He wanted to run downstairs, put his arms around her and hold her until she thawed. By that time, he knew, he'd be way past thawed and want to take her back to his place and do some serious holding.

Fat chance now.

Timmy's hand shot up in the air. "I got the answer, Mr. Nicholson."

Nick's mind wasn't on his class; he only half heard Timmy.

If only it were so easy to find the answer to helping Hollie. Lying sprung to mind, but that would set a really bad example, and he'd never get on staff at the high school. Of course if they heard about him baby-sitting during class while Hollie ran around town, he could kiss that goodbye now, anyway. And how much could he enjoy the job knowing Hollie would be in serious hot water with the judge?

"Whose turn is it to baby-sit?" He turned and saw Timmy's hand up in the air, waving frantically to get Nick's attention. None of the boys had volunteered previously. "You sure?" he asked doubtfully.

Timmy glanced at his paper. "Uh-huh."

Nick sighed. Well, if he could baby-sit, why not Timmy? He had two younger siblings at home and undoubtedly had enough experience. Over the loud, unrestrained vocal objections of every girl in the class, Nick carefully placed Christopher into the arms of a very surprised Timmy and left the room at a fast clip.

When he didn't see Hollie or the police in the hall, he burst into the main office.

"They're inside," the secretary, poised in front of her computer monitor, said without looking up. She'd been the secretary when Nick had been a student there, and her attitude said she'd seen it all. Now Nick knew it was all a facade, because nobody could say they'd ever seen a situation like this before.

"Check on my class in a few minutes, will you?"

"No problem."

He turned to his immediate left and aimed toward the closed door, the top half of which had Principal stenciled on its frosted glass. He could see the images of several people on the other side, filling the small room to capacity.

Without hesitation, he charged into Ed's office, prepared to call the man "Mr. Nelson" to his face for the rest of his life if it helped Hollie. Two police officers, dressed in their winter blues, stood with their hands on their hips, staring at each other as if they weren't sure how to proceed.

Hollie, ashen faced, perched on the edge of a chair against the wall, her reindeer-socked ankles wrapped tightly around the chair's front legs. Her position clearly dared anyone to try to move her from that office before she was good and ready to leave. Nick certainly wouldn't want to be the one to try it.

The two officers, one of whom Nick had played football with in high school, turned toward him with curious expressions, as if wondering, *What next?*

The principal gave him his old I-thought-I-told-you-to-behave look, still unchanged from years ago.

Hollie slowly looked up at him with big, sad, moist eyes. Eyes that clearly said she knew she was in deep trouble, all of which could have been prevented if he'd just talked to her about Joey's truancy instead of his father. The simple notes he'd sent home with Joey had come back dated and signed. Perhaps, Nick admitted to himself now, he should have looked more closely at those signatures.

He'd been really good at improvisation in high school. He hoped he was even better now.

"I can explain." The words rushed out of his mouth. His brain went into overdrive, trying to figure out just how he was going to explain anything when he felt the way he did now.

All he wanted to do was save Hollie—from his father, from the police, from another appearance in court where his dad would decide who-knew-what. With direct eye contact, he included both officers and the principal in his hastily prepared speech as he tried to buy her more time.

"I'm afraid it's my fault—"

"No!" Hollie vaulted out of her chair.

There was a stubborn bent to her mouth. He'd seen it before, several times in his classroom over the past few days, only it was more pronounced now. A sudden urge to kiss it away shook him to the core.

"You see," he continued instead, holding up his hand in a silent plea for her to remain quiet for once and let him help her, "I'm responsible—"

"Stop it, Nick!"

He grinned inside, in spite of the scenario. She had a good, commanding "mother's" voice that warned him not to mess with her. If he were Joey, he wouldn't have crossed her. He took a closer look at the two cops and decided they weren't in a hurry to do anything for exactly the same reason.

"Where's Christopher?"

"He's fine. Timmy's baby-sit...uh, Timmy's in charge. And the secretary will check on him in a minute."

Officer Grandowski, formerly the East Bay fullback to Nick's quarterback, removed his navy blue uniform hat, scratched his head and gave Nick a sympathetic look. While he wasn't outwardly grinning, Nick knew Ski had an innate sense of humor that would enable him to retell this tale long past the Christmas parties. Something along the lines of how last week it had taken a court order to get Hollie into the school and today they couldn't get her out without serious physical pressure.

"Mrs. Landon insists on waiting here until her son returns," Grandowski informed Nick. "Do you think he'll come back here?"

"Of course he will," Hollie snapped, then resumed her chair-hugging straddle. She muttered, "If he knows what's good for him."

"He always has," Nick replied. "He's almost as good at sneaking in as he is at sneaking out. You've got a little boy about the same age now, don't you, Ski?"

Ski's grin told Nick he was well aware of Nick's ploy to garner his sympathy through association. "Uh, he's a little young for this stuff."

"You mean he hasn't busted out of day-care yet?" his partner asked.

Not one to relinquish control easily, the principal cleared his throat meaningfully. "I think you should return to your classroom now, Mr. Nicholson. These officers have everything under control."

Nick didn't want to leave Hollie here alone. She was perched on the edge of the hard wood chair again, her legs still wrapped around it—as if that would stop Ski and his partner from just picking her *and* it up when the time came to cart her off to court. She gripped the edge of the seat so tightly with her fingers that her knuckles were colorless.

He wasn't a parent, but he knew she was probably worried whether Joey had really skipped school or if something had happened to him. Or both. And she had to be really concerned about what was going to happen next.

"How did you know Hollie was gone?" he asked the officers. He was curious, stalling for time, and pretended he'd never heard Ed's "suggestion." Nick hadn't spent all those years on the stage for nothing.

"Hollie?" Ed asked pointedly.

"Uh, Mrs. Landon." He nearly added "sir," but decided he'd save that for when he really needed it—like if the two officers tried to drag Hollie out. Not that Nick would let them, but he might need Ed to back him up.

"The school nurse called 9-1-1," Grandowski said. "Something about a crazy woman trying to kidnap a little girl from the nurse's office."

"I did not!" Hollie denied.

Grandowski held up his hand, but it did nothing to stop her.

"I was looking for Joey," she said scathingly. "I didn't have time to stop and explain the details to her."

"Please, Mrs. Landon, I understand," he said in a reassuring tone. "We're not making any formal charges on that."

"Better not," she muttered.

Nick wanted to pull up the other chair and sit beside her. He wanted to take her in his arms and hold her until Joey came back. He wanted to make the police go away and make everything go back to normal.

Well, not exactly normal. He wanted her back in his classroom every day until Christmas break.

"Of course," Grandowski continued, "I can't say whether the nurse is going to pursue this."

Hollie's head snapped up.

"What do you mean?" Nick demanded.

"Well, she was scared. She said something about calling Judge Nicholson direct to complain about putting—" he lowered his voice in an aside to Nick, his old buddy "—criminals in school with the children."

Hollie's chair slammed back into the wall as she jumped to her feet again. "I am not a criminal!"

Grandowski's partner grimaced at him. "Jeez, why don't you just announce it on the PA system?"

"Sorry, Mrs. Landon."

"Why aren't you out there looking for my son? Maybe he's hurt. Or...or maybe someone picked him up." She paced the small amount of floor space left in the office already filled to capacity with a large desk, two chairs, assorted file cabinets and five adults.

"I'm sure—"

"Never mind." She tried to shoulder her way past Grandowski, but he didn't move aside.

Nick watched as she fisted her hands on her hips and glared up at the man. She'd done the same to him often enough in the classroom, but while there was a spark in her eyes, it wasn't the same bright, fiery one he'd grown accustomed to. Not like when she and he squared off. Now her eyes were cold, nearly lifeless, definitely humorless.

And that's when Nick suddenly knew she'd *enjoyed* every minute she'd challenged him. Every hour. Every day. Every last thing she had done to drive him nuts had been in earnest, but carried off with a sharp sense of humor.

He could barely wait to get this straightened out and take up the challenge again.

"I want to go back to the classroom," she said firmly, as if daring either officer to question her.

"I'm sorry. You'll have to stay right here."

"Yeah, she needs to get back." Nick questioned his sanity for wanting to help her when she'd enjoyed tormenting him so much, but he did it, anyway. He'd analyze it later.

"My baby might need me."

"Your baby?" Grandowski asked with a frown that invited her to explain.

Hollie continued, "The kids have all been good with him, but Nick or I have always been nearby." Both officers gave her a blank look.

"You know—" Nick held his hands about two feet apart "—a baby. A little kid. Wears diapers. Kind of helpless without his mother."

They still looked blank.

Ed cleared his throat. "Mrs. Landon brings her infant son to school with her. I believe he's in Mr. Nicholson's classroom."

"And I have to get back to him," Hollie added.

"You're not going anywhere just yet," came a voice from the doorway.

The officers spun around, clearly caught off guard as they hadn't heard the door open behind them. The principal's head snapped up. Nick hung his, knowing this new development, this intrusion, was the last thing Hollie needed.

Grandowski was first to recover his power of speech. "Judge Nicholson." He stepped away from his partner to make more room for the judge to enter the office.

Hollie sank into the chair. Her head fell back against the wall. "Oh, God. What next?"

Nick didn't care who was watching, he stood beside her and laid his hand on her shoulder.

"Next, maybe someone can explain to me what's going on," his dad intoned in his official judge's tone. He glared at Nick.

"Look, she didn't try to kidnap anyone," Nick said in her defense. For a father and son who rarely talked, he thought they were doing an awful lot of it since Hollie had come into their lives.

"That's reassuring," his dad replied.

Nick gave himself a mental pat on the back. The two of them were finally starting to communicate on the same wavelength.

"Who said she did?"

"Uh—"

Hollie brushed his hand off her shoulder. "Never mind, Nick. I think I can hang myself without your help." She rose and faced the judge. "Why are you here?"

"I promised my son I'd reconsider my ruling."

Nick thought her smile lit up the room.

His dad continued, "So, before I did that, I thought I'd come by today, unannounced, and see the results for myself."

He perused the office, the principal, Nick and Hollie and two of East Bay's finest, as if waiting for one of them to explain why the situation didn't look quite the way he thought it should. Like two of them should be in the classroom and two of them should be in the patrol car.

Nick watched helplessly as Hollie's smile faltered. She had a really expressive face. He'd have to warn her not to play poker for money.

Hollie turned toward him, her expression an adorable mixture of uncertainty mingled with surprise. "You asked him to reconsider?" she asked softly.

Nick was pleased to see at least one crease on her face relax a little. "I said I would."

"I know, but...I guess I thought you were just saying that to get me to quit bothering you."

His dad cleared his throat impatiently, and Nick realized that when Hollie had spoken to him in that soft, grateful voice, he'd forgotten everyone else was in the room. He felt an even stronger urge to protect her, which was pretty darned confusing considering she'd done everything possible since Monday morning to make his life difficult.

The judge singled out the principal. "Mr. Nelson, might I borrow your office for a few minutes?"

"Certainly, Judge."

The two officers filed out, the principal right behind them. He reached back in and grabbed Nick by the arm, but Nick shook him off and closed the door on him, effectively putting an end to that matter.

Hollie, alone now with Nick and the judge, squelched the urge to reach up and knead her tight neck muscles. It wouldn't help, anyway. She feared she was going to get a lot more knots before this day was over. Better to keep her wits about her and do whatever she could to save her family.

"So...did you?" she asked Judge Nicholson. "Reconsider?"

"I gave the matter a great deal of thought."

Hollie thought she'd burst if he didn't get to the point. Nick didn't look much more patient. He scowled at his father as if he were ready to shake the answer loose.

Unfazed, the judge continued as if he were in his courtroom and he had all the time in the world. "I carefully considered what kind of message that would send to the community. To the whole state, as a matter of fact."

"The state?" Hollie suspected the man thought a little too highly of himself and his importance.

"Ah, yes," he said with a smile she didn't think she liked. "You haven't read the paper?"

"I've been a little too busy," she retorted through tight lips.

"It's been on the evening news. They're even reporting that I might send you to jail. I could, you know, if I wanted to."

The suspense was killing her. She wondered how much he'd add to her penalty if she screamed at him to get on with it. "No one's interviewed me."

Nick grinned, and she thought she must be confused. He looked at his dad as if he'd just found new respect for the man.

"That's because they've been camped out on Dad's porch until now. A news van pulled up outside right behind you."

She was too impatient for this dillydallying. "So, what's the verdict? Are you going to let me go home?"

Should she state the obvious—she'd been in the classroom as per the judge's order and Joey had *still* managed to cut school—or would she be putting her own neck in the noose?

The judge wasn't distracted. "As I was saying, after much serious deliberation—" he glanced at Nick "—I decided to let you go home. You may pay a fine instead."

Hollie couldn't help herself; she threw her arms around the neck of the man who had made the difference—Nick.

"Thank you, thank you, thank you," she said, squeezing him tightly, barely controlling herself enough not to kiss him again.

She felt Nick's arms circle her. He held her longer than necessary, probably longer than appropriate, but he just felt so darned good, she didn't care. She was free, thanks to him. She was going to be really busy from now until Christmas, but she'd find time to bake him a double batch of double-chocolate-chip cookies.

She let him go and tugged her reindeer-tracked sweater back down around her hips. "Thank you, Judge. I'll write you a check as soon as I get home."

"Not to me, you won't. To the City of East Bay. Five hundred dollars."

He might as well have had a gavel in his hand. He might as well have hit her with it. The amount staggered her as hard as if he'd raised the wooden hammer and done just that.

"Five hundred..." She couldn't even say the rest. She glanced at Nick for help.

He didn't look too surprised.

"You knew?" Her voice was no stronger than a whisper.

His hand moved aimlessly in the air as she stepped away from him. His lips moved, but he said nothing.

"You knew he was going to fine me five hundred dollars and you didn't tell me?"

"I didn't know for certain."

"A hint would have been nice."

"I called the bank this morning and checked my balance. If you don't have it, I could lend it to you."

Her lips were so tight she could barely speak. "Didn't know for certain, huh?"

"Mrs. Landon—"

"Oh, shut up." She quickly realized she'd just snapped at a man who held the future of her family in his hands. She added, "Your Honor."

"I can withdraw the money as soon as school's out this afternoon," Nick offered.

Hollie's hands balled into fists. She squeezed tears of frustration back so the judge wouldn't see her cry. "I can't accept it."

"You have to!"

She shook her head. "No, I don't. It's against my principles to borrow money I don't know I can repay."

"Don't be foolish."

"Borrowing five hundred dollars would be foolish. I'm not about to set that kind of example for my children." Hollie's chin came up stubbornly. She glared at the judge with the same cold, hard look she'd bestowed on the cops.

"I'll continue to come to school every day with Joey instead."

The judge shook his head.

Confused, she asked, "What?"

"The condition of my ruling was that you were to keep Joey here all day, every day. Mrs. Landon, you failed again."

The "again" really rankled. Right up there with "failed." She already felt bad enough and she didn't need an outside observer passing sentence on her abilities as a mother.

"It's obvious you have no control over your son's whereabouts. If you won't pay the fine, I'll have the two officers outside take you in on contempt charges."

"Wait!" Hollie searched her brain frantically for a compromise.

There had to be a better way. If she paid five hundred dollars this time, and Joey skipped again, then what? Another five hundred? A thousand? As if she could spare *that*. And there was a dangerous precedent here of letting the legal system establish a dollar amount as an acceptable resolution for truant kids.

"There must be some other arrangement we can come to. Maybe, after Christmas when I'm done with the Snowflake Ball, Joey and I could do some community service or something."

The judge pursed his lips in thought, which gave Hollie a moment of hope. "I'll tell you what, Mrs. Landon. I'll give that serious consideration while you spend a few hours in a jail cell and reevaluate how you handle your son."

"Jail?"

"Joey hasn't been listening to either of us, and they say one picture's worth a thousand words. Maybe when he comes back and finds you behind bars, it'll get his attention.''

''Fine,'' she snapped. She'd make sure the media got a picture of her and Christopher going to jail, even if it was only for a few hours. ''I'll go get my baby first. Then we'll just see what those reporters have to say about that.''

Chapter Nine

Hollie flung open the door of the principal's office so hard that it smacked against a file cabinet. The sound of breaking glass was a small, but hollow, reward. It only served to remind her that her life was shattering in a similar fashion.

She stormed down the hall toward Nick's classroom. He was right beside her.

"I can find my own way," she spat out.

"Quick," he whispered urgently. He leaned so close that she could feel his breath tease her hair and warm her ear. "You gather up Christopher. Don't take more than you can carry. I'll get my motorcycle."

She glanced at him nervously.

His arm circled her shoulders and held her close in his confidence. "I'll meet you at the back door in, say, ten minutes?"

"Nick . . ."

In a quick, nervous glance, she was both relieved and disappointed to see a smile tugging at the corners of his lips. Would she have done it if he'd been serious? Run off with him?

The thought was more than interesting. What was downright intriguing was the way her body reacted to the thought of roaring off into the unknown with Nick.

She wouldn't have gone, of course. She could never have left without Joey, even though the little brat—she thought the word with a healthy dose of motherly love—was responsible for getting all of them in this mess in the first place.

She was momentarily diverted from her somewhat shaky future as she wondered, if she'd taken Nick up on his offer, if he'd really have gone through with it. According to gossip she'd overheard in the grocery store checkout line, that's exactly what he'd done right after his senior year of high school. He hadn't even hung around for the graduation ceremony. Was he still the type of man to run when things didn't work out the way he wanted?

"Better relax or you're going to scare Christopher."

He was right, she realized. She slowed her pace slightly as they walked down the long hall, Nick's arm still around her shoulders. She took a deep, cleansing breath and tried, without success, the same visualization she'd used to relax during childbirth. *That* had been a piece of cake compared to this. "It's not working. I can't relax."

"Yes, you can."

His hand slid away from her shoulder as he grabbed her arm gently but firmly, effectively stopping her as he turned her to face him. When he glanced back at the two police officers, Hollie noticed they had the courtesy to stand aside and allow them a moment of privacy. Apparently *they* weren't worried that Nick might meet her at the back door with his Harley.

"Look, I'll talk to my dad again."

"No, thanks!" She was sure her expression matched the horrified tone she heard in her refusal. "And don't stand there looking so innocent. It's your talking to him that's gotten me this close to jail already, thank you very much."

"I'll go to the mayor, then."

"Who's that? His brother?"

A slow grin spread across his face and slowly weakened her knees. She folded her arms across her chest in an attempt to block all nonverbal communication with him, to get a hold of herself and stick to the business at hand.

"No, she's an old girlfriend." He waggled his eyebrows as if that said it all.

"God, Nick, don't ever think you're not just like your father." She stormed away, hoping some distance between them would help her focus.

"Hey, that's not fair." He kept pace with her, an easy thing to do with his long legs.

She grasped the doorknob and yanked the classroom door open. Nick's hand landed on the wood above her head and slammed it shut again.

"Stop it," she hissed as she turned on him. She found him closer than comfortable. One move in the wrong direction and they'd be mashed up against each other. Instinctively she backed against the door. He followed until his chest was no more than a finger's width from her breasts. His head dipped to her level until she saw golden flecks in his deep brown eyes.

She wondered if she stomped on his instep if she'd be charged with assault.

"Don't even think about it," he said in a low voice. "You need to calm down before you go in there."

As if she could ever relax with him that close.

"I don't need to be calm to gather up my stuff and leave."

She was going to say more—she had lots to say to him—but he made a little shushing noise and laid his index finger along her lips. It was the gentleness of his touch that silenced her. His closeness. His quietness. She couldn't think while inhaling his unique scent of leather and fresh pine, and staring at his neck, studying how it seemed so strong as it disappeared beneath the band of his T-shirt and widened out into shoulders broad enough to help her through this.

"You need to be composed so you don't upset my class," he said in a quiet tone meant, she was sure, to instill the same in her. "I don't want them frightened. They need to know the police are their friends."

"Well, they're not mine today," she muttered. She stifled the urge to fold her arms across her chest, to block him out again, but he hadn't left enough room between them to do that without touching him. It would seem like more of a caress than what she was going for.

He traced her bottom lip with the tip of his finger. She wanted to reach up and slap it away, but her hand wouldn't move.

"Relax," he said.

She took a deep breath. Against her better judgment, the pine scent soothed her, reminded her of Christmases past. "Do you work at a Christmas tree lot at night?"

"Huh?"

"Uh, nothing." She fidgeted from one foot to the other. "I'm ready now."

"Sure?"

She nodded, lost in his warm hazel eyes as his arm circled her waist. Every nerve ending tingled and she resisted the urge to fling herself against his chest. But just barely.

Her maternal ear could hear the children on the other side of the door. No screams, no yells, no sounds of them getting out of control and tossing things around. There was nothing pulling her away from Nick and into the room right that second.

His hand brushed against her hip. She elected not to move away from it.

"As much as I'm enjoying this—" he grinned "—I can't open the door unless you move about an inch to the left."

She sidestepped to her left, right smack into his hand.

He groaned. "I meant my left."

"Oh, sorry."

"I'm not." Again, that wicked grin that drove her to distraction.

She moved the other direction, though not too far. The heat of his gaze as he looked into her eyes kept her rooted within inches of him.

Officer Grandowski adopted the principal's throat-clearing method of getting their attention.

"Yeah, yeah," Nick replied without breaking eye contact with Hollie. He tugged the door open, forcing her toward him as he inched backward. "Don't be in such an all-fired hurry to lock a lady up."

Without enough room to maneuver, her foot bumped the toe of his boot, making her stumble. With a smooth sweep of his other arm, he steadied her by pulling her into the warmth of his body—which did nothing to steady her nerves.

If Christopher had wailed at that moment, she'd have had no trouble pulling away from Nick. As it was, the children had all scurried to their seats the instant they'd known someone was in the hall right outside their door—that had been pretty obvious when Nick slammed it shut—and Christopher was being an angel. Hollie didn't have the strength to step out of Nick's grasp.

"You're going to make *me* do this, aren't you?" he asked.

His unsteady grin gave her a renewed sense of power. "Well, it is your arm around my waist."

She watched, mesmerized by her effect on him as he closed his eyes, took a deep breath and warred with himself for the strength to let her go. She slowly ran her hands up the front of his T-shirt, tracing the muscles beneath.

He groaned. The warm circle of his arms disappeared as he grasped her hands in his. "Not fair."

"Add it to the list."

"Later," he promised.

She snickered. "Yeah, like I'm going to kiss you in jail. Get real."

She let him off the hook as she took the responsibility to pull away from him, then turned and entered the class-room. He followed on her heels. The girls and boys quickly surrounded them with a dose of reality.

Uh-oh.

Joey skipped into the school parking lot to find a police car parked near the front door. There was another car be-side it he didn't recognize, but he did know the man stand-ing next to it. Judge Nicholson, huddled up inside his overcoat, his collar turned high against the cold breeze, looked just as mean as he did in the courtroom.

This was bigger than grounding, bigger than losing his video game privileges for a whole month. A whole year, even. He was in deep doo-doo and he knew it.

"Young man," the judge said when he saw him.

Double uh-oh. He knew that tone of voice, even if he didn't have a dad. His mom was really good at it.

"What . . . what're you doing here?"

"I came to see you and your mother—" the judge's eyes were colder than the December wind "—but you weren't here. You know what that means, don't you?"

Joey felt his whole body go hot and cold at the same time. He had an overwhelming urge to run to the bathroom. He wouldn't have noticed that tears started to stream down his face, toward his shaking lower lip, except they burned on his cheeks.

"Your mother and I were just about to leave."

Joey glanced at the police car. "No, you can't make her go!" He wanted to kick that mean old judge in the shins. "I don't want you to take my mommy away. Christopher needs her. It's my fault. Punish me."

The judge tipped his head slightly to one side as he listened. Joey thought his eyes grew a bit warmer.

"Where've you been, Joey?"

If he told the judge *why* he'd skipped school, everything might be all better, but he couldn't. "I can't tell."

"Why not?"

"It would ruin my mom's Christmas present."

"But, Joey—"

"No! I want to get her something special. I want to earn it all by myself." He swiped his face with his coat sleeve.

"You have to tell me, son."

He could lie, but that'd make his mom even madder than going with the judge. His shoulders slumped.

"Can—" he hiccuped "—can you keep a secret, sir?"

If he could, Joey decided he'd come clean on everything. He could even take the judge home with him and show him that the Baby Jesus statue was safe and sound. He'd been trying to fix His finger so when Mr. Nicholson got Him back, he'd be happy. And if he told everybody else half the truth, he just might be able to pull it off and surprise everyone.

INSIDE THE CLASSROOM, Timmy quickly deposited Christopher in Hollie's arms, then waved his hand in front of his nose with a theatric flair that made Hollie wonder if Nick had picked the wrong lead for the Christmas play. "About time you got back. He needs to be changed."

"Where's Joey?" Michael asked.

"Why are the police here?" Linda asked.

Mary Margaret pressed her forehead to the windowpane. "Who's that man talking to Joey?"

"Where?" Hollie, along with everyone else, rushed to peer out the windows.

"Looks like he didn't sneak back in quite so well today," Nick commented by her ear.

She felt the heat from his body warm her back and the heat from the radiator warm the front of her thighs. She didn't know which was hotter. She knew which was more dangerous, though.

"That's the judge," Michael said importantly.

"Oh, no," Mary Margaret wailed. "Mr. Nicholson, are they going to arrest Joey?"

"I'm sure they're not." His deep voice rumbled in Hollie's ear as he tried to reassure all the children.

"Who'll take his part in the play?"

Hollie blocked out everything they had to say. She was far more concerned that Joey and Judge Nicholson had met up with each other at the worst possible time. They stood together at the end of the walk, Joey gazing earnestly up at the older man.

The wind whipped at them. The judge grabbed his hat and held it on his head, bowed toward Joey, who was apparently talking a blue streak if his hands waving around in the frigid air were any indication.

Nick's hand landed gently, reassuringly, on Hollie's shoulder. "You want me to change Christopher?"

Dumbstruck, she turned away from the window and looked up at him. Baby-sitting was one thing, but Joey's own father had never even changed a wet diaper, and now

Nick, completely unrelated to Christopher, was willing to go one better for her?

After her husband had died, she'd entertained the idea of another relationship. She'd even tried dating. Twice. It was awkward and uncomfortable. It had been impossible to get to know someone well in a short time before they'd started pressuring her toward the bedroom. She'd been completely turned off by the whole rigmarole.

And now, after a few days in Nick's classroom, the guy offered to change a diaper. He wasn't anything like any man she'd ever met. A long-term relationship with him would never be dull or boring. He'd never pressure her into anything. The way she felt whenever he touched her only happened once in a lifetime, she was sure.

Too bad Nick was the guy the other teachers thought would be run out of town by Christmas, if not sooner. And they knew him better than she did.

"Yeah, well, it's for extenuating circumstances," he said. "I figure you'd probably stick the poor kid with a pin in your hurry to get down there to Joey."

The corner of her lips tugged upward in delight. "A pin, huh? You're behind the times, big guy. You'd better have Mary Margaret supervise."

Nick saw Mary Margaret's nose glued to the window as she continued to monitor Joey and the judge. "If I need any help, I'll ask Linda."

She slipped Christopher into his arms, trying to ignore any and all electrical currents that flowed from Nick's chest, through her fingers and right to her heart. She wasn't very good at it, though.

She grabbed her coat out of the closet and zipped it up on her way out. Now if she could just straighten things out with her older son and the judge. Besides needing to do that for

Joey's welfare, she had the added incentive of wanting to smooth the way for her and Nick.

In only a matter of days, she'd spent more time with him than any other single adult in the past twelve months, except maybe her neighbor, Terri. And Terri was more like a sister. There wasn't anything that smacked of "sibling" in the way she felt when she thought of Nick. Which was most of the time and not just when he had her pinned up against the door.

She raced past the two very surprised policemen, charged out the front door of the school and vaulted down the stairs, oblivious to any patches of snow and ice that might upset her balance. She had more important things on her mind just then.

"Ah, Mrs. Landon," Judge Nicholson said when he saw her running toward him. He reached down and took Joey's hand in his, as if he were ready to haul him off to juvenile hall right then.

The sight made her heart sink.

"No, wait," she pleaded, suddenly engulfed with guilt. What a rotten mother she was! How could she have been thinking of Nick when her son took priority? How could she make it up to Joey? "Please," she begged.

The two police officers, who'd shadowed her all the way down the steps and out the door, stepped forward in case they had to restrain her.

"Joey and I are going to take a little drive," Judge Nicholson said.

Well, if begging didn't sway the ogre, maybe threats would.

"My son's not going anywhere without me, and I'm not going anywhere without a law—"

Suddenly Nick was beside her, his hand on her arm offering her strength. She drank of it heavily. The only reason she heard his voice was because it was so soft, so calm.

"I think he has more to say, Hollie."

"I don't care," she snapped. The cold wind whipped at her skin, drying any tears she might have shed. "This isn't right."

"Me'n the judge are going somewhere, Mom."

Hollie thought of grabbing her son's hand and pulling him away from the judge, but Joey had a look in his eyes she'd seen before. Usually right before her birthday or Mother's Day, when he was trying to hide a present from her. Nick moved so he was standing behind her, his hands on her shoulders as if he thought he might have to stop her from acting like a mother lion and attacking his father before she got all the facts.

"Joey and I've been talking," the judge said. The corner of his mouth twitched ever so slightly. "We've, uh, decided there's some more information that I need to consider before making any decisions today. Perhaps I'll reconsider letting you continue to attend school every day."

Hollie waited for either him or Joey to explain. When they didn't, she prompted with an exasperated, "Well?"

"It shouldn't take us long." He looked down at Joey. "Less than an hour, you think?"

Joey nodded up at him. Was that pride she saw in her son's eyes?

"With your permission, of course, Mrs. Landon."

Hollie was stumped by the judge's query and Joey's response to the whole situation. She looked over her shoulder at Nick as she felt his hands squeeze her reassuringly. "He's your father. What would you do?"

"If there's any chance he won't haul you into court when he gets back, I'd let him go."

Hollie was puzzled. But if there were any reason not to trust the judge, she was sure Nick would have told her.

"I'll let you know my decision as soon as we return," he promised.

That's what I'm afraid of.

"Okay." Then, if he didn't agree to let things continue as they had been—and she was mortified that that suddenly seemed like a good option—she wondered if he would consider flogging instead of a fine, an overnight stay in jail or whatever else he might have in mind for her. "One hour."

"We'll be prompt." The judge smiled.

It was something Hollie was sure happened so rarely that she actually felt a little reassured by it.

The judge and Joey turned and walked away, the older man hunched over in an effort to ward off the chill. They chatted as they walked together, and the wind blew their words away so no one could tell what the two of them found so interesting.

Nick's hands kneaded Hollie's tightly strung shoulder muscles with absentminded intensity, until he'd evidently applied too much pressure, he noted, as she twisted out of his grasp and stepped away.

"Sorry." He dropped his hands to his sides. He'd never forgive his father for treating Hollie like a neglectful mother, who let her son run wild and rule the roost. He'd met few women with such strong, maternal instinct. And yet she managed to balance it enough to produce a kid who was more well-adjusted than most of his two-parent students.

Joey reached for his seat belt, and the judge waited for him to secure it before he drove away. Nick got the feeling that if he hadn't, Hollie would have run out in the parking lot and read him the riot act.

"He'll be fine," he assured her.

She stuffed her hands into her pockets.

Nick not only wanted to tell his father off, he wanted to take Joey aside and explain to him how his actions were affecting his mother. He wanted to tell him to knock it off, or else. He knew he didn't have the right.

And that bothered him, too.

HOLLIE STOOD BY the windows, holding Christopher as he slept in her arms. He was clean, dry and full.

When she'd returned to the classroom, expecting that Nick had reneged on his offer to change the baby, she'd discovered otherwise. Linda proudly told Hollie she'd put on the diaper herself, and admitted she'd done it after Nick had cleaned his bottom so fast even Christopher had seemed confused.

She stared out the windows as she slowly paced their length up and down the side of the schoolroom. The parking lot was below her. Her station wagon was parked crooked. The police cruiser was gone. The judge's car hadn't returned. Nothing moved in the frigid air, except for the tops of the bare trees swaying in the wind.

Nick's voice as he conducted his class was a soft, low murmur in the background of her thoughts. He soothed her nerves. She drew new strength from him.

She wondered how life could turn so funny that one day she was hard at work on the Snowflake Ball, and the next she was stuck in her son's fourth-grade classroom—and he wasn't even on the premises.

Her attention was caught by a car pulling into the parking lot. It stopped in front of the school without regard for parking in a designated spot, much as the judge had done, but it wasn't his. Hollie bent over the portable crib, laid Christopher down and tucked a lightweight blanket around him. He was in such a deep sleep, he didn't even wiggle. Not even when the door opened, Joey walked in and everyone started talking at once.

"Where'd you go?"

"Didja bust outta jail?"

"Enough," Nick warned his class.

Hollie took a deep breath. She looked at Joey, saw he was physically all right, but the good spirits he'd been in earlier when he'd left with the judge had been replaced by a little-boy scowl. She focused over his shoulder to see what kind of mood the judge was in. Only he wasn't there.

Her in-laws filled the doorway behind Joey.

Usually, whenever she saw Al Landon, she saw what her husband would have looked like if he'd lived another thirty-five years. They'd shared the same tall, angular build, hidden today beneath a dark brown winter coat. The same dancing blue eyes, except today Al's gaze was cold and steady. His hair was as gray as his mood.

The only thing her husband had inherited from his mother was what everyone always noticed first—her smile. Normally it lit up her face to the point where no one noticed much else about her. Today Hollie saw her tightly permed gray hair, her thin lips, her wringing hands.

Hollie watched in stumped silence as Nick introduced himself by first name and shook hands with her frowning father-in-law. Then all three of them turned as a unit and stared at her as she cuddled Joey to reassure herself that he was really there.

"Where did you go?" she asked him quietly. This was, after all, their business, not everyone else's. In spite of the fact that the judge continued to make it public information with his antics.

"Home."

"Why, honey?"

"I had to show Judge Nicholson something I've been working on. It's a secret, Mom."

"Joey, you can't have any secrets about this. It's too important."

"It's for Christmas." His small little voice choked on a sob. "It'll be ruined if I tell."

Hollie was dumbfounded. *Christmas?* What the heck did Christmas have to do with Joey and the judge?

"Young man—"

"Aw gee, I can't tell. Don't make me. You'll see later."

"But—"

"You told me how important it is not to lie, Mom. You told me I have to keep secrets if they don't hurt anybody. I'm not lying and I'm not hurting anybody. The judge isn't going to make you go to court. And he isn't going to make you pay the fine. Just wait, please."

Hollie had never heard so much logic from a nine-year-old. Either Joey was in earnest or he was a little con man. She preferred to think the former.

She straightened his hair and strove to deflate the issue. "Where's your hat?"

He pulled it out of his pocket and grinned. "Guess I forgot it, huh?"

She took one last, long look in his eyes. He'd always been trustworthy before. She trusted him now.

"Grandma and Grandpa brought me back."

"So I noticed." She rose, then bent down and whispered in Joey's ear. "Did they forget how to smile?"

"Uh-huh." He went the long way around her to go hang up his coat.

Hollie pasted on a bright smile. "Mom, Dad, what are you doing here?"

She exchanged the customary hugging ritual with her in-laws even though it felt as though she were embracing two trees for all the warmth she received in return.

"What's all this nonsense we've been reading about?" her father-in-law demanded of her. His yellow knit cap was in his hands, getting the life choked out of it.

"Reading about? But, Dad, you live in Kansas."

"We have newspapers in Kansas," he snapped.

His strong, clear voice was filled with more anger than Hollie had thought possible. This was the man that had stood by her side, day by day, while her husband fought a losing battle against disease? The same man who thought her giving him another grandchild on her own was some of the best news he'd ever had?

She was shocked—by his reaction as much as by the fact that East Bay's local news had traveled two states westward. And who knew where else? If Judge Nicholson was getting *that* much exposure, would he be as likely to back down? To give in? To change his ruling? No one liked to admit they were wrong in front of others. She thought it might be particularly hard for someone who was used to as much power as the judge.

She felt, more than saw, Nick move toward her. He seemed to be doing a lot of that, poor man. Lending her his strength in a quiet, self-assured manner whenever she needed it. Which lately turned out to be quite often.

"We decided to come see for ourselves," her mother-in-law, Bea Landon, said. It wasn't an explanation as much as a criticism. "We were going to wait at your house for you to come home this afternoon—we know where you leave the key—but Joey was already there. With that...judge, no less." On her lips, *judge* sounded like a dirty word.

Nick took Hollie's hand in his as he ushered all the adults out of his classroom and into the hall, then closed the door behind them. He released her hand, but not before he tossed her a private wink that went a long way toward renewing her.

Bea Landon sized Nick up, her surprise quite obvious as she took in his black leather jacket and the worn jeans that hugged his thighs. "You're Joey's teacher?"

"Yes, ma'am."

"Well . . ." Her eyes clearly said she'd discount his attire just this once because she had more important business at hand. "I'm asking this because you're his teacher and you see my grandson every day, you understand. Do you think he's being well cared for?"

"Mom!"

She tossed a quelling glare in Hollie's direction while she awaited Nick's answer.

"You have no right to come here and bother him with a question like that."

"I have every right."

Nick looked at Hollie as if he wanted to reach out and hold her, to comfort her in the face of this unexpected attack. Instead, he stuffed his hands into his pockets. "Mrs. Landon, I have nothing but the highest regard—"

"Stay out of this," Hollie snapped.

Nick looked shocked. "I was just going to reassure her that Joey—"

"She has no right to be checking up on me."

Hollie heard voices down the hall, strangers to the school discussing which way to turn, right or left.

"Now see here, Hollie," Al Landon began, "they're our grandsons."

"Then don't change that. Be their grandparents. Call them on the phone every week. Come visit them and cuddle them. Take them to the zoo. Read them stories. But don't go checking up on me."

Bea stood straight and stiff, totally unmoved by Hollie's plea. "We have to do what's best for the boys."

Hollie had always admired her mother-in-law and she realized, if Bea's overprotective attitude hadn't been directed at her right then, she'd have supported the woman wholeheartedly. There was no doubt Bea loved her grandsons.

"May I help you?" Nick asked.

Taken by surprise, Hollie followed his gaze and looked over her shoulder. The next step in her bid for freedom had arrived. A small group of her students, some of which regularly drove an hour to meet with her, stood hesitantly behind her.

"Hollie, is all right?" Ling asked in her halting English. The petite Chinese woman, in her mid-thirties, was flanked by four other adults of various ages and nationalities, two men and two women.

"Yes, Ling, it's all right," Hollie reassured her with a warm smile.

"Hollie," Nick said with a low, warning rumble.

"This is Nick," Hollie told her visitors. "We'll be using his classroom today." She turned to him then, neither surprised nor fazed the least bit by his stormy look. She smiled. "Nick, this is my class. Ling, Amini, Ana," she introduced the three women, and then the two men, "Karl and Tat."

Nick smiled broadly and, barely moving his lips, asked, "What the hell are they doing here?"

Hollie heard whispers beside her as her English-as-a-second-language students compared interpretations.

"They're here because this is what I do on Thursdays. Class, this is Joey's and Christopher's grandmother and grandfather."

Her students adored her children and were pleased to meet the grandparents, both of whom traded in their stony faces for looks of complete bewilderment in response to enthusiastic rounds of "Ahh!" and "Hello!"

"Not this Thursday," Nick said.

"Why should they miss class because your father sentenced me to fourth grade?" she asked in what she thought was a perfectly reasonable tone.

"Because it'll disrupt *my* class."

"Nonsense." She smiled at her students to reassure them that all was well. "We'll be good, won't we?"

They all smiled and nodded and said, "Yes."

She turned back to Nick. "We'll need more chairs, though."

"Good luck finding them."

"But, Nick," she reminded him sweetly, "I can't leave to go find any. Remember? Apparently, since I'm still here, I'm back to square one with your father." She sighed theatrically. "Stuck here in your classroom every minute of every school day except for when I nurse Christopher."

In truth, it felt like a great weight had been lifted from her shoulders. She'd still needle Nick to rehash the issue with his father some more, but she had a whole new perspective of the situation. She'd watch Joey like a hawk. Follow him to the door of the boys' room, if she had to.

"Hollie, I think we'd better take Christopher back to the house with us," Bea said.

These were the only grandparents willing to accept her sons. Hollie was eager to mend fences. She checked her watch and smiled warmly at the older woman.

"Mom, that'd be great. If he gets thirsty, there's a bottle of juice in the refrigerator that'll hold him until I can get home. And there's baby food on the shelf next to the refrigerator. Oh, and the diapers—"

"I'm sure I can find everything."

Hollie was sure she would, too. She reached for the doorknob as she turned to her quiet students. "Karl, Tat, Nick is going to find some more chairs for our class. Would you go with him and help him? Ling, Amini, Ana, you can come with me."

She opened the door and led the way into the classroom as if she had no doubts that everyone would do just exactly as she said.

Nick stood his ground for a moment, along with the Landons and Karl and Tat.

"I'll get the baby," Bea finally said, and disappeared through the doorway.

Al Landon looked at Nick. He stuffed his knit cap halfway into his coat pocket. "I guess I can help you get those chairs before I go."

"Is she always like this?" Nick asked him in a man-to-man kind of way.

"It's one of the things my son loved about her." Al smiled then, something Nick hadn't thought to see today. "Frustrated the hell out of him sometimes, too."

Nick was reassured that he wasn't the only one constantly off balance in Hollie's presence. Now if they could tell him *how* she did it, maybe he could cope better. Something he was going to need to be able to do if he were to keep his class's attention while Hollie sat in the back and conducted her own class with five very interesting-looking people.

HOLLIE AND HER CLASS usually worked on grammar, vocabulary, current events, reading, conversation and anything else her students needed to get by in the everyday world of the United States. There was slang to contend with, idioms that defied literal translation. There were customs to explain, and they shared their own in return.

They were fascinated by Nick's fourth-grade class. Some of their own children attended public schools in East Bay and surrounding cities, and now they were able to see first-hand what their children were growing up with. Hollie wisely let them listen in and, when they had questions—which was often—she quietly clued them in as to what was being said.

She saw Nick with new perspective. She didn't have Christopher to occupy her. She wasn't working on the Snowflake Ball decorations.

He moved around his class with a comfortable grace, instructing them, fielding the children's questions with answers that were short enough not to bore them and long enough to spark more interest. Her eyes followed his long stride as his boots thumped on the wood floor. She noticed the way the black leather hugged his broad back as he stretched his arm out and wrote on the board, the warmth of his smile when he enjoyed the impish humor only a fourth-grade child could display.

The subject was science. All five of her students had had some upper-level education in their respective countries. Science wasn't new to them, but having it presented to them in English was. Many of their questions they could answer for one another.

When Nick passed out the sex-education booklets to the first student in each row, Hollie quickly decided it was time to steer her little group, seated in a semicircular huddle in the back of the room, toward a conversation about how they dealt with education in their respective countries. It would give them a chance to practice speaking their English and, as they had grown into a family unit of sorts over the past six months, to learn something interesting about one another. Interesting enough, Hollie hoped, to distract them from what was going on in the rest of the room.

The last child in each row had an extra booklet. They glanced at one another in silent question, then got up and passed the material to Hollie's students.

Her gaze snapped up at Nick to find him unsuccessfully trying to hide a smile. His shrug reminded her of a naughty little boy trying to lay the blame elsewhere even though he'd been the one caught with his hand in the cookie jar.

"Didn't want them to feel left out," he said to her, as if she needed any explanation. "Page thirty," he told her students.

Timmy took one look at the page and shot his hand up in the air. "Hey, Mr. Nicholson."

Hollie didn't have a booklet. Nor did she want one. But when she looked over Ling's shoulder and saw a reproductive diagram, she wanted Nick's head. On a platter.

Her semicircle of students huddled tighter as they discussed what they were seeing in their hands.

"Yes, Timmy?" Nick responded.

"How come a worm doesn't have a penis?"

The girls groaned. The boys laughed. Hollie's students whispered frantically as they tried to figure out the question. Then they looked to her for an explanation.

Nick was looking at her, too, she noticed, as if waiting to see how she was going to handle this mess she'd gotten herself into today.

Chapter Ten

So, she was a teacher, hm? Nick thought Hollie looked as though she wanted to bolt from the room. He could almost read her mind.

Uh, Nick, I decided to make Joey tell all. I'll be going out into the hall to do that now.

He couldn't help himself; he grinned. If he had to, he'd pull rank and remind her she couldn't go out into the hall except to nurse Christopher—and *he* was at home. That pretty well left her stuck right here, right now. And her students were waiting for clarification on a word that was new to them.

His grin faded when he saw her pick up a piece of paper and a pencil and start to draw. That was too easy. And he still worried about what the kids were telling their parents when they went home at night. That Mrs. Landon was sitting in class drawing penises?

"Uh, Hollie..."

"Almost done," she stalled him sweetly. "There!" She held it up for her five students to see.

"Let me see, too," Timmy said.

Nick felt his heart skip a beat.

"Me, too!" echoed around the room.

He was sure his heart stopped and he had Hollie to thank for it. She was needling him again, he knew. And darn it, it was working. He should have pressured her father-in-law for some quick pointers in how to deal with this maddening woman.

"That's a worm," Hollie told her students.

His heart started beating again. Hollie turned the pad so the children could see what she'd drawn, though Nick thought they suddenly showed less interest. Even Timmy had forgotten his question. Or was that just how he saw it?

It seemed he couldn't trust his own instincts anymore since she'd been sentenced to his classroom. He felt as if he were always one step behind when he needed to be ahead of her. Even when he tried to leap ahead, like passing out enough sex-education booklets to get her students involved, she used it to her advantage.

And he wanted to continue to see her after Christmas? He should have his head examined. Except he knew it wasn't his head that was affected. It was his heart. He was dangerously close to losing it to her. And except for getting him to get his dad to rescind her sentence, she didn't even need him.

Well, then, it was up to him to convince her she did.

PLAY PRACTICE WAS Nick's favorite time. Not because the school day was nearly over, but because the theater was his first love. It had to be, or how else could he cope with the lack of help and the excess of things to be completed by Sunday night?

At the top of his list was finding Baby Jesus. While he waited for the students to run off a little excess energy before practice began, he pulled the props out backstage and thoroughly searched the area. He went through both the boys' and the girls' locker rooms, poked around in the trash cans and opened every locker. Nothing.

His proverbial goose was cooked if he didn't have a complete nativity by the time the curtain rose. Not only would the high school not hire him, he'd be lucky if they didn't run him out of town for losing East Bay's fifty-year-old statue of Baby Jesus.

A quick survey of the props, as he heard the children killing time waiting for him, revealed that he had a long couple of nights ahead of him. He pulled out a drop cloth, several cans of paint and brushes. Maybe he could get a head start. He thought briefly about having the children help him, but decided supervising twenty-five nine- and ten-year-olds, all with wet paint in their hands and no other supervision, would be courting disaster. He tacked Hollie's torn sketches to the wall beside his own, then tore his down, crumpled them into balls and sent them flying into the wings.

"Okay, kids, settle down. Let's get started."

Hollie and her students, speaking quietly among themselves, entered as a group through the double doors and strolled down the center aisle to the third row of folding chairs.

"Nick, I have to leave, but my students want to know if it's all right if they watch."

"You're leaving?" Besides feeling lonely already, he'd hoped she would take pity on him and make some new, wrinkle-free nativity sketches. "You always stay."

"I know, but I have to go feed Christopher."

"I thought your mother-in-law was going to do that."

She stared at him pointedly. "Think about it, Nick."

"But you said there was juice and baby food—"

"Think about me, too, Nick. *I* need to go nurse."

"Oh." He jumped off the stage. "Could I talk to you for a minute? Over there?"

She glanced at her watch. He knew she wasn't on a time schedule, but he got the point just the same.

"It'll only take a minute." He led the way across the floor in front of the stage to the side aisle, and she followed. "I've got a lot to do," he explained in a quiet voice that he didn't want to carry back to her students. He didn't know how much English they understood and he didn't want to hurt anyone's feelings. "I can't direct the children and answer their—" his glance scanned the five adults "—questions at the same time."

"But, Nick—"

"I've got three days left. Three days to polish their lines, paint the props, find Baby Jesus and get Him painted—"

"Nick!"

She fisted her hands on her hips, pulling her top tight across her full breasts. Nick forgot what he'd been saying. He wondered what size she'd be after she weaned Christopher. On her slender frame, he'd guess—

"Are you listening to me?"

"Huh? Oh, yeah. I don't have the time. They can come back tomorrow when you can stay and answer their questions."

"Karl drives an hour to come here once a week. Amini drives forty-five minutes. I can't tell them to come back tomorrow."

"It's kids' play practice, Hollie. What's the big deal?"

"It's educational."

"Look, Hollie, I think it's wonderful that you tutor foreign students. I think it's very brave of them to travel so far from their homelands and try to learn a new language. But I don't think I should have to spend my time—what little I have left—answering their questions because you can't be here."

"Fine."

He recognized that tone. It was her too-agreeable one, the one that always meant he, Nick, was about to be bettered.

"I'll tell them not to ask any questions."

"Yeah, right," he muttered. In his classroom, he'd seen how curious they were. He doubted they'd remain quiet.

"Cool!" drifted from one of the children over to where he and Hollie stood.

Nick recognized it as a tone which indicated something was up. Something unplanned for play practice. His head snapped up to see Tat, paintbrush in a steadily moving hand, facing one of the backdrops.

"Hey! Don't—"

Hollie punched him in the gut. Not with all her strength, he knew, but hard enough to make him stop in midsentence. His reflexes handled the rest as he took a quick step backward, slightly hunched over with his hand guarding his stomach from further attack.

"Relax. Tat's an illustrator for children's books," she told him.

"How was I supposed to know that?"

"As a courtesy, you could have asked my students to introduce themselves to your class."

"I didn't know how much English they could speak."

She favored him with a sweet smile. "I think you're about to find out how well they can paint."

Nick looked up on stage and found the rest of the adults discussing Hollie's sketches, pointing and gesturing to fill in the gaps in their conversation. They all had paintbrushes in their hands. He had visions of a stage set being ready on time, even if the kids weren't.

"Well . . ." he mused.

When he turned back to Hollie, all he saw was the door swinging shut behind her retreating form.

"YOU LIKE?" Tat asked.

Nick had been standing behind Tat for five minutes, admiring his work when he should have been telling one of the wise men that the word was frankincense, not Frankenstein. "I like."

Tat looked pleased. "Good. I finish now?"

"Yes, please."

They'd been painting for an hour. An hour during which Nick had been totally engrossed by two completely different things, neither of which was set design. It was a constant struggle to get his mind off Hollie and onto the children.

"Baa-aaa."

The children broke into peals of laughter.

Nick started to pin Danny with a glare, but lost it when he saw the youngster had borrowed some geriatric's curly white wig and had it on his head. "You're supposed to be a silent sheep." The reprimand lost all power as Nick gave in and chuckled.

"But, Mr. Nicholson, my sheep *feels* hungry." Danny said it with emotion, the same way Nick had coached them for weeks to deliver their lines.

"Well, be sure to feed your sheep before the play."

"But—"

"Ever heard of Silent Night?"

"Yeah."

"It means the animals."

"Oh."

Nick couldn't believe how kids could be so difficult and so easy at the same time.

He wondered how long Hollie's in-laws were going to stay and if they would baby-sit part of tomorrow, Friday, while Hollie sat in his class. That would give her more time to work on her Snowflake Ball decorations. That would probably also mean she'd find more time to take over even more space in his classroom.

Before her arrival, he and the children had decorated in their own limited way. Green construction-paper Christmas trees sported painted-on ornaments and glitter glue. White cutout snowflakes, also covered with glitter glue, danced on the windows. Sun-catchers, made of melted plastic beads, stuck to the windows with little suction cups until it was time for them to be taken home as gifts. Amazing what had been invented since he'd been in school.

Then Hollie had come on the scene. Every available surface in the room was now draped with red and green and gold fabric swatches in prints and solids, colorful, lacy ribbons—crinkled up with wire in them, no less—red velvet bows and sprays of green holly. They weren't decorations for his room; they were supplies for the annual ball. But just having them laying around had added a certain three-dimensional joyousness to the children's artwork.

And even when Hollie wasn't in the room, they reminded him of her. In the mornings before she arrived, for instance, when Nick always got there early so he could prepare for the day. This morning he'd sat in his desk and daydreamed of her. He wondered if any of those green holly things could pass for mistletoe.

In the evenings, he went back up to his classroom and tried to put some order into it after seven hours of rambunctious children. Lately he'd just walked around and touched Hollie's stuff. Her portfolio. Her darned sewing machine, he thought with a grin. The baby swing that tick-ticked like a metronome as it lulled Christopher and, unfortunately, several of the older children into a nap.

"Mr. Nicholson!"

Nick focused on a dozen children circled around him. "What?"

"We're finished."

"You are? Oh, you are. Yes, and a fine job you did, too."

"I fell off the stage," T.J. said.

Nick hadn't seen that. "But the point is, you got right back up there and finished."

"No, I didn't. I broke my ankle."

Nick shouldn't have, but he let himself look down at T.J.'s ankle.

"Gotcha!" rang through the gym at his expense.

"Okay, you got me," he admitted. Thank God they didn't know where his thoughts had been.

Joey glanced at the clock. "My mom'll be back real soon, Mr. Nicholson."

"In a hurry to go home and see your grandparents?"

"No. They were real mad." His grin told Nick that Joey's attention wasn't so easily deterred.

But Nick's was—right back to Hollie.

If her in-laws were so mad earlier, would they be giving her a hard time at home now? Was she going to come back with tears in her eyes? Looking drained and tired from the strain?

How could he help?

The door opened. The adult ESL students continued to paint without interruption. The children turned to see who was there.

Hollie entered the gym, tired from four of the longest days in her life, to find Nick looking at her with what appeared to be mixed emotions.

He looked happy, she thought. And why shouldn't he be? He was here in a gym with twenty-five little actors and actresses, eager to get their lines down, and five terrific volunteers. What did he have to be stressed out about? Grumpy in-laws? Not likely. The way he and the children were laughing when she'd opened the door, it sounded as if they hadn't a care in the world.

He looked concerned, too, though. Certainly not for his props; they were coming along beautifully. Certainly not for the children; they were all fine. His eyes had been on her instantly as she'd come through the door. He hadn't been engrossed in directing the play, supervising the painting or hunting for Baby Jesus.

Had he been watching the door for her return?

She was about to dismiss that idea entirely when she saw something else in his eyes. She couldn't give it a name, but it made her blood run hot. And when he smiled at her, she questioned her sanity when she'd told him he couldn't come visit because she was going to be washing her hair.

Stupid, stupid, stupid.

No, she realized, what was stupid was second-guessing herself. All it took was for her to remember the kiss she'd given him this morning—the one he'd returned. If she'd agreed to see him tonight, she'd be wanting him under her Christmas tree long before Christmas.

HOLLIE'S DOORBELL RANG sharply at eight o'clock. Or maybe it just seemed sharp because of the headache she'd developed due to her in-laws' sniping comments. They couched them carefully in their conversation so she couldn't retaliate without making a scene in front of Joey.

When she'd pulled Bea aside, the woman had the nerve to smile sweetly at her and say, "Oh, you're just imagining it. I guess you've had a hard day at that school. Do you have to just sit there all day?"

No, Hollie wanted to say, *I chase the teacher around the desk during recess. We make mad, passionate love in the coat closet during lunch break.*

And then she'd smiled. Her in-laws shared their own worried glances, and the sniping continued.

So when the doorbell rang, Hollie said a quick prayer of thanks, figuring it was Terri coming over for a visit. Hollie would get to climb out of the boxing ring and go to her own corner for a while.

Joey ran through the living room on his way to the door. "I'll get it!"

"No you won't, young man," Hollie ordered. "You know better."

"But it could be Brian."

"Brian's mother isn't about to let him walk over here in the dark."

Hollie flipped on the porch light and peered through the peephole. Instead of Terri, which would have been nice, neutral territory, she got a head and chest view of Nick standing on her porch.

"It's Nick...uh, Mr. Nicholson," she announced to the room in general as she unlocked the door.

"Nicholson," Al Landon mused aloud, as though the name sounded familiar but shouldn't be attached to Joey's teacher.

Hollie opened the door into her parquet-floored foyer, but remained in the doorway and blocked Nick's entrance.

"Hi." His smile was warm.

She remembered what she'd just been envisioning about chasing him around the desk and making love with him in the coat closet. Dangerous territory when he was standing in front of her looking far too sexy for her own good.

She kept her voice very low. "I told you not to come to-night."

A grin tugged at the corner of his lips as his eyes roamed her dry hair with an intensity that made her feel as if his fingers were combing through it.

"Well, it looks as though you're done washing it."

"I'm just getting ready to."

His full-blown grin was short-lived, as if he realized he might get punched in the gut again for it. His hand covered his mouth, figuratively wiping his smile away.

Hollie missed it more than she thought was safe.

"Besides," he said, "that was before all the trouble you had with Joey today. I thought you might need a friendly face around the house tonight." He looked over her shoulder into the room. "Hello, Mr. Landon, Mrs. Landon. How are you tonight?"

Hollie had no choice; she stepped aside and let him into the room. If she didn't, she'd come off as rude and undoubtedly hear about that, too.

Al folded up the newspaper he'd been reading and stood. "Your name's Nicholson?"

"That's right."

Hollie closed the door, unprepared for the chill that suddenly suffused her father-in-law's whole demeanor.

"You're related to Judge Nicholson?"

"He's my father."

Bea plopped down onto the nearest chair. "Oh, my! His son!"

"Well, gee, Nick, nice of you to stop by." Hollie wasn't sure whether to be angry with him or grateful that someone had finally taken the wind out of her mother-in-law's sail.

"Anytime."

"Hey, Mr. Nicholson, how come you're here?" Joey asked.

"Yeah, Nick, how come you're here?" Hollie echoed innocently. Better for Bea and Al to be mad at his unfortunate ancestry than at her son's.

"I wanted to drop your sketch pad by in case you needed it."

Hollie looked at his empty hands. She looked at his jacket and remembered the last time he'd hidden something in there. Last night. She hoped he hadn't brought another ruby rose; she didn't need sharp-eyed Bea making suppositions about Nick's feelings for her. Or vice versa.

Although Hollie wasn't too clear herself about her feelings for him. If he'd been anybody except the judge's son...

"Where is it?" Joey asked.

Hollie cleared her throat easier than she did her memory of the kiss that had come with the rose. "Yeah, Nick, where is it?"

He patted his jacket and came up empty. "I guess I left it on my motorcycle."

Bea watched them like a hawk. The frown puckering her eyebrows indicated she didn't believe the sketch pad story for a second.

"I'll, uh, go get it," Nick offered.

"Oh, that's okay," Hollie said as they inched toward the front door. "I don't need it tonight." She lowered her voice, not enough to raise Bea's suspicions, but quiet enough to keep the conversation more personal. "I'm glad you stopped by. I forgot to thank you today for your offer."

"My offer?"

"The loan, remember?"

"Oh, yeah." He shrugged as if it had been nothing to him.

It certainly had been more than that to her. She wouldn't have accepted it, even after a few hours in jail, but he couldn't have so much to spare that he just went around offering five hundred dollars to women in need.

"What loan?" sharp-eared Bea asked.

"My mom needed money to pay the judge," Joey volunteered.

After all Hollie had preached to Joey the need for honesty in this world, she could have cut out her own tongue. Obviously there was a right time and a right place for something a little less than the whole truth—now, for example—but she hadn't ever told him that.

She should open the door and let Nick escape, but she was a chicken. She needed him as a buffer.

Her eyes never left Nick's as she backed away from the door. "It's awfully cold out. How about some coffee before you go? I'll just go into the kitchen and make some."

Nick followed on her heels. "I'll help you."

Bea and Al followed, though Hollie got the impression Bea dragged Al along behind her.

"What's all this about money for the judge, Hollie?" Bea asked.

Hollie turned on the water and carefully measured it into the carafe. Nick busied himself with searching through her cabinets, pulling out a can of coffee and a filter when he found them.

"Hollie, I'm not leaving this kitchen until you tell me what's going on. Do you have to pay a fine, too?"

"No, Mom, I don't. The judge was going to change my sentence to a fine, but I couldn't afford it, so Nick offered to lend me the money. That's all. No big deal."

Nick stayed within arm's length of Hollie. She wasn't sure whether that was too close or too far.

"And you took it?" Bea exclaimed, making it sound as though she'd accepted drug money.

"No, Mom, I didn't. The judge changed his mind."

And when she saw Judge Nicholson again, she'd give him a piece of her mind for discussing it with her son without consulting her first. Right now, she needed to change the subject.

"So, Nick, how's the play coming?"

"Fine."

"How are the props coming along?"

"Fine."

She scowled at him. At this pace, she'd use up all her ideas in about forty-five seconds. That wouldn't be long enough to bore her in-laws into leaving the room and giving Nick and her some privacy.

She persevered. "Have you found Baby Jesus yet?"

"Nope."

"I'm going to go do my homework now," Joey announced as he zipped out the kitchen door.

"He's sure a good kid," Nick commented.

Hollie basked in the warmth of his gaze, her in-laws be damned. And that's when she saw it. A new ruby red rose, leaning crookedly in a glass of water, graced the windowsill by the kitchen sink.

She glanced nervously at her mother-in-law and dreaded the lecture if Bea ever made the connection between the rose and Nick, but the two of them were totally engrossed in conversation.

"And I'm not just saying that because you're here," Nick told the older couple. "Joey is a really good kid. He just made a couple mistakes."

They scowled back.

Hollie inhaled deeply, believing she could smell the rose from across the room. Needing to smell it, to savor it, to thank Nick properly—with another kiss that did as much to melt her bones as his.

"Hollie's a great mom. I'm sure you know that."

"So, you're the judge's son, hm?" Al clearly didn't expect an answer. He turned his back and walked out of the room.

With her father-in-law in the combination living and dining room and her mother-in-law in the kitchen, Hollie had nowhere to be alone with Nick over a simple cup of coffee. Except her studio.

She handed Nick a steaming mug. "Would you like to see my sketches?"

Dumb, Hollie. Really dumb.

"Uh, I mean of the Snowflake Ball," she tacked on hastily. "They're in my studio."

"I'd love to."

"Mom, there's plenty of coffee. Help yourself."

"Snowflake Ball, hm?" Bea mused. "I think I'd like to see them, too. If you don't mind?"

What could Hollie say?

For the next hour, every word Hollie said to Nick was overheard by someone. Shortly after nine, she sent Joey to bed and grabbed her coat out of the foyer closet.

"I'm going to walk Nick out. I'll be right back."

Nick jumped up off the couch like a jack-in-the-box suddenly released. And he looked just about as happy as one when Hollie opened the front door.

She stepped out onto the porch without pausing to button up her coat. She needed to get away from all the prying ears. She needed some breathing space.

She needed to be alone with Nick.

They walked in silence to his motorcycle, which was parked in the driveway behind her car. As he retrieved her sketch pad, she watched the moonlight play over his shoulders and back, snugly encased in his black leather jacket. The breeze tousled his dark hair.

"You're shivering." He tucked the pad beneath one arm, Hollie beneath the other. "Let's get out of the wind."

She dug her feet in. "I'm not going back in there yet."

"Is your car locked?"

"No."

He took a step in the direction of her car, the pressure of his arm urging her to go with him.

Hollie glanced around the neighborhood. "Nick, we can't."

He grinned. "It's a car," he said pointedly.

She knew he meant "not a bedroom."

"Tell that to the two little old ladies across the street. They've been peeking out their front window since you pulled in my driveway."

He looked across the street. "I don't see anyone."

"Of course not."

"Then how do you know they're watching?"

"I just do, Nick. They have nothing better to do. And they like to talk over the fence, too."

His grin widened. "Well, then, if they're going to talk, they may as well have something to talk about."

She was carried along with his strong stride toward her car. "But, Nick . . ."

He turned and engulfed her in the circle of his embrace. His arms were strong, his body hard, his breath warm as he dipped his head and covered her lips with his own. The kiss was fleeting, lasting just long enough for her to forget the spectators and want more of him.

He braced his hips on the rear quarter panel. She leaned in to him, sacrificing her own balance as she came to rest against him, effectively sandwiching his body between hers and the station wagon.

He needed no coercion, no flirtatious comment, from her to spur him on. As he pulled her body up along his, she realized neither of them had zipped up their coats. There was no bulkiness between them.

The two old ladies across the street pulled back their window curtain and stared openly. Bea flashed Hollie's porch light. A few snow flurries fell.

"We'd better get in your car," Nick murmured between kisses that turned Hollie's knees to mush.

"Why?" she asked against his lips, then smiled because it was such an intimate thing to do.

"I don't want you to catch cold."

"Is it cold out here?"

He chuckled.

"I hadn't noticed."

She didn't argue when he dragged one arm from around her body and unlatched the back door of her station wagon. She didn't delay when he turned her and aimed her for the interior. She did notice the frigid vinyl beneath her rear and scooted out to the very edge.

"What's wrong?" Nick asked.

"Cold seat."

There was just enough moonlight to pick up the twinkle in his hazel eyes. He settled back and patted his thighs invitingly. "Warm lap."

She actually considered it. What had gotten into her?

Her station wagon had never felt so tiny as when Nick leaned toward her. His broad shoulders seemed to fill the whole back seat, like a wall. A nice, warm wall that closed in as his lips met hers again.

She inched toward his lap. Her hands landed on his biceps and smoothed their way over the leather until she could feel the bare skin of his neck. Her fingers threaded through the hair over his collar and teased the sensitive area behind his ears.

He slipped his hand beneath her knee and tugged one leg over his. His hand splayed over her other thigh, then circled beneath it and tugged that leg onto his lap beside the other. As he lifted her effortlessly, he maneuvered his way beneath her until her hips settled snugly, intimately, into his possession.

"Nick," she murmured.

Her hands never stopped moving. His hair was thick and lustrous. The column of his neck was firm and strong. His breathing escalated as her hands slipped down to find his nipples hard.

And what liberties she took, he took in kind. She nearly cried out when his hands covered her.

"You've got on too darn many clothes."

She giggled.

"What?"

"One minute you want me to zip up my coat, the next you want me out of my sweater."

His tongue traced her bottom lip, and she forgot about talking.

Then everything stopped.

"Is this all right?" he asked tentatively.

She was sure the look she gave him was an absolute blank.

His hand tugged at the hem of her sweater. His fingers grazed the skin beneath.

"I mean, with you nursing and all."

With her hip pressed intimately into the cradle of his pelvis, she knew how much it was costing him to stop and ask the boundaries of a nursing mother. While she had none on that score, it provided a wonderful opportunity for sanity to return. And with it, the cold.

She tugged the sweater out of his hand and down. She dragged his hand up to her mouth and kissed his knuckles.

"When?" he asked in a breathless tone.

"Nick, I don't think this is a good idea," she prevaricated.

"You can't...do this?"

She felt herself blush and thanked God they weren't beneath a full moon. "I just don't think we should."

He grinned. "You mean you could, if the time were right?"

If she admitted to that, she'd be admitting to the fact that the time might eventually be right for them. She wasn't ready for that step.

"Hollie." He traced her bottom lip with his tongue again, teasing it to the same throbbing state as the rest of her heated body.

"Yes," she admitted.

His hands grasped her bare flesh beneath the sweater, encircling her waist as he lifted and turned her until she straddled him.

"You're in control, then," he said. "Call a halt whenever you want."

He pulled her close, working his lips down her neck, across the soft spot of her throat, over her collarbone. At the same time, his hands inched upward, heating her skin with featherlike brushes until he reached her bra. When his fingers reached around back for the clasp, her eyes flew open.

She started laughing.

Nick's head fell back on the top of the seat. "You're bruising my ego here."

"Sorry." She tried to stop, but couldn't.

"I've never gotten this reaction before."

"It's not you," she hastened to assure him.

"What, then?"

The wave of her hand took in the circumference of their surroundings. "We've steamed up all the windows."

He pulled her lips down to his. He tugged her hips into a tighter straddle against his obvious erection. "I'd like to steam up a whole bedroom full of windows."

She wedged her hands between their chests and pushed herself away. "I know."

"You could put me out of my misery and tell me 'some-day.'"

"Maybe," was the best she could do. She was caught up in a moment, she knew. A moment didn't make a future.

She pushed open the back door and climbed off his lap, though her feet weren't steady beneath her. She slipped slightly on a wet spot, and, seated in the doorway of the station wagon, Nick reached out a hand to steady her.

Snowflakes drifted down and perched momentarily on her dark hair before melting. Nick thought they looked like stars nestled there.

"Wait, you forgot your sketch pad." He reached down onto the asphalt driveway where he'd dropped it.

"Oh, yeah."

He knew she'd feel pretty stupid going back into the house without it. As if she'd had ulterior motives when she came outside in the first place. Which she might have, but she certainly wouldn't want to admit it to the Landons.

He turned on the edge of the seat, his feet on the drive-way, his body filling the doorway as he offered her the pad. If he got up, he knew he'd just drag her back inside the station wagon, and it wasn't what she wanted. It wasn't what he wanted, either, because as much as he needed to make love to her, their first time together should be something to remember—and not because it was a quickie in the back seat of a car.

"Thanks." She accepted it and turned to go.

"Oh, one thing, though."

She turned back to him. In her eyes, he could read desire to kiss him one more time warring with knowing what her reaction would be.

He knew what would send her running. He glanced at the pad in her hand, smiled crookedly and said, "I like your work."

Chapter Eleven

Friday, December 20

Hollie spent the better part of the night trying to get to sleep. It didn't help any that, before climbing onto the spare sleeper sofa, she'd opened her sketch pad to see how incriminating the evidence had been and found that Nick had, indeed, found his likeness within. And not just once. Besides Nick decorating a few impromptu Snowflake Ball sketches, there was one of him with a smoldering fire in his eyes, burning just as hot as when he'd dragged the rose down her skin.

She toyed with the idea of skipping school the next morning. It hadn't worked as a kid when she'd wanted to avoid the teacher because she hadn't done her homework the night before, but she was almost willing to give it another try. Except then she'd be stuck at home with some very disgruntled in-laws. Bea had made it quite clear the night before that she hadn't approved of the amount of time it had taken Hollie to get her sketch pad back from Nick. Al had maintained a stony silence.

At five o'clock Hollie got up, snuggled into her purple polar fleece robe, made a pot of coffee and tackled the Snowflake Ball in her studio. A lot of her supplies were at

East Bay Elementary, but there were still enough materials at home to keep her busy for days. If only she *had* days.

It was Friday again. A week since her life had changed irrevocably. A week since she'd found out she disliked one Nicholson and was falling head over heels in love with the other. And that one knew she was sketching him as if she had nothing better to do.

"Mom! Mom, turn on the radio!"

She heard Joey long before he ran into the studio in his pajamas, his hair sleep-tousled, his face aglow with the possibility of a snow day.

"Turn on the radio!"

"Okay," she whispered.

"Why are we whispering?" he queried with a low tone to match hers. Christopher had gotten so he could sleep through almost anything the past couple days.

"Because we don't want to wake your grandparents."

Joey looked out the window longingly. Large snowflakes floated down to a lawn already blanketed with a fresh coat of white. He glanced back down the hallway with a frown. "If it's a snow day, I get to go shovel driveways."

"Won't do any good until it stops." She wished for the comfort she and Joey used to experience in the company of his grandparents.

"I could, uh, get a start on it."

Hollie further rumpled his hair with her hand. "Maybe your grandparents won't be so grumpy today. You used to like to do puzzles with them."

He shrugged.

She grabbed him playfully by his pajama shirt. "Just promise me you won't split and leave me here holding the bag."

He giggled and tried to wriggle free. "Nuh-uh."

She wrapped her arms around him and a short wrestling match ensued. "No promise, no radio."

He caught his breath. "But, Mom, I need to make money shoveling snow. I want to buy Christopher a Christmas present."

"I didn't say you couldn't go. Just ask first so they can't complain that you disappear whenever you want to, you wild little hooligan, you," she teased.

He was laughing so hard he could barely say, "Mo-om!"

"Promise me or I'll raspberry you."

He tugged down his pajama top to protect his bare tummy. "All right! I promise."

Hollie kissed him soundly on top of his head and released him.

Joey quickly regained his dignity and moved to the shelf in front of the radio. "What station?"

"Third button over."

He was out of luck. Hollie wasn't sure which was better for her—school with Nick or home with the in-laws, but she got school. She put her work aside and got herself and the boys ready.

The phone rang just as they were going out the door. Hollie would have ignored it, but Bea answered.

"Yes, she's still here."

Hollie waved to her mother-in-law, trying to clue her in to the fact that she and both boys were already all zipped up.

"Who shall I say is calling?" Bea turned to Hollie. "It's Mrs. Fagan calling long-distance from Florida. Something about the Snowflake Ball."

Hollie bounced Christopher in her arms as she took the receiver. She had to make this quick before he realized he was getting hot. "Mrs. Fagan? Is everything all right?"

"I was going to ask you the same thing, dear."

"Why, yes, of course."

"I talked to my maid last night, and she said none of the decorations have arrived yet. Frankly, Hollie, I'm worried whether you might need help with this job."

Hollie heard that as "whether this job is too big for you."

"Everything's fine, Mrs. Fagan. Everything's done—" she noticed Joey was listening intently "—except for a few small items, and sitting in my studio. It's all going up this weekend."

"The ball is Monday evening."

"And it'll be the most beautiful Snowflake Ball ever." The whole Fagan family had done the decorating in the past. "No offense intended, of course."

"None taken, dear. We're flying in first thing Monday morning. Will we see you then?"

"Uh, no. I'm tied up until Monday afternoon."

"Tied up?"

If the news hadn't hit Florida yet, Hollie wasn't about to be the one to enlighten them. "Yes. I'll see you then. And, Mrs. Fagan? Don't worry. It'll be beautiful. I promise," was the last thing she said before she hung up.

"Mom?"

"Get in the car, Joey."

"But, Mom, how come—"

"Christopher's getting hot all bundled up in here. Let's go. Mr. Nicholson's waiting for us."

She'd hoped to distract Joey by mentioning his teacher. All she succeeded in doing was distracting herself.

"How come you told Mrs. Fagan you're almost done?"

Darn. He'd heard that.

"Well, the trees and the pine roping and all the poinsettias will be delivered while we're at school today. I've already arranged *all* of that." She struggled to make it sound like as much as possible. "And the mistletoe. You know about mistletoe, don't you?"

He shook his head. He'd known last year, but she thanked God he'd forgotten since then. She launched into a long, slow explanation of the mistletoe tradition, and by the time she was done, he made no more mention of her little white lie.

She hadn't forgotten it, though. Nor had she forgotten how important this job was to her future if she wanted any more jobs to keep a roof over their heads and food on the table. If she had to, she'd dip into her nearly zero savings and hire some teenagers to help her over the weekend.

All the distraction helped one thing. For a whole thirty minutes, Hollie forgot how mortified she'd been that Nick knew she'd been sketching him instead of the Snowflake Ball.

She had the rose safely tucked away in the diaper bag. She wanted to get it to school, and away from her mother-in-law's prying eyes, before it dried out. And she *wouldn't*—no matter how much Nick expected it—kiss him for this one.

NICK, HANDS WRAPPED around a steaming mug of coffee, stared out the classroom window and anxiously watched the snow fall.

Sure, everyone wanted a white Christmas, including him. But too much of a good thing would keep Hollie at home, and he didn't want that. And too much would keep the ESL students, who had volunteered to return and finish up, from making the trip. One of them, he thought her name was Amini, had even tackled the children's costumes. Nick had thought he would have to get by with the same old ones this year; he was a director, not a seamstress. But Amini had taken one look at the set designs, one look at the clothing and, twenty minutes later, turned out a rather spiffy wise man.

Tat had a few questions on painting the props. Nick had shown him as best he could what he wanted, but that old saying about one picture being worth a thousand words applied double when they were dealing in shaky English. If Hollie would work up a couple more sketches dealing with problem areas, which also happened to be the areas she hadn't sketched previously, all would be well.

He hoped she wouldn't have any problems driving in the snow. He'd go pick her up, but that would only work if he had a car and if he could get away with saying her house was on his way to school. If he showed up on his motorcycle to drive her in her own station wagon...well, he imagined that would go over about as well as a blizzard.

Nick kept busy until the children started trickling in, and then he posted a pair of boys at the window to let him know when Hollie arrived. When she did, he went down to help her with her stuff.

He didn't know what he'd expected, but it certainly wasn't her ducking into the back seat of her station wagon to avoid him.

"You came down to help?" Her question was barely discernible, coming as it was from the inside of the car. "How nice."

He didn't think she sounded grateful at all. She passed the diaper bag out to him and, somehow, managed to do it while she kept her back turned. She gathered up Christopher, pivoted on the seat and scooted out until her feet touched the ground.

"Here, let me take him," Nick offered, shouldering the bag like a pro and extending his arms.

"That's all right. I've got him."

"It's slippery."

"I'm wearing good boots."

His arms felt empty, held out as they were for either the baby or her arm, both of which were refused him.

She got out of the station wagon without difficulty, stole a quick sidelong glance at him, then averted her eyes again as she headed for the school.

"Well, I'll just get the car door for you," Nick muttered, then slammed it soundly.

What had happened since last night? They'd shared some pretty hot stuff in that back seat.

Oh. The back seat. Was she embarrassed?

Hollie? No way. Angry?

Not likely. It had to be something else.

He followed her into the school and up the stairs, wondering how on earth she could look sexy beneath a heavy winter coat. The same red coat she'd worn the day she'd stormed out of the courthouse with Joey. He'd liked her in it then, too.

He followed her through the hall, wishing she wanted to walk beside him as they waded through scores of children. He darned near followed her right over to her chair to demand why she was avoiding him.

"Here, Mom." Joey held out the burgundy leather bag she'd given him to carry upstairs.

She glanced nervously in Nick's direction. "Just put it down over by the window, honey."

Sticking out of the top of the bag was her sketch pad.

Ah-hah! Nick understood she wanted it as far from his prying eyes as possible.

He smiled to himself. So maybe that parting crack he'd made last night hadn't been the wisest thing he'd ever said. His father had always been right when he'd predicted Nick's mouth would get him into trouble someday. But Nick wanted her to know that he knew he was on her mind a lot these days, and that he liked it.

He'd wait until morning recess, to give her some time to adjust to being around him again, before he asked her to do the sketches he needed.

WHEN THE BELL RANG, most of the children donned their outerwear and rushed outside to play in the snow. Playful little-girl shrieks and boyish calls floated in through the glass as the children boisterously vented their excess energy. Joey, and a few others who'd either forgotten or didn't have their boots, stayed indoors.

"Hollie?"

She paid close attention to tying the red velvet ribbon in her hands into a perfect bow to match all the ones she'd piled onto the adjacent desktop. Better that than watching Nick wiggle his jeans-clad hips into the junior-size desk, putting him on an even eye level with her. The desk was at an angle to her chair, and his knee nudged hers. Her arm twitched in response, and she had to yank the velvet ribbon out of its crooked bow shape and start over.

"I'd like to ask you a favor."

"I'm really busy, Nick. You know the Snowflake Ball's on Monday, and I'm way behind."

Under the guise of getting a better look at what she was doing, he held the finished bows in place with one hand and scooted the little desk closer, putting them more side by side. If she moved her arm too much—a required element in bow making—they'd bump elbows.

"How do you do that?"

His husky voice reminded her of roses and back seats.

Her fingers faltered. Was she supposed to go over or under next? "What?"

"How do you get perfect bows every time?"

"The velvet has wires in it."

"It still looks hard."

"A child could do it." A child wouldn't be so easily distracted by a hunk whose only concession to winter weather was a T-shirt with long sleeves.

He remained silent as he watched her do another bow. And another.

She sighed and lowered the velvet to her lap. She took a deep breath, locked eyes with him and asked softly, "All right, Nick. What is it you want?"

He perked up visibly; his back straightened, his eyes brightened, the corners of his lips curved upward.

"And that 'all right' means I'm willing to listen only," she admonished. "I've still got too much to do to start granting favors."

Nick was careful not to break out in a smile. She was looking at him; he felt victorious. Her eyes met his in a steady gaze that turned progressively warmer.

"Tat had some questions last night about painting the props. I thought maybe you could do a couple more sketches so he'd know exactly what I want."

The warmth receded instantly, leaving her eyes a cool green that reminded him of a holly bush—a touch-me-not beauty with enticing red berries protected by prickly leaves.

"Just a couple?"

He thought she said it as if he'd asked her to spend hours on them. "You do them so quickly. It would take me all day."

She looked down at the ribbon twined through her fingers and sighed. "Yeah, I know how you feel."

Nick reached out and fingered the velvet stiffened with wires he couldn't see. He could compare that to Hollie, too, but then he'd have to admit he'd gone over the brink.

"Is that really so easy a child could do it?"

"For my house or yours, yes. For the Snowflake Ball, I don't think so."

"Well, how about something else you have to do by Monday?" He popped out of the desk and started perusing the sketches on one of his bulletin boards.

Joey, apparently bored with what he was doing, wandered to the back of the room to see what was up.

"Nick—"

"Like these stars, for instance. Could the kids and I do these for you while you do the sketches for us?"

"I don't think—"

"We'll call it art class. And it'll be a great lesson in cooperation. Come on, Hollie. Say you'll do it."

Joey looked from one to the other, as if he were at a tennis match.

It was no secret that Hollie's goal was to get out of school entirely, not to help Nick with his play. She felt it important to teach a child to set goals and stick to them. But sometimes living up to one's principles needed to be balanced with cooperation. Was Joey old enough to grasp that concept? She certainly hoped so.

"I guess you and the kids *could* handle a few of the simpler projects."

"You're gonna let us do some of the Snowflake Ball?" Joey asked, his eyes wide with amazement.

"Well, Joey, sometimes we can continue to work for what we need *and* help someone else at the same time," she said, carefully choosing her words so Joey would know she wasn't giving up and giving in.

"It's called compromise," Nick added.

"It's called cooperation," Hollie corrected, her eyes daring him to help her again.

"Yeah, I get it," Joey responded to both of them with his own sly smile.

The room quickly filled with cold, energized fourth-graders pouring in from recess. Hollie was unable to ask

Joey what was behind that grin of his; the moment was lost.
She wouldn't soon forget it, though.

Joey had picked up on the compromise-cooperation issue far too quickly, far too comfortably, for her peace of
mind. She wanted to know what he'd been up to and when.

"ART CLASS" TOOK most of the day. Nick bounced back
and forth between Hollie and the children, consulting the
former and supervising the latter. He had to give the children guidance, give Hollie some input regarding Tat's
questions the night before and get Hollie's instructions on
the Snowflake Ball decorations to pass back to the children. All in all, a very confusing, energizing arrangement
for him. Kind of like he imagined it would be to direct a
dozen bright East Bay High School students in one of their
two annual plays.

His attention was so centered on what everyone in the
classroom was doing, that he didn't notice when the principal came into the room and, for several minutes, stood
quietly by and studied the whole scenario for what it was.

Sparkling silver snowflakes and gold stars had been cut
out by the hundreds and attached to invisible nylon thread.
They would be hung later at the mansion. Right now they
were temporarily draped from the overhead light fixtures so
they wouldn't get crinkled and so the children could enjoy
the fruits of their labor.

Bright red, green, gold and blue glass balls decorated
every desktop. The children embellished the small, me-
dium, and large globes with a sprinkling of glitter. Not one
had been dropped. Not one had rolled off a desk and been
broken. As they dried, each one got a tiny, glistening gold
bow attached to its hanger.

A Christmas CD played quietly on the stereo. Some of the children sang along, but most, like Hollie and Nick, were too engrossed in their work to notice the music.

"What in tarnation is going on here?" The principal's demand boomed through the room, echoed off the walls and sliced through everyone's concentration except Hollie's.

Nick heard at least three glass balls hit the floor and shatter. Three children instantly turned to him with horrified expressions on their faces for what had just happened. Mary Margaret's eyes glistened. The Christmas music suddenly sounded flat and joyless.

"It's all right," Nick assured them softly. "He just scared the daylights out of you," he said so the principal couldn't miss his meaning.

"Mr. Nicholson—"

"What can I do for you, Ed?"

The principal's scowl was furious as he ignored Nick and strode directly over to Hollie's chair.

"You kids go ahead and keep working," Nick said to reassure the children. He patted several small shoulders and backs as he quickly moved through their ranks to the back of the room.

"I thought it was time I dropped in to see how Mrs. Landon's presence was affecting the class."

"She's been here all week," Nick said dryly.

"I knew there would be a breaking-in period. I didn't want that to influence my report."

"Your report?"

Hollie's head shot up from her sketches, giving the principal his first view of what she'd been working on so diligently.

"Yes, my report. Judge Nicholson expects a full accounting." Ed glanced at the play sketch at Hollie's fingertips, the ball ones on the bulletin board and what the children had accomplished so far. The evidence was laid out and hung out in front of him. For all he knew, they'd done the red velvet bows and the tree skirts, too, *and* covered the one hundred little gift boxes in gold foil.

"These projects are not part of the curriculum."

"I decided to have art today."

"And what about the rest of the subjects? You know— reading, writing, geography."

"We did one or two of those already."

Ed's jowls shook. "Mr. Nicholson—"

"I like to combine subjects and encourage questions as they arise."

"And sex education?"

Nick grinned, in spite of biting the inside of his lip to keep from doing so. "It pops up from time to time."

"Not good enough, Mr. Nicholson."

"We're doing fine here, Ed. The kids are learning everything, I promise you."

"*Mr.* Nicholson, get back to your regular subjects immediately. Or you'll be suspended."

Even the CD quit when the principal slammed the door on his way out.

Nick said nothing at first. No doubt about it, Ed had it in for him now. He'd already broken so many rules by trying to be good that he doubted he could do much worse trying to be bad.

He waded back through the round-eyed children, started the CD over and broke out into a jovial rendition of "Deck the Halls."

"Time for music class," he announced.

Hollie rolled her eyes. Nick burst out laughing. The children smiled again and resumed glittering the ornaments while Nick helped Mary Margaret clean up the three broken ones.

He had nothing left to lose, so why worry? Sure, Ed could suspend him. But how would he keep Nick from coming and directing the children in the play?

He couldn't. Short of calling the police to remove him from the premises. Since Linda was the police chief's daughter, Nick wasn't too worried about that happening.

A sobering thought reared its ugly head. Nick had nothing left to lose *here*. There was still that matter of the high school position he wanted, though. There wasn't exactly a position open, but he'd been sure once they saw what he could do that they'd let the coach be a coach and hire Nick as the drama teacher. He knew the other guy would be eternally grateful.

Of course, when he directed the annual fourth-grade Christmas play without the antique Baby Jesus in the manger, his goose was as good as cooked, anyway. He only had one solution, and it depended on Hollie.

She held up her final sketch. "There, that does it."

"Uh, Hollie..."

Her frown was quick. "What's wrong with it?"

"Nothing," he said just as quickly. "It's great. Thanks."

"But?" She turned it this way and that, studying it from every angle.

He slipped it out of her grasp so he'd have her full attention. "But...I need to ask a favor."

"I'm not redrawing that, Nick."

"It's perfect."

"Then quit crinkling it."

"Oh." He smoothed it out against the wall and idly tacked it to the bulletin board, spearing the pushpin right through Joseph's eye.

When he looked back, Hollie's arms were folded across her chest. She had that Mom-says-no look about her.

"It's a simple favor, really."

Her toe tapped on the floor. "Is that why it's taking you so long to spit it out?"

"I haven't been able to find Baby Jesus yet."

Her spine relaxed, her arms unfolded, the guarded look left her eyes. Even the toe tapping stopped.

"Where have you looked?"

"You name it, I've looked in it. Every gym locker, every trash can, every box in the supply room, every file cabinet drawer in the entire school. The storage area for the tables and chairs. Behind the folded-up bleachers in the gym." He stuffed his hands into his jeans pockets.

He could tell by the sympathetic look on her face that she felt as bad about this as he did, but he knew she didn't understand the high-school-job ramifications on top of the immediate disaster.

"Well, we have until Sunday night, right?"

"He's gone."

"Maybe He'll turn up."

His patience was growing thin. "It's not like He's been kidnapped and we're going to get a ransom note."

"Then you need a substitute."

"Exactly what I was thinking."

Her expression grew wary in direct proportion to his spurt of enthusiasm.

"Only not just any substitute will do. The school has, er, had...a beautiful, fifty-year-old statue. A dime-store doll just won't cut it, but no one would think twice if a rebel like me used Christopher."

Her chin raised to a stubborn angle. Obviously she remembered him bringing this up once before. "No."

He didn't know the children had been listening until they crowded around.

Joey asked, "Use Christopher for what?"

Hollie answered before Nick could open his mouth. "He wants to put Christopher in the manger for the play."

"Cool."

Her eyebrows arched and her arms barricaded themselves across her chest again. "It's not cool."

"He's perfect for the part," T.J. said with a grin.

"Yeah," Timmy added.

"Yeah," Nick echoed, drawing Hollie's fiery eyes back to him. He flashed her a crooked grin. "No one'll care that he's a little old for the part."

"Please, please, please, Mom."

The high school board would never know he'd lost the statue. They'd think he was an innovative, daring director. They'd roll out the red carpet.

"No."

"I'll give up all my Christmas presents if you let him be in the play with me," Joey begged.

Hollie stared at her son as if wondering who he really was, then quietly, firmly, repeated, "No."

"But, Mom—"

"But, Mrs. Landon—"

"But, Hollie—" Nick sputtered right along with all the children. "He *is* perfect."

She looked as though she couldn't argue with that. "Sure he is. But if this were a perfect world, I'd be at home working on the Snowflake Ball decorations, not sitting in your classroom."

"Ah," Nick said as it dawned on him that she was still challenging him to help her get out of her sentence. A kind of you-help-me-and-I'll-help-you compromise. Or was it just another type of out-and-out blackmail?

"I can go visit Santa at the store and tell him not to bring me a Harley T-shirt. Okay, Mom? Please, Mom?"

"Yeah," Timmy said innocently. "He's kind of like Jesus, anyway. They were both in maculate conceptions."

"Immaculate," Mary Margaret corrected.

"Hey, Mrs. Landon, does that make you a virgin again?"

Nick heard the gasp at the door the same time as everyone else whirled around to see who it was. Over their heads, Nick grinned at the principal.

"Hi, Ed. Welcome to the fourth-grade sex-education class."

Chapter Twelve

Hollie felt pretty good about all the decorations that had been cut out, glued, glittered and strung during the day. When dress rehearsal rolled around that evening, she packed both boys and her in-laws into the station wagon and, prepared to stay the whole time and lend Nick a hand, she drove back to school.

"Careful now, Hollie," Bea cautioned from the back seat. "I get carsick when you take those turns too fast."

Hollie eased down below the speed limit. She'd left five minutes early, knowing exactly how this would go.

"Mo-om. I can't be late. I'm Joseph."

"We're fine," she assured him.

"Joseph's really important, Mom. I can't be late."

Her mother-in-law groaned ominously. Hollie was grateful the mansion would take the entire weekend to decorate.

The first dozen parking spaces in the school lot were full, as Nick had scheduled the dress rehearsal after dinner in order to make it special for the children. He'd said he didn't want it to be just another after-school practice complete with finger-gagging, teasing and ad-libbing. He'd hoped the "donkey's ass" comments would be suppressed in front of the parents.

It seemed to be working, too, she noticed as she shed her coat and settled Christopher in his car seat on the floor, safely surrounded by chairs so he wouldn't be stepped on. Bea immediately rescued him from his seat and cuddled him on her lap. That was fine with Hollie. It was good for both of them and freed her to go backstage and offer her help to Nick.

He looked different tonight. Energized. She stood in the wing and watched him—a rugged bad boy gleefully supervising two dozen innocent children who hung on his every word and then, when he was done giving orders, scattered in six different directions.

She dodged the quickly moving children. She had to move fast to catch and keep up with Nick. The bells jingling on her socks would have embarrassed her, but there was so much chatter, she doubted if anyone else heard. "What can I do?" she asked.

His smile was broad. When Hollie worked on her designs, she tended to tune everything else out. Nick's face, however, was a mirror of everything he enjoyed. And he certainly seemed to be glad to see her.

"You can help the girls into their costumes."

"Right." She had difficulty turning away to her assigned task. She wanted to memorize the sparkle in his eyes, the laugh lines framing them and that rebellious lock of hair that fell over his forehead; she could capture it all later with her pencil. When she did manage to turn to her assigned task, she bumped into the judge. She recoiled away from him.

"Dad." Nick sounded as surprised as Hollie was wary. "Come to watch me direct?"

"No, I came to see Joey."

"Well, you're right on time, then. We're just about to start—as soon as all the costumes are pinned up."

Hollie headed toward the girls to do her part.

"Hey, Judge Nicholson! Whatcha doin'?" Her son certainly didn't seem to dread the man's visit.

"Hello, Joey. Mrs. Landon—"

Hollie froze in midstep, turned slowly and faced the judge.

"—if it's all right with you, could I have a talk with Joey when he's finished?"

"Can he drive me home, Mom?"

Hollie's mouth dropped open as she watched her son slip his hand into the judge's. "He's a busy man, Joey. I don't think he—"

"Oh, that'd be fine with me," Judge Nicholson agreed quickly. "It'll give us time to talk. If it's all right with you, Mrs. Landon?"

Hollie gave him the barest of nods.

"Fine, then. You go on now, Joey, and get ready for your rehearsal." Without waiting for anyone's reaction, the judge took a seat and waited patiently for Joey.

Hollie felt Nick's warmth as he eased up behind her.

"I wonder what they're up to," he mused.

She threw one hand into the air, figuratively saying, "Who knows?" with a high degree of exasperation.

"Hollie." Bea's voice was heavy with censure as she suddenly appeared, holding Christopher. "You shouldn't have agreed to let him go with that man."

"He'll be fine, Mom." She wondered if she sounded at all convincing. Nick's warmth reminded her that he, for one, was sure Joey was safe with his father.

"He won't lock him up, if that's what's worrying you," he told Bea.

"What's going on?" Al Landon asked as he joined them.

Hollie shrugged.

"If you weren't so busy, you'd know what's going on with your children," Bea admonished.

Hollie sighed. She leaned backward, sucking up positive vibes from Nick. She resisted the urge to snap at her mother-in-law. "My children are fine, Mom."

Nick's arm felt like heaven as he moved to the side and slipped it around her shoulders. When she glanced up at him in surprise, she saw a determined set to his jaw that clearly told the older couple to drop the issue or they'd be dealing with him, too. Other than influencing his father to change his ruling, she didn't want or need him fighting her battles.

"Nick," she warned softly.

He turned her toward the stage. "The girls are waiting on you." He gave her a slight push in their direction.

She reached out and took his hand. She wasn't about to leave him to handle her problems with her in-laws. She tugged him along, trying not to pay any attention to how good his hand felt wrapped around hers. How strong and comforting and masculine. How right.

She toyed with the idea of inviting Nick over on Christmas afternoon. By then the boys would be tired out somewhat, her in-laws had plans to spend Christmas Day with out-of-state relatives, and she could have some friendly, adult company. She wondered if he preferred turkey or ham.

She thought of nothing else as she pinned costumes securely. She didn't even feel the pain when she pricked herself twice. Bea had to repeat Hollie's name to get her attention after the last costume was finished and Nick had everyone in place.

"Hollie, I'm talking to you."

"Oh. What is it, Mom?"

"Al and I decided it's the best thing to do."

"What's that?"

"We're going to stay through Christmas."

Hollie promptly forgot about Nick, and she wasn't too happy that she'd been forced to do it. She'd been enjoying it immensely. Probably too much for her own good.

She'd dreamed of a quiet Christmas morning, just her and her two boys. Small. Intimate. Memorable. Christopher's first Christmas. Joey's first Christmas with a little brother. Her first Christmas with two sons.

Those dreams disappeared in a vapor.

She could have argued with the older woman, but they were her grandchildren and, living out of state as she did, she seldom got to see them. The boys needed to get to know their grandparents, too. And it wasn't as if Hollie *had* to have Nick over for supper.

She bit her tongue and pasted on a smile.

"OKAY, THAT'S IT for this act," Nick announced. "This is when the curtain will close, so if any of you are too far forward, you're going to get hit with it. Keep your eyes open, okay?"

They all nodded energetically. The same as they had the last time he'd told them. He knew they'd forget by Sunday night, even if he told them Sunday afternoon.

He took a black marker to the rolled-up towel in his hands and quickly drew two eyes, a tiny little nose and a mouth. As an afterthought, he added two eyebrows. It was supposed to be Baby Jesus, in spite of his artwork. As it was, Joey would crack up when he saw it. Especially when Nick reminded him to look at it "adoringly." All the better for Nick to get his point across to Hollie about letting him borrow Christopher.

"Okay, get ready for the next act." They scurried to their places. Nick walked over to the manger and came to an abrupt halt as his gaze landed on its contents. "What's that?"

Mary Margaret sighed. "It's Barbie."

"I know that," he snapped. He took a deep breath to regain his composure, though how he was supposed to do that with a long-haired, anatomically correct fashion doll in place of Baby Jesus, he wasn't certain.

He looked to Hollie for advice. She grinned and shrugged. Some help she was.

"I guess it'll do *for now*," he said pointedly in Hollie's direction. "Until we can find something...or *someone* better."

"No, Nick."

He hopped off the stage and stormed up to where she sat in the second row. "It's a damn fashion doll," he muttered so only she could hear.

Her grin was crooked, too cocky for his way of thinking.

"I know what it is," she said.

He recognized that look in her eyes—the one that said she was having fun at his expense again.

"It has breasts."

"Well, they're not real ones."

That gave him pause.

"It's just a doll, Nick."

"If the parents get wind of it, they'll probably think I've been using it as a model in sex-education class."

He watched her bite her lip. He hoped it hurt.

"I'm sure they won't."

"Come on. Let me use Christopher."

Her eyebrows arched. "Has your dad changed his mind about my coming to class yet?" she asked pointedly.

He exaggerated his sigh for effect, but she showed no signs of giving in. Not that he could blame her, but he had to try. "One call..."

She waited for him to finish. Probably not out of patience so much, he thought, as from the effort it was taking her to keep from laughing.

"One call from one parent and . . . and I'll . . . I'll . . ."

"You'll what?" she prompted.

"I'll take my phone off the hook." He spun on his heel and stalked back to the stage.

Tsk, Tsk, Tsk.

Nick didn't have to hear it; he could feel it. He turned around to see three members of East Bay Elementary's school board watching the dress rehearsal. They shook their heads. Frank's double chin wobbled dangerously. Nick knew they might just as well have pointed at the manger, empty of the correct Baby Jesus, and yelled, "Incompetent!"

East Bay was not a huge city. If he were to be considered for the high school staff, he knew he had to impress the heck out of the elementary board. Unfortunately, he'd never been good at redeeming himself. He'd been better at leaving town.

"Okay, kids, good job. Hang your costumes on the hooks."

Out of the corner of his eye, he saw the three board members rise and shrug into their coats. They were deeply engrossed in a heated conversation, and, from their darted glances in his direction, Nick could only assume he was the main topic.

He tried to remember every lesson in tact his dad had tried to teach him years ago. After all, Nick had returned to East Bay because it was a town that still taught values to its children. They came with the same set of strings as when he'd grown up there. He couldn't have one without the other.

"Gentlemen." He nodded in their direction as he closed the gap between them. He added a smile. "It's always nice to see members of our school board take an interest in what we're doing." He nearly gagged, but it did get the requisite pleasant looks in return for his effort.

"Mr. Nicholson," Frank Andrews, the eldest of the three, muttered.

The other two, in their thirties, knew Nick from when he'd played football with their younger brothers in high school. They both responded with a neutral, "Nick."

"You have to do *something*."

Nick hadn't known Frank had a cane until the man pounded it on the gymnasium floor. It echoed around the room, keeping time with the man's double chin.

The other two men nodded in agreement, but they looked more eager to stay out of Nick's reach than to support their agitated leader. Though Nick knew, if push came to shove, they no doubt would. They might be afraid of him, but they had to live in this community whether he stayed or left again.

"Gentlemen," he repeated, pasting on his most pleasant stage smile. "I assure you, this was just a dress rehearsal."

"Cut the crap, Mr. Nicholson. We heard the Baby Jesus statue is missing."

Nick wondered which little monster let that cat out of the bag. "He was indisposed this evening."

"Indisposed?"

"Yes. I think His understudy handled it quite well, though, don't you?"

All three visitors glanced at the manger, then at the happy-faced towel rolled up under Nick's arm.

"Which one?" Rick asked with a snicker.

Frank glared him into silence.

"Need I remind you that you are a substitute teacher, Mr. Nicholson?"

"Heavens, Frank—" Nick placed his arm around the man's shoulders and urged him toward the double doors "—I thought I made it quite clear when I took the job that it was only temporary."

Frank sputtered—Nick's only reward for playing the part so well.

"Thanks for stopping by, gentlemen."

He resisted the urge to toss them through the doors. It was enough just to get them out of there.

He turned to find Hollie, standing in the middle of the aisle, staring at him as if he were from another planet.

"Who are you and what have you done with my son's teacher?"

He strutted toward her. "Besides being a great director, I'm also a darned good actor."

"I can see that."

He grinned down at her.

"And everyone in town thinks you're bad through and through."

"Everyone in town?"

"Well, everyone at the grocery store."

"Ah, yes. Mabel, my favorite checker. You don't think she'd like to head my fan club?"

She snickered. "Not even when pigs fly."

He strutted past her. "You should hear what she has to say about you."

Hollie followed on his heels, as he'd hoped she would. She didn't, however, inquire as to the rumors.

"Aren't you even curious?" he asked as they walked side by side up the steps and back to the wings.

She bent to pick up an angel costume and hang it on a hook. "Oh, I've heard."

"It doesn't bother you?"

She shook her head. "All I have to do is look at Christopher and I know I did the right thing."

"Are you planning on doing it again?"

A laugh escaped her throat, and she clamped her hand over her lips as if embarrassed by her honest response. When she'd composed herself, she said, "I'm not insane, Nick. My husband and I planned on two kids."

"So you did it for him?"

"I did it for me." Her chin raised a notch. "And I don't regret it for a moment. They're my whole world."

Nick reached up under the guise of straightening a costume on the hook nearest Hollie's head, then let his hand drift down tenderly over her dark hair. He toyed with a lock near her shoulder, feeling its silkiness, arranging it just so. Debating on the wisdom of choosing his moment. The kids were all gone, her in-laws were out front. They were as alone as they'd ever been.

Her eyes were soft as they met his. His thumb eased her chin up as he dipped his head and let his lips brush gently over hers. He paused to enjoy the picture of her standing there, eyes hooded, waiting for him to initiate another kiss.

He was astonished by his reaction to her. As an actor, he was used to getting in touch with his emotions—when he wanted to. He could turn on the charm, the laughter, the tears, the passion. He could turn them off just as quickly. Except when he was near Hollie.

He tried to identify his present reaction as he kissed her again, though it was darned hard with his lips devouring hers, his arms crushing her to him. Like? Lust? Hormones? Admiration?

All of the above. And one more emotion he'd never felt before. One he'd given up on. One that scared the daylights out of him.

Love. Pure and simple.

He had nothing to gain by falling in love with her.

"Mr. Nicholson!"

And everything to lose, he added as he looked over his shoulder to find Frank standing behind him. He suspected chances were stronger than ever that he'd be leaving town soon in search of another job. He held no illusions of Hollie piling herself and her two kids on his motorcycle with him.

Nick turned to face the man, shielding Hollie behind him. "Frank," he greeted with great control in his voice, "I thought you'd left."

"It's quite obvious what you were thinking, Mr. Nicholson."

When the man didn't continue, Nick prompted him with, "Did you forget something?"

"I most certainly did. I forgot to tell you we might not be needing you after the Christmas break."

"I see. And when will you know for certain?"

Frank glanced at Hollie, who refused to remain out of sight behind any man. "Sunday night. Maybe sooner," he warned.

FINALLY!

Joey had cut a deal with the judge. In exchange for explaining why he'd cut school, where he'd been and a promise not to do it again, Judge Nicholson had agreed to drive him over to Old Lady Simmonds's house.

It had been more than a week since he'd shoveled her driveway and walk. He hoped she remembered she owed him five dollars. He wanted to buy his mom something pretty. He'd told her he needed money for Christopher's present, but he didn't. It was for her. It was a little white lie.

After the whopper she'd told Mrs. Fagan on the phone, he didn't think he was going to go to hell for it.

Old Lady Simmonds had an awfully bad memory. She was always getting her days of the week mixed up. That's how come he could shovel her snow and she never pressed him as to why he wasn't in school. She just figured it was Saturday, and he let her. His mom said it was rude to correct adults.

"You remember your promise, don't you, Joey?" the judge asked as they walked side by side up Old Lady Simmonds's front walk. There was more snow on it, but Joey didn't think he'd be getting a chance to shovel it again for a while.

"Uh-huh. I won't skip school anymore. Ever."

"Good boy. Because your mom wouldn't like a gift that caused you to disappoint her. She'd much rather you stay in school and get good grades. You get good grades, don't you?"

"Yes, sir. *A*'s and *B*'s."

"Good."

Oh, yeah, it was almost Christmas; he'd better be really honest. "And one *C*. But I'm doing all my homework now."

"So you understand about not disappointing your mother?"

"Uh-huh." He sure wished he had a dad to explain these things to him. "I told her I didn't want any Christmas presents this year."

The judge stopped in midstride. "Why would you do that?"

Joey tugged on his hand. "Because Mr. Nicholson—the other Mr. Nicholson, my teacher—he wants my little brother to be in the Christmas play with me, but my mom said no."

"My son wants a real, live baby in the manger?"

"Uh-huh. So I begged my mom to let him do it."

Joey looked up to see why the judge wasn't moving anymore. He had a really strange look in his eyes. Kind of like how his mom looked at him when she knew he wanted something, and she said he couldn't have it, but then later she surprised him with it, anyway. He didn't know who the judge was thinking about and he didn't really care. He wanted to get that five dollars and get to the store.

"I know there's not really a Santa Claus," he said with a grown-up air.

"You do?" The judge still sounded far away.

"My mom told me, but I have to pretend for my little brother. She says I have a guardian angel, though."

"That's nice."

"I'm going to ask my guardian angel to get me a dad."

Mr. Nicholson would be nice. He made Joey's mom smile. He brought her flowers. He kissed her when he thought no one was looking, and she got that same dumb look on her face that made him gag in the movies. Mary Margaret had been practicing that look on him, but he hadn't kissed her. And he wasn't going to, either.

He really needed a dad to talk to about these things.

"Maybe I could ask Santa, too, just in case? Huh, Judge?"

Chapter Thirteen

Saturday, December 21

For the first time in more than a week, Hollie woke up raring to go. No court today. No school. She had a mansion to decorate, not much time in which to do it and very little help.

She found Joey sitting cross-legged on the couch in front of the television, still in his jammies, entranced by his favorite superhero. "You're supposed to be getting dressed."

"But, Mo-om—"

"I'll be glad to watch him," Al offered. He eased himself down onto the cushion next to Joey and cuddled him beneath his arm as if sharing cartoons together was their usual, good-buddy, Saturday-morning routine.

Hollie almost hated to ruin the picture. "Gee, Dad, thanks. Any other time and I'd take you up on it, but I'm afraid Joey has work to do."

Bea, carrying two cups of coffee from the kitchen to the living room, pushed her way through the swinging door with her hip just in time to hear the tail end of their conversation. "You make him work for you?"

"Only when I'm behind schedule because I have to be in school with him."

Joey kept his eyes riveted to the television—anywhere as long as he wasn't making eye contact with his mom.

"Dressed. Now," Hollie ordered, "while I get Christopher ready."

Joey slid slowly off the couch and shuffled out of the room, leading Hollie to believe it would be quite a while before he was ready unless she kept after him.

"At least we can take care of Christopher for you today," Bea offered.

"Gosh, Mom, I can't." Hollie was starting to feel guilty, even though she had no choice in the matter.

Bea's spine went rigid. She raised her chin up a notch. "Why on earth not? We raised three children of our own, you know. And I think we did a pretty darned good job."

"Yes, Mom, I know. It's not you. Don't take it personally. I have to nurse Christopher, remember?"

Bea's jaw dropped open. "You mean to tell me he doesn't ever get *any* formula?"

"That's why I've been taking him to school with me."

Bea opened her mouth to object.

"And please don't tell me to buy a breast pump. I've already been through that discussion with Terri."

A rosy-pink blush crept up Al's neck.

"I wouldn't think of it, dear." Bea exchanged a silent look with her husband as she set both cups on the coffee table with an uncustomary clatter. "Wouldn't think of it at all."

Hollie knew their feelings were hurt. As aggravating as they'd been this visit, she didn't want any hard feelings to come between them and her family. Perhaps she could make amends.

"You know, Mom, Dad, if you think you'll be bored sitting around here all day, you might want to come hang some decorations." She made the invitation sound as inviting as possible without patronizing them.

"Oh my no, thank you," Bea declined for both of them. "Do you think Terri would mind if I went over for a visit?"

"Her number's on the fridge. Call and see if she's up."

Ordinarily, Hollie would tell anyone to just stop by and see Terri. She hated being holed up on crutches and she still didn't have a release to go back to work at the law firm. But Bea had been so snipey that Hollie wasn't sure she'd wish her on anyone.

Hollie didn't have time to wonder what her in-laws were going to be doing with their day. They could visit Terri or they could come help her; it didn't matter. She was going to be lucky to get through all she needed to do today.

She refused to admit that, if it weren't for the fact she was going to be busy all day, she'd miss sitting in Nick's class and annoying him to no end. She'd miss that frown he got when he couldn't decide whether to take her to task for her latest class interruption or ignore it and hope it would go away. She'd miss that crooked grin when he'd found a way to get even with her.

So much so that she decided, if she didn't totally exhaust herself hanging decorations, she'd call him that evening.

AT TEN O'CLOCK, while precariously perched on the fourth rung of a stepladder, Hollie found out what the Fagans' doorbell sounded like from inside the mansion. It amazed her what people spent their money on. Big, booming, it sounded as if she were standing in a cathedral listening to "We Three Kings" echoing out of organ pipes. She would have to suggest Mrs. Fagan soften the blow on the night of the ball, maybe pick some light, fluffy tune like "Jingle Bells" and turn it to a low volume.

Joey, standing at the bottom of the ladder and handing more snowflakes up to her, hummed the rest of the tune—or what he could remember of it.

All the Christmas trees—one for each of the three floors—were in place for Monday night's ball. Bare, but in place. Hollie wasn't expecting any other deliveries, so when "We Three Kings" started over, she told Joey, "Ignore it."

"What, Mom?"

"Just keep handing me those snowflakes."

"I am. Ignore what, Mom?"

"The doorbell." She reached high overhead for the beam and suspended three glittery snowflakes so they drifted down to various levels.

"Can we put on some different Christmas music?"

"That's not music." This was the only part of the job she hated. She steadied herself with one hand on the top step of the ladder while she reached down with the other without looking. "Hand me another bunch."

"What's that playing, then?"

"The doorbell."

She shouldn't have told him. The last thing she heard as he jumped over a box of ornaments on his way out of the room was "Cool!"

When she got three more loud renditions of the kings bearing gifts, she descended the ladder, stomped down two flights of stairs and into the foyer. Heaven help whoever dared interrupt one of only two days she had left to work.

"Mom, look, it's Mr. Nicholson. And some of my friends." Joey beamed as if he hadn't seen them in a week instead of just yesterday.

Real snowflakes decorated the top of Nick's dark head, and she wondered if he ever zipped up his leather jacket. Or if he ever wore anything heavier than a T-shirt beneath it.

When he stepped inside, brushing snow off his leather collar, the huge foyer seemed to shrink to the size of a closet.

Hollie forgot she'd been about to read the riot act to whoever was at the door—until Joey, Timmy, T.J. and Michael scuffled over whose turn it was to push the button next. As "We Three Kings" began again, she clapped her hands over her ears and shouted, "Stop!"

She couldn't hear Nick's chuckle, but she could see it. His smile was warm enough to melt chocolate and his eyes twinkled merrily as he pulled all four boys inside, safely away from the doorbell, and shut the door firmly. By the time the music stopped, he'd given the boys a stuffed paper bag and sent them running up the stairs. He handled them with such ease; she thought he should have half a dozen of his own.

"What...what're you doing here?" she asked, bewildered as to why her demand didn't sound like one.

His fingers, still cool from being outside, circled her wrists as he tugged her hands away from her ears.

She listened for a moment. "Oh, thank God," she murmured into the silence. She stepped closer to him, drawn like a magnet, not knowing if he pulled her or if her feet moved forward on their own. She didn't think they were under the mistletoe she'd hung, but she didn't want to break eye contact long enough to look up and find out.

"Does that mean you're happy to see me?" he asked.

"What?"

"You said, 'Thank God.'"

She couldn't remember what she'd been thanking God for, but she didn't think it was for putting her so close to Nick that, if she took a deep breath, their chests would touch. Although that might be worth it.

"Oh, no, I think it had to do with...something else. What're you doing here?"

His hand tunneled through her hair and cupped the back of her neck, heating her skin everywhere he touched. She only caught the last half of his explanation.

"...Karl and Tat have taken over the props, thanks to your sketches. And I thought you might need some help over here, so I borrowed my dad's car and picked up the boys. I know if you hadn't been in my class all week, you'd probably be done by now."

If she hadn't been in his class all week, he wouldn't be here. She might never have met him outside of some parent-teacher thing. She never would have known how generous he could be, how much he loved children, how much teaching drama meant to him. And she never would have fallen in love with the man inside East Bay's leather-jacketed, motorcycle-riding bad boy.

"How did a nice guy like you get such a bad reputation, anyway?"

His eyebrows puckered together. He glanced over his shoulder theatrically. "Shh, don't let on."

She giggled at his antics, as he'd obviously intended. "Really, Nick, if people could only see you with the kids..."

His skin had warmed up, she realized when he clapped his other hand lightly over her mouth. He smelled of fresh pine. She wondered if, even in the middle of summer, he would still remind her of Christmas trees. Or if she'd be in touch with him so many months from now. If things didn't work out for him here in East Bay, there was no telling how far he'd have to go to find another job.

"That's our little secret," he whispered.

Her little secret was what she wanted under her tree this Christmas. And she didn't care whether he came gift-wrapped or not.

She covered his fingers with her own. As she dragged them slowly, tantalizingly, off her lips, she covered them with soft kisses. The twinkle left his eyes then, as they locked with hers and heated to a soft golden brown.

"Hollie..." His voice held a ragged edge.

"Don't worry. Your secret's safe with me."

He glanced over her shoulder. "Not anymore." The twinkle returned along with his crooked grin.

Hollie didn't have to turn around. Her instincts told her there were four little boys staring at her back. After hearing the questions they'd asked all week in sex-education class, she couldn't delude herself with the thought that they were too young to notice the heat sizzling between Nick and her. They'd seen enough movies that she didn't think they'd buy the I've-got-something-in-my-eye-and-Nick's-trying-to-get-it-out routine.

"Maybe we'd better hang up some stars or snowflakes or something," Nick suggested. "Want to give us some direction on what to do?"

"Oh, yeah."

She glanced around the foyer, annoyed with herself for taking so long to get her bearings, but she had to physically step away from Nick in order to do so. He followed her up both flights of stairs, so close as to make her extremely conscious of him just behind her derriere.

"Wow. You've got to do this whole house this weekend?"

Hollie sighed as she surveyed everything that hadn't been done yet. "And this is only the ballroom. See why I bugged you all week?"

His grin was as crooked as ever as he asked, "Does this mean that if we get done, you'll behave in class on Monday?"

"Put it on your wish list, Nicholson."

The twinkle was back full force. "I already have. So, where do we start?"

Hollie didn't need anyone to ask a second time. Yes, it was her job to decorate for the ball. Yes, her reputation could be made or broken by how it all came together, but it would surely be mud if she didn't get done on time. Or if she came so close to the wire that she gave Mrs. Fagan heart failure.

She picked up a handful of snowflakes and climbed the ladder. "Why don't you start the boys on the trees? They can go as high as they can reach."

"Awesome!" voices chorused behind and below her. "We get to do the trees!" The boys tore into the boxes of ornaments. T.J. stuffed the brown bag back into Nick's arms.

"What's in there?" Hollie asked.

"Something for later."

"You're staying through lunch?"

"No." His grin was one that reminded her of Joey when he was up to something. "Well, yeah, I can stay all day."

"What's in the bag, Nick?"

He held it behind his back.

"Don't make me get down off this ladder, buster."

His grin erased all thoughts she'd had of little boys. It was all man and it said, "Come and see for yourself."

"Nick . . ."

"Come on, Mr. Nicholson!"

"What's in the bag, Nick?"

"It's marshmallows, Mom. Mr. Nicholson says when he was a little boy, he used to always—"

"Not on these trees!" she ordered.

"It's tradition." His argument lost all power when he couldn't keep a straight face.

"Not at Mrs. Fagan's Snowflake Ball, it's not. Save them for your own tree."

"I don't have one." He stuck out his lower lip in perfect imitation of any one of his students.

Hollie snickered. "You can't fool me, Nick. I've been in your classroom, remember?"

Heck, yes, he remembered. It had started off as a dull holiday season until she'd arrived wearing Christmas sweaters, blouses with Santa Claus buttons and little gold bells on her socks that she loved to jingle in front of Christopher's nose. On Friday the thirteenth, when his dad had sentenced her to the classroom, Nick had thought she was the lump of coal in his stocking.

Now he knew she was the best present of all. And he wasn't at all sure if he could keep her.

HOLLIE TURNED OFF the incandescents, plugged in the Christmas lights and a few strategically placed spotlights. The ballroom glowed. Stars shimmered and twinkled overhead. Snowflakes floated on the air. The gaily decorated tree put the ones in the department stores to shame. It was easy for her to imagine crackling flames in the fireplace and soft music prodding guests to mingle and dance.

Nick gave a long, low whistle of appreciation when he entered the room. He strolled a large circle around the dance floor, his hands resting comfortably on the snug hips of his jeans as he did so. His eyes roamed from floor to ceiling and back again in order to see that every nook and cranny, every pillar and every beam, carried off the intricately mixed themes. Red, green and gold for Christmas were touched off with glittering silver snowflakes everywhere.

"It's even better than your sketches. Oops—" either he flushed slightly, or his face picked up the glow from a red bulb "—I meant that in the best possible way."

"Three dimension's always better."

"The Fagans should give you a whopping bonus for this."

"I'll be lucky if Mrs. Fagan doesn't think I've been goofing off all week and give me a bad reference for being so slow. How are the boys doing?"

His grin made her forget she was tired.

"What?" she asked, not sure she wanted to know.

He glanced at his watch.

"There'd better not be marshmallows on one of the trees downstairs, Nicholson."

"Nope. We ate them."

"So what about the boys?"

"Boy, you really get caught up in your work, don't you?" He turned his arm so she could see his watch. "It's after eight, Hollie. Do you even remember eating?"

"Uh..."

"Tell me if any of this rings a bell. Al and Bea bringing pizza?" He paused, but didn't receive confirmation. "You eating half of a large all by yourself?"

She shrugged apologetically, hoping she hadn't ignored him completely since he'd come to help her decorate. Or eaten more than her share.

"You giving Joey permission to go ice-skating with the other boys?"

"Now, *that* I remember. He earned it. And Bea promised to read Christopher a story and tuck him in."

"Good. You had me worried there for a minute. And now—" he executed an imaginary drumroll "—the stairs are done and waiting your approval, madam."

Her mouth dropped open. "You did them yourself?"

"Come see."

He took her hand in his as naturally as if they'd done it a thousand times before. He tugged; she followed.

The stairs were swagged with boughs of pine, dotted with red bows and tiny white lights. A colorful, stuffed collection of Santa's elves spread from the landing and perched on the edges of the treads going down.

Hollie was in awe. Both because of the artistic way Nick had carried off her theme and because he'd worked for hours to make her deadline easier. If the school board had any brains, they'd hire him full-time and never let him go. If she had any brains, she'd quit annoying him in class and do the same thing.

"Nick, it's beautiful."

"I just followed your sketches. See, there's an elf twisting red and white pipe cleaners to make candy canes. And there's one wrapping gifts."

He moved closer to Hollie as he pointed out each one in turn. So close that, instead of his artistic interpretation of her sketches, she noticed his warmth as his chest brushed against her shoulder. The slight stir of her hair beneath his breath tickled her ear.

Those thoughts ground to a halt as she noticed two elves in a dimly lit, recessed corner on the landing. Her eyebrows puckered as she peered closer. "What are those two doing?"

"Kissing."

"Elves don't kiss." She bent down to turn them to innocent positions.

He tugged her back up before she could. "Sure they do."

"They do not."

"You just don't know your elves." He turned her in his arms and held her against his chest. "After all, I'm one of your elves and I've wanted to do this all day."

His lips covered hers with a gentleness she hadn't expected. A gentleness she couldn't—didn't want to—pull away from. A gentleness that was matched by the pad of his thumb skimming her cheek. And then he pulled back—just an inch or so, just far enough that she knew he was giving her space to make a decision.

"You kiss pretty well for an elf," she whispered raggedly against his lips.

"Oh, yeah? You know how elves kiss?"

When his head dipped again, she inched backward, taking him by the hand and leading him into the ballroom. On the way, she flicked off the lights on the landing. Nick kicked the door closed behind them, throwing them into a fantasy world of twinkling lights and glittering stars that heightened all her senses.

Behind the closed door, Nick dragged her back into the circle of his arms. He crushed her against his chest, the pressure teasing her sensitive nipples with the promise that they might as well be skin-to-skin for all the restraint she wasn't feeling. He smelled of fresh air and a whole forest full of trees, leading her to wonder what it would be like to make love outdoors. He tasted of red-hot peppermint. His kisses made her want to live the dream of unwrapping him beneath her tree. As her feet moved toward the only tree available, he took the lead, seeming to read her thoughts.

He pushed gold-foil-wrapped packages aside and eased her down onto the round, quilted skirt as if she weighed no more than one of the empty stockings hung from the mantel. She reached up then and pulled him down on top of her, accepting his weight as if she couldn't imagine him crushing her.

She traced his bottom lip with her tongue and tugged his head down. She felt his hesitation melt away as he wedged a knee between her legs and eased himself into the cradle of her hips.

"Oh, God, Nick."

He quickly levered himself up on his elbows. "Am I hurting you?"

She wove her fingers through his thick hair and pulled him back to her. "The only way you could hurt me now is if you stop."

"You're sure?"

She hooked her legs around his thighs and squeezed him close, pressing him against her so he'd have no doubts—nor clear thoughts—of his own.

His low, throaty chuckle echoed through her chest. "And what would you like Santa to bring you this Christmas?"

"A sex-education teacher."

He moved against her. "As if you need one."

"It's been a long time."

"I hear it's like riding a bicycle."

"Shut up and show me."

Minutes later, they parted only long enough to shed their clothes. She tugged his T-shirt over his head. He tossed her bra over his shoulder. She unzipped his jeans and lost all coordination after the backs of her fingers brushed against his erection. He helped her out of every last stitch, and she had no idea which way her panties flew or where they landed.

He cupped her swollen breasts, making her gasp at the pleasure he gave. She reached down and circled him intimately, and discovered he was being patient with her, withholding his own pleasure, giving her time to adjust to something she hadn't done in a long, long time.

She didn't want to wait. She told him so, but not with words. With her lips, as her kisses heated his skin. With her tongue, as she traced his bottom lip, then plunged inside. With her fingers and her hands, as she urged him closer. With her body, as she arched up to him.

Nick's gentleness gave way to something far more primal as he responded with a fiery possession that threatened to set the tree above them ablaze.

Ornaments, set in motion by his shoulder and her feet, bobbed out of control above them. Tree branches swayed. Gold-foil-wrapped packages slid aside to frame them as they finally came to rest in each other's arms.

Nick rolled off Hollie, pulling her onto his chest where he wouldn't crush her. A red glass ball plopped onto her head and bounced off, sending them both into peals of laughter.

Hollie lay her head on his shoulder and peeked upward. "My God, it's still standing."

"What?"

"The tree."

His chuckle rumbled deep within his body, and he liked the pressure of her body playing against it. When she handed him the ornament, he reached above her and re-hung it. He squeezed the hanger tightly around the branch so, in case he recovered shortly, it wouldn't get knocked off again. Then he inhaled deeply and savored the feel of how he could raise her body merely by expanding his chest.

His fingers traced aimless patterns on her bare back. He could feel her relax, her bones softening as her body melded itself to his.

He wanted to tell her he loved her, but he didn't want the first time to be in their version of a bed. He didn't want her to have any doubts that he spoke the words only in the throes of passion. He'd pick a better time.

"TURN HERE," Nick said from the passenger side of the station wagon. Hollie had made him use the seat belt, against all his protests that the kids weren't there and would never know, and in spite of the fact that he'd said he really wanted to scoot over and sit next to her.

"This isn't the way home," she said.

"I know. I want to show you something."

"What?"

"You'll see. Turn right here." Nick checked his watch. Quarter to ten. "I've still got fifteen minutes."

"The high school?" she asked as she flipped on her blinker. "Fifteen minutes for what?"

"To show you something important. Park by the door."

The lot was full, obviously a big night at the high school. "There's no space."

"So double-park."

"Nick, I can't—"

"Sure you can. Pull over there."

She took only a minute to do as he asked, aware that Nick was in a hurry to show her something that meant a lot to him.

The board outside the school advertised East Bay High's holiday stage production, and she knew Nick's goal was to be on staff and direct one himself, so she guessed that's what they were doing there. In spite of the fact that he seemed to think this was going to be some kind of surprise.

As soon as she closed the car door, he took her by the hand and, much like a whirlwind, sucked her along behind him into the commons.

"Hey, Pops."

Pops glanced up at the wall clock. "I almost gave up on you, boy." He wheezed and waved Nick and Hollie on their way into the connecting auditorium.

Nick opened one of the double doors just wide enough for them to slip into the back of the dark room. Hollie went first, then pressed herself up against the back wall while she waited for her eyes to adjust.

She'd never been in a play back in her high school days. Like being on a ladder, the thought unsettled her. Standing up in front of all those people and delivering lines did not look like fun, although she would have liked to have a hand in the backdrop. They called that a castle wall?

Her hand was still in Nick's. She could tell by his grip that he was excited when the lead man spoke, as the young man was obviously very comfortable in the role. She could tell when he winced for the leading lady, who stumbled over her line just before the kiss. And, her hand still snugly in his, he clapped along with everyone else when the court jester stole the show.

When her eyes adjusted to the dim light, she turned her attention to Nick's profile instead of the stage. If he hadn't been holding her hand, she would have thought he didn't know she was there at all. He was enthralled by the production in front of him. He whispered the next line the leading lady stumbled over.

"She just doesn't understand what it means," he whispered to Hollie. "I could have made that easier for her."

And she had no doubt he could have; she'd seen what he'd accomplished so far with Joey's class.

For the next ten minutes, she felt as if she were Nick's anchor, the only reason he didn't rush up front and tell everyone how it was supposed to be done. That would certainly perpetuate his bad-boy image.

She said as much to him when they were back in the station wagon and on their way to her house.

He laughed, but it sounded forced. "As much as I was tempted, that wouldn't be the way to get hired. And I'm not about to jeopardize that. Not for anything."

His words were intense, and she believed him.

When they turned into her driveway, the porch light flipped on. "I guess Al and Bea are still up."

Hollie opened her car door, illuminating Nick's sexy grin in the dome light.

"Too bad." He took her gloved hand in his. "I'm glad they picked up the boys earlier." He unsnapped his seat belt and let it fly back into the retractor as he scooted across the seat toward her. He dipped his head and leaned close. "Hollie, I lo—"

Knuckles rapped sharply on the window on Nick's side and sent them both jumping into the air. Nick bumped the head liner.

"Need help carrying anything in?" Al asked, peering in through the window. In spite of his offer of help, his expression was tight-lipped and grim.

Hollie popped out her side, trying to hide her ragged breaths, but not having any luck since everyone could see them in the cold air. "Uh, no, Dad. Thanks, anyway. Want to come in for some coffee, Nick?"

"You bet."

They followed Al into the house, where Bea stood in the center of the living room, as if waiting for them.

"Hollie," Bea said as tight-lipped as her husband. "We need to talk to you."

"Okay, just let me get some coffee started first."

"This involves Joey."

Hollie noticed Bea waited expectantly, as if she thought Hollie should go get him up. "He worked hard all day, Mom. If you want to talk to him, it'll have to wait until morning."

Bea's chest rose and fell with barely suppressed emotion. "I thought I'd do some cleaning while you were gone today. I found the school's missing Baby Jesus statue in your studio."

The missing statue had ceased to be a secret long ago, thanks to bigmouthed fourth-graders. Hollie's studio, on the other hand, was her private territory.

"In my studio?"

"In the back of the closet inside Joey's backpack."

The implication outweighed her privacy. She took a deep breath and unbuttoned her coat as she gathered her thoughts. An immediate answer would be nice, but Joey, she was sure, had been fast asleep for quite some time. It would take a lot to wake him, and if she did, she knew she'd be up the rest of the night. They'd both worked hard all day; they both needed their sleep so they could put in several more hours tomorrow. Her future and that of her boys depended on her finishing the job.

She looked at Nick to see how he was handling the news that his statue had been found. His expression gave nothing away.

"Well, I guess this certainly does involve Joey," she said slowly. "I'll speak to him first thing in the morning."

"Now, wait just a minute—" Bea said.

"Bea," Al warned softly, "remember your blood pressure."

"What raises my blood pressure is her just letting him sleep when he's got a lot of explaining to do."

"He's worked hard, Mom. He needs his sleep. And frankly, so do I. Morning will be soon enough."

She felt Nick at her side and was surprised how much comfort she derived from his presence.

"It's not right, Hollie," Bea criticized. "You should punish a child as soon as you find out he's done wrong. Otherwise he'll never learn."

"It's my decision, Mom."

"We want to take the boys off your hands until you can get your life back together. We can take them back home with us."

Nick's hand landed on Hollie's shoulder, but he didn't think she felt it just then. Bea tilted her head back and looked down her nose at him.

"You must be out of your minds," Hollie said in a deceptively soft tone.

He listened in disbelief as her mother-in-law continued.

"You think so? You, a single mother with two children…no steady income…one boy in trouble with the law already…you sentenced by a judge…one more mistake and back to court…"

Nick thought it all sounded pretty bad when the old lady laid it out like that. He could feel Hollie's shoulder tremble beneath his hand. "Mrs. Landon—"

"Stay out of this, Nick," Hollie said quietly.

He'd never been good at doing what he was told to do. He'd known since the second he'd realized he loved her what he would eventually do about it. So he stepped up the timetable a little.

"Marry me, Hollie."

She wheeled on him. "What??"

"Marry me."

"Absolutely not."

"Why not? Then you wouldn't be a single mother anymore. You wouldn't be doing everything alone." He knew this would be a good time to tell her he loved her but, for chrissakes, not in front of her late husband's parents.

Hollie stepped away from his hand. "It's the principle of the thing."

"The principle? Lady, your principles are in danger of landing you in deep—"

"Nick, I think you'd better go."

He couldn't believe she was throwing him out. Not after what they'd shared under the Christmas tree. Not after he'd taken her to watch the play with him. Not after he'd made such a monumental step in their relationship as to propose marriage.

He glared at Al and Bea. "And what about them?"

"They're Joey and Christopher's grandparents. They may stay as long as they behave themselves. And as long as

here's no more talk about 'taking them off my hands' for
a while,'' she said pointedly in their direction.

Nick brushed past Hollie, purposefully making contact
with her to try and bring her to her senses. She didn't change
her mind, however, and Al pulled the front door open to
hasten him on his way. So much for planning on spending
the night on Hollie's living room couch. So much for his
plan to share breakfast with her and the boys the next
morning.

"He needs a ride back to the Fagans', Dad," Hollie said.

Nick waited on the front porch while Al bundled up in his
coat, hat and gloves and let himself out.

"I don't need a ride," Nick told Al when he stepped onto
the porch.

"Why didn't you say so sooner?"

"Because I wanted to talk to you out here. Away from
Hollie."

"There's nothing you can say to make Bea change her
mind. Lord knows, I've tried."

Nick wasn't but a couple of inches taller than Al, but he
felt as if he were towering over the older man as he leaned
very close and retorted, "Try harder."

"Now listen here, young man, you have no right—"

"Neither do you. You pack up your wife and get the hell
out of town."

"Are you threatening me?"

"Hollie and those boys belong together. If you can afford to take them *for a while,* then you can afford to help
her out."

Al's expression was cold and tight. "You're out of line."

"That's nothing new for me."

Nick stormed off the porch and headed across Hollie's
yard, shortcutting his way back to the Fagans' where he'd
left the car he'd borrowed from his dad. The hike in the

frigid night air would do him good, not that he noticed the cold; he was too steamed. He'd been more careful than he used to be, though; he'd taken care to intimidate Al Landon in private so it was just the older man's word against his. Maybe he'd finally grown up; maybe his punch-the-other-guy-out days were over.

If Hollie's principles were going to prevent her accepting his help—and he'd learned all week long that she was a firm believer in principles—he'd do his best to help her without allowing his bad-boy image to hurt her case further.

Chapter Fourteen

Nick didn't want to call too early Sunday morning and get
Hollie out of bed, but he didn't want to wait so long that her
mother-in-law would be up, either. He paced the floor until
7:00 a.m., then figured she probably was up with Christopher by that time. He dialed her number.

Bea answered on the first ring. Her hello was clipped and
short, and Nick knew she'd been waiting for him to call.

"I'd like to talk to Hollie."

"She's busy with the baby."

"I'll wait."

"Then she has to talk to Joey. I'm sure you remember we
have a behavior problem on our hands over here."

Nick stifled the urge to throw the phone across the room.
"Since it's my statue you found, I'd say it's safe to assume
I'm well aware—"

"I'm sure she'll be busy all day."

Click.

Nick's frustration was vented in a roar that rattled the
roof. He resisted the urge to punch the receiver through the
wall. Instead, he grabbed his helmet, stuffed it beneath his
arm and stormed out the door. This time he wouldn't take
no from his dad. Not even if it took him all day.

"THE PLAY'S TONIGHT! The play's tonight!" Joey bounced into the kitchen, excitement over the impending play replacing any thoughts he should have had of another day of decorating the Fagans'.

Hollie's mind, on the other hand, was focused on everything except the play. She had a mansion to finish decorating. She had a son to question and discipline. She had a baby who was fussy from yesterday's strange break in his new routine. She had in-laws she wasn't quite sure what to do with.

Ever since her husband had died, her every example had been geared toward teaching Joey the importance of family. They'd left all the family photos up on the wall in the hallway. They'd added Christopher. They wrote the grandparents regularly.

Last year, when Hollie had gotten pregnant, Joey had questioned the sudden absence of her parents. It had been difficult to explain to him that they wanted nothing more to do with her radical choices in life, but it had been the springboard to a discussion of just how important the family they had left really was.

"Hey, Mom, the play's—"

"Tonight. I know, sweetie." She jiggled Christopher on her lap and cooed at him until he smiled.

"Can I go skating today?"

She shook her head. "We have to finish the Fagans', remember?"

"Aw, Mo-om."

Bea, dressed in a long robe, her hair in curlers, entered the kitchen. Her lips were pressed together more firmly than last night, if that was possible.

Hollie rose to leave. "But first, Joey, we need to go have a chat in my studio."

He grabbed an apple out of the basket on the table, sneaked a wary peek at his grandmother's grim expression and hurried out of the room behind his mom and little baby brother.

It got worse when he walked into the studio to find his backpack in the center of the room, on the floor, open. The Baby Jesus statue lay on his mom's black office chair.

Uh-oh.

He turned and saw his grandmother hovering just outside the door, her arms folded across her chest, her toe tapping on the hall floor.

"Mom," he whispered. "Can I close the door?"

He saw her chew the inside of her cheek, but she nodded. He slowly pushed the door shut, afraid all the while that his grandmother would put her hand out and stop him, but she didn't.

"Well?" Hollie prodded.

He hated that. It meant *he* had to decide where to start explaining.

"I'm waiting, Joey."

"Well, when I was at play practice, and Mr. Nicholson was painting Baby Jesus, I noticed His finger was broken." He pointed at the digit in question. "So I found the other piece in the prop room and I was going to bring it home to glue it."

He risked a look at her face. He was pleasantly surprised to see she wasn't turning purple.

She traced the fine line where he had joined the two pieces. She sighed. He hated that sigh. It meant she thought he hadn't been thinking things through again. She'd had two favorite topics lately—principles and consequences. He thought this was going to be the latter.

"But, Joey, Mr. Nicholson has been worried sick. This is a very important night for him, and he's nervous about it going well."

Joey didn't think Mr. Nicholson ever got nervous about anything. Except, now that Joey thought about it, maybe having his mom in the classroom.

"I was going to bring Him back—right after the play. Then Mr. Nicholson wouldn't have to worry. But..."

"*After* the play?"

She hadn't started yelling yet, so he got up the courage and continued.

"I thought it'd be really neat. You know, me and my little brother in a play together. And you could take our picture and hang it on the wall with the others so we could tell him about it when he gets older. Just like we're going to tell him about my dad and how he wanted another baby so much that you made him special."

Was that a tear he saw in his mom's eye? If so, he was almost home free.

"So I hid Baby Jesus. I was going to return Him after the play. Honest."

Not only a tear, but a proud smile. He knew that smile. He *was* home free.

"But, Joey, I never said Christopher could be in the play."

"I know, Mom, but it's real important to me. And it will be to Christopher, too, when he's old enough to understand."

Hollie was back to chewing her lip. "But there's that one scene where Mary Margaret would have to carry him across the stage—"

"She won't drop him. She takes care of him sometimes in the classroom and she's never dropped him."

"I know, Joey, but she'll be wearing that long skirt she's not used to. I just can't take that chance."

Joey stuck out his lower lip and tried to think of a way around this unexpected obstacle.

Hollie said, "You did all this just so you could have Christopher in the play with you?"

He was embarrassed when a tear ran down his cheek. He looked down at the floor and said quietly, "I love him so much. It's the only thing I want for Christmas."

"What about the Harley T-shirt?"

He heard the smile in her voice. He glanced up to see her eyes were bright, too. "I don't need it."

"Did the judge know about the statue?"

Joey nodded. "He brought me home the day Grandma and Grandpa got here, and I showed him that Baby Jesus was okay. And he said he couldn't think of anything nicer to give Mr. Nicholson than what he wanted the most—and that's to have a great play and get to go work at the high school. So we agreed it could be our little secret."

If his mom thought that was all the judge knew, that was for the better. For now. She'd find out the rest on Christmas morning, and then she'd cry some more and hug him and tell him what a little man he was growing up to be. And how his dad, up in heaven, would be so proud of him.

"I'll tell you what," Hollie interrupted his rambling thoughts. "You call Mr. Nicholson and tell him what you did."

Joey hung his head. *So close. Well, there was still Christmas morning to look forward to.*

"And then you can tell him that, if Christopher doesn't cry or anything, he can be the baby in the manger. But you have to use the statue for the moving parts."

Yes!

Joey threw himself against her, wrapped his arms around her waist and Christopher and hugged them for all he was worth. "Thanks, Mom! I'll go call Mr. Nicholson right now."

He tore across the room and pulled the door open. His grandmother blocked his way.

"Then get dressed," Hollie added. "You, too, Mom."

"Me?"

"Yes, you and Dad, both. I told you last night you could stay here, but now I've decided that's only if you want to spend time getting involved in your grandson's life—not his book bag."

"B-but..." the older lady sputtered. "Going out in this cold weather just makes my arthritis worse."

"You're coming with us if I have to drag you myself."

Wow, what a mom!

"DAD, YOU'VE GOT to do something!" Nick said for the hundredth time that day.

"Trust me, Nick."

"Trust you?" Nick thought that was absurd, considering the changes in his life since he'd trusted his dad long enough to ask his advice about a truant Joey. "Look where that's gotten me so far."

"It's better if Mrs. Landon works this out with her in-laws. Hiring an attorney for her would just complicate the issue."

"They're trying to take her children away from her."

"They were upset. Mrs. Landon appears to be quite capable. The wisest thing you can do right now is to give her some time to bring them around."

"If you think she's so capable, why'd you stick her in class with me and threaten to take her back to court?"

The judge turned away and hid a smile. "She needed a push."

"A push? You call that a push?"

They went around and around until late that afternoon. Nick got nowhere with his dad.

He rode over to the Fagans' house. When he saw the Landons' car parked behind Hollie's station wagon, he sat at the curb for several minutes and gave the matter more thought. If Hollie's in-laws were there with her, maybe they were helping. He went on his way—just in case his dad was right.

There were plenty last-minute details for him to tend to. He checked costumes and props and electrical equipment. Parents showed up to help, and he got his first glimpse of the finished program. In his element, he started to relax. It was all coming together. He could almost taste that job at East Bay High, especially when he saw the board members arrive and take front-row seats.

Hollie arrived a little early, preceded by Joey and the statue. Nick didn't care about it anymore. He wanted to know if she was all right with her in-laws.

"Hey, Mr. Nicholson."

"Hey yourself."

Over the top of Joey's head, Hollie's slow, confident smile warmed Nick to the core. She was all right. Maybe his dad had given him good advice. He could return his attention to the play at hand, knowing he'd get a few more minutes with her again when it was over.

"I took Him home and fixed His finger." Joey held the Baby Jesus statue up to show off his work.

Nick examined the repair. Not only had Joey glued the finger, he'd done some nice touch-up painting, as well. "You had Him all this time?"

Joey swallowed visibly. "I tried to call you today, but you weren't home. I wanted my baby brother to be in the manger."

"Your mom said no."

"She changed her mind."

"She did?"

"Uh-huh."

Nick's eyes never left Hollie while Joey did all the explaining.

"She said Mary Margaret had to carry Him, but that Christopher could be in the manger."

"As long as he's quiet and doesn't ruin the play," Hollie clarified.

NICK WAS DETERMINED the play would start on time.

"Mr. Nicholson."

He recognized a plaintive tone when he heard one. He turned to see Linda holding up two fingers. "I told you that you don't have to do that anymore," he said.

She hopped from one foot to the other. "But I have to go."

What would he say if he had parenting experience? *Hold it?* Or, *Didn't I tell you to go before we left?*

"Go. Hurry," he ordered. "Anybody else?"

"I feel sick," Kevin whined.

Nick felt the boy's forehead. He didn't know what he hoped to gain by that, but it certainly wasn't Kevin's supper on his boot.

"Oh, sick!" echoed through the entire fourth-grade class, which had been assembled in a relatively orderly fashion until then.

Nick stood rooted to the spot. He'd been behind plenty of rising curtains and seen plenty of adults with the same reaction as Kevin. "You sick?" he asked, just to be sure.

"No, I feel better now."

"Good. Everybody outside." He didn't have to tell them twice. "Angie, go to the bathroom, get Linda and meet us at the front door."

As Nick herded the children to their outdoor positions, he used the nearest bush to clean his boot. The only difference between kids and adults was that adults who threw up from stage fright tended to do it off to the side. Fortunately there was a willing parent on hand to take care of the floor tonight.

"Okay, we're all here," he said as Linda and Angie took their places. He checked Joey and Mary Margaret last. "Whoa, what's that doing here?"

The children giggled. "It's Baby Jesus," T.J. said.

"Yeah, but He hasn't been born yet." He plucked the statue from Mary Margaret's arms and stuck it under his leather jacket. He tried to zip himself up, but besides there not being enough room, he looked nine months pregnant.

"I can put Him under my costume," Mary Margaret offered.

"Uh-huh," Nick said sarcastically. "And when He falls out at the wrong time, then what? No thanks. Stick with your pillow." He wanted to be innovative, not suicidal.

"Mr. Nicholson, I'm cold."

"Me, too," echoed through the line.

"Okay." He set the statue aside and got preoccupied with a couple haloes that needed straightening, and he had to reposition two boys in line so they'd quit boxing with each other. Then he opened the door to the building. "Angels first. Remember, flutter around, smile at people. You're good angels."

Joey and Mary Margaret were the last ones to enter the auditorium. They went slowly. Halfway up the aisle, Mary

Margaret clutched her stomach when the pillow started to slip.

Nick snapped his fingers as he remembered the most important part of the play. "Oh, yeah." He ran back to collect the statue.

In its place was a small, round pillow.

He groaned. "Oh, no." Just to cover all bases, he crossed his fingers *and* said a prayer.

As the little couple made their way up the aisle, Mary Margaret hung on to Joey's arm with one hand and her belly with the other. Joey kept a wary eye on her as he paused from time to time to ask a member of the audience if there was any room in their inn.

Nick couldn't see the board members' faces, but he could see Hollie. She had her hand over her mouth to cover her laughter. He panned the audience to see open amusement. They were loving it. He breathed a sigh of relief. So far, so good.

He joined Hollie in the wings, where she held Christopher until he was on. From there, Nick moved around, cued the children when needed and repinned costumes between acts.

Finally, Christopher was on. Nick watched two of the board members lean close and whisper between themselves. Then to the next two, like the old telephone game.

Hollie slipped her hand into his. "Do they like it?"

He squeezed it back. "I can't tell."

Five minutes into the act, an unused prop in the wings got knocked over and fell with a resounding crack. Christopher, startled and wide-eyed, looked around for something familiar. He didn't find it among the costumed children. He screwed up his little face.

"Oh, no," Hollie whispered.

Nick's thoughts exactly.

Christopher shrieked. The actors were distracted. The board members shook their heads. Nick clenched his fist as his future flashed before his eyes. He'd be back on the road doing rinky-dink theater projects to make a buck until he was old and gray. No one would ever give him a chance again.

Hollie watched her two sons. This was an important night for Joey. Above all other Christmas presents, he wanted his little baby brother to be in the play with him. She looked up at Nick to see how he was taking this.

Not exactly in stride. His jaw was clenched. His grip on her hand hurt, but she knew he wasn't even aware of her fingers in his fist. He raked his hand through his hair as Christopher settled into a series of fussy, crabby whimpers that had every mother in the audience squirming.

She looked back at Joey and, without a doubt, knew what she had to do. This was only one hour of his life balanced against Nick's future. Joey would have to understand. He would have to learn to put other's needs first when appropriate. She would have to find some way to explain it to him.

"I'll get Christopher," she whispered consolingly to Nick as she extracted her hand from his.

"No. Wait."

His hand landed on her shoulder. When she patted it reassuringly, then lifted it off, he grasped her arm gently, but firmly.

"You can't," he said simply. He shook his head as if even he couldn't believe what he'd said.

She glanced down at her clothes—twentieth-century Christmas apparel, not in keeping with the play. "Oh, of course. You want to pull the curtain for a minute?"

"No. Leave him."

"Leave him?" He was making such a fuss. "But, Nick—"

"It's too important to them."

Mary Margaret glanced at Hollie and Nick. The question on her face clearly said, *Help! What do I do now?*

"But, Nick, the children worked so hard to get ready."

"Yes, they did. It's their play, really, you know."

What she knew was that Nick, since she'd known him, had always put his students' needs first.

He smiled at her, touched her chin with his fingers in a gesture meant to be reassuring. It distracted her, not an easy thing to do when her baby was unhappy.

"And they all wanted Christopher to be a part of it with them. So let him stay."

Joey smiled softly and whispered soothing noises to his little brother as he bent over and scooped him up. Held against Joey's chest, Christopher stared at him wide-eyed, then seemed to recognize his touch and voice. He gurgled and waved his arms. The audience smiled at one another like proud parents.

Hollie stood hand-in-hand with Nick as he watched the board members' stern expressions.

He groaned. "They hate it."

WHEW!

Joey was relieved when the final curtain closed. His mother beamed proudly at him from right wing, his teacher from left.

He'd seen them standing hand-in-hand earlier. Maybe there *was* a Santa Claus.

NICK BREATHED A SIGH of relief after the final curtain call. Christopher was safely back in Hollie's arms. Funny, that's where Nick wanted to be. He hadn't gotten to thank her for offering to take Christopher off stage. He hadn't even gotten to stand with her more than a few moments. Not nearly enough. He knew how protective she was of her children, how she'd fight for them like the toughest lioness. And yet . . . she'd stepped forward to save the play for him.

Parents, grandparents, brothers, siblings, aunts, uncles, neighbors—they all filled the space between him and Hollie. He couldn't get to her; it was worse than trying to wade through a Christmas sale at the mall. They all wanted to hug their little fourth-graders at once.

Kind of what he had in mind for a certain fourth-grader's mother. To hell with the antiquated, narrow-minded school board.

"How'd I do, Mom?" Joey asked.

"You did terrific!" She held Christopher in one arm and hugged Joey with the other, turning it into a three-way, family thing.

"Look at Grandma and Grandpa."

She watched in amazement as they exchanged pleasantries with people who were total strangers to them.

"I guess there's no common bond like grandparenthood," Hollie murmured.

"Does this mean they're happy again?"

Bea and Al hugged Joey. Bea kissed his cheek. Al patted him on the back.

"Now, Bea, tell Hollie what we decided," Al prodded.

Bea's happy smile turned to one of embarrassment. "Everyone's been congratulating us on the boys. It's quite obvious Joey loves his little brother. There, I said it."

Al prodded her in the ribs.

"All right." She slapped his hand away. "Joey acted very responsibly." She turned on her husband. "God, why don't you just say, 'I told you so.'"

Al grinned. "I'm too wise for that."

Hollie caught his wink over the top of his wife's head. She mouthed a thank-you to him.

"There's more," he said.

Bea took a deep, fortifying breath. When Al bent down and kissed the tip of her nose, she visibly melted.

"Maybe we could move closer to you and baby-sit sometimes. If... if that's all right with you?"

Hollie hugged her. "Thanks, Mom."

Bea and Al were quickly engulfed by more grandparents. Joey disappeared with his classmates.

"Well, Christopher, it's just you and I." She looked for Nick and found him working his way through the crowd in her direction.

She wondered how her in-laws would handle a continuing relationship with Nick. Hell, if the board members fired him, she wouldn't have to worry about that. He'd leave town. Not that she thought he'd propose again anytime soon, anyway. She realized that proposal had just been his way of wanting to help her out and not a declaration of love. And it wasn't as if they wouldn't be seeing a lot of each other again come tomorrow morning. She was due back in his class for the last day before Christmas break started. That should be long enough to bring him around.

"Mrs. Landon," Judge Nicholson interrupted her thoughts.

"Oh, hi, Judge. Uh, Your Honor."

He smiled broadly, as if used to that reaction. "It was a wonderful play, wasn't it?"

"Yes, it was."

"I was concerned about Nick trying something new, but I think he made a wise decision, don't you?"

"Uh, yes."

"He takes after me, you know."

"No, I didn't know that."

"Yep." He turned to go, then doubled back. "Oh, you don't need to go to school with Joey anymore."

"I don't?" She was sure she looked as shell-shocked as he felt.

"I think Joey and I have everything ironed out now. Merry Christmas."

Too bad Nick couldn't say the same for him and the board.

Chapter Fifteen

Christmas Morning

Nick answered his doorbell to find his dad on the porch wi[th]
a pastry box in one hand and a sweater box in the other. [H]
knew it was a sweater because he had a box the same si[ze]
and shape for his dad. Only the wrapping paper was diffe[r]
ent.

"Merry Christmas, son."

Nick grinned, in spite of the fact that he still didn't ha[ve]
a clue as to his immediate future. He opened the door wi[de]
and let his dad in. "Merry Christmas to you, too. I did[n]
think the bakery would be open this morning."

"It's not. I went last night." He handed over the cher[ry]
Danishes and shrugged out of his coat. "Busy place. A[nd]
of course the topic of conversation was the Snowflake Ball[.]

They settled at the kitchen table. Nick poured coffe[e]
"I'm glad for Hollie that the Fagans were happy with t[he]
job she did."

"Not just the Fagans, although they've already hired h[er]
for next year. But, if everything I heard last night is tru[e,]
Mrs. Landon's already got enough jobs to keep her aflo[at]
all year."

"At least somebody does."

His dad's eyebrows rose.

"Heck, that sounded bitter, didn't it?" Nick raked his hand through his hair. "And I'm not. She deserves the jobs."

"Like you deserve to teach drama?"

"Yeah."

"Look at the bright side."

"Which is?"

"Maybe she'll hire you."

"Uh-huh. Like that's every teacher's dream—to work as a decorator."

They ate in silence for a moment before his dad asked, "What will you do if you don't get the job you want?"

Nick shrugged. "Go looking."

"Do you know where?"

"Some place small. Quiet."

"Like East Bay?"

Nick nodded. "Like East Bay." Then he couldn't resist the urge to tease his old man. "Someplace without a grinch for a judge, though."

"Bah, humbug."

The phone rang, and they exchanged a look that said, "This might be it."

Nick adopted a positive attitude as he answered it. "Merry Christmas."

"Nick? This is Mr. Nelson."

"Good morn—"

"Oh, hell, Nick. This is Ed."

Nick instinctively turned his back to his dad, as if that could keep bad news private.

"I heard from the board this morning. It's time for you to clean out your desk."

"OPEN IT, Mom!"

Hollie, surrounded by scads of torn, discarded Christmas wrap and empty boxes, sat on the carpet in front of the fire. Bea and Al were similarly ensconced in their chairs. Christopher was content to sit in his swing and bat at the colorful new activity toy that was attached to the front of his seat. Joey had played Santa's helper and passed out all the gifts.

He dropped to his knees in front of her. "I saved the best till last."

"You did, huh?" Hollie teased him by unwrapping the tiny, odd-shaped package one corner at a time. After each corner, she shook it next to her ear and tried to guess what it was. "A TV?"

He giggled. "No, Mom."

"A dishwasher?"

"Mo-om."

"I know! Is it something I need?"

"It's something to make you pretty."

"I'm not pretty?"

"Mo-om! You're beautiful!"

She dropped her jaw and feigned shock. "You think I'm beautiful?"

Joey reached for the gift to help her open it. She playfully snatched it back.

Then, when she did get it open, her mouth dropped open for real when she held in her hand the prettiest golden barrette she'd ever seen. Her initials were engraved in script on the outside.

"Oh, Joey."

"Put it on."

She didn't need urging. She pulled her dark hair back and caught it in the clip with practiced ease.

"Yep, Mom, you're beautiful."

She brushed a tear of joy away.

"Even when you cry. Aren't you going to ask me how I got it?"

She glanced at her in-laws.

"Don't look at us."

"They didn't help you?"

He shook his head proudly. "I did it all by myself. Aren't you going to ask me how?"

"How?"

"I raked leaves for Old Lady Simmonds. And then, when it snowed, I shoveled her walk."

"When..." It only took her a second to come up to speed. "Oh, Joey, that's where you were when you were cutting school?"

He nodded. And he didn't look in the least apologetic. She wondered if Nick knew. Probably the judge did, since he and Joey had gotten pretty buddy-buddy.

The doorbell rang. It wasn't "We Three Kings," as at the Fagans', but it sounded pretty joyful in the middle of their cozy little Christmas celebration. Joey, the only one with any energy left after getting up at five o'clock, sprang up onto the couch and peered out the picture window.

"It's Mr. Nicholson! And his dad."

"I wonder what they're doing here?" Bea murmured to Al.

Joey vaulted off the couch and ran to the front door. He tossed a worried look over his shoulder at Hollie. "Is he coming to say goodbye?"

Hollie wished she knew. If he were unemployed, a man like Nick wouldn't want to stay that way for long. The scuttlebutt at the grocery store was that the board was divided in their decision, but being swayed toward dismissal. Many people had called to tell her how beautiful the mansion had been for the Snowflake Ball and to promise to pass her expertise on by word of mouth. While her business would always revolve around holidays and special occasions, and never be lucrative, it would successfully support her and her sons. But no one who had called, including Nick, knew what his future would be.

"Well, let him in and we'll find out," she said as cheerfully as she could to Joey.

"Merry Christmas," Nick and his dad greeted as the door opened.

It wasn't as cheery a greeting as she'd hoped. Pretty neutral, as a matter of fact.

"What're you doing here?" Joey asked bluntly.

"Joey!" Hollie stage-whispered.

"Oh, yeah. Come on in."

"It's all right," Nick answered as he ruffled Joey's hair with his free hand. He had Hollie's ruby red roses in his other.

Hollie was on her feet, cinching her purple bathrobe tighter and taking the judge's coat. She noticed the roses right away, and her knees shook. He didn't have to tell her he was returning the flowers she'd left in his classroom so she'd have something to remember him by. They'd remind her of the days they'd battled in the classroom. Of her pranks. Of his caring.

Joey asked, "Why'd you bring my mom's ratty ol' flowers off her desk?"

Nick put himself smack dab in front of Hollie. She forgot to breathe.

"Because," he answered Joey, even though his eyes never left Hollie's, "I'm offering her the same ratty ol' proposal."

Hollie's lips formed a silent *Oh*. She glanced around at her audience for the briefest of moments before her eyes were drawn back to Nick. Tall, strong, broad, he stood before her, holding her roses. They didn't look so ratty.

He grinned. "The florist was closed today, but I figure it's the principle of the thing."

"Yeah, Mom. It's the principle, like he says," Joey threw Hollie's own words—the ones he'd heard time and again—back at her. "So cooperate, will you?"

Nick slowly unzipped his leather jacket, revealing, instead of another flower, a red bow right smack in the middle of his chest. For once he was wearing something other than a T-shirt.

"New sweater?"

"Yeah. Dad gave it to me."

"And you left the bow on it?"

His eyes twinkled merrily. "Ah, the bow. No, that's for you."

"From your dad?"

"Not likely."

Hollie wasn't sure whether to go back to the proposal they were in the middle of or untie the bow that was being offered her. If he was proposing, was he leaving East Bay? And would she follow him if he were? Could she, with two small boys?

"Open it, Mom!"

She glanced at the judge, who failed to give anything away by his expression. Years of practice, she supposed. She glanced at her in-laws, who were openly curious, too. She glanced at Joey and wondered if this was something he and the judge had cooked up and dragged Nick into.

"Yeah, Hollie, open it," Nick urged.

She reached one hand tentatively toward the bow. As her finger touched his chest, as she felt his strong heartbeat, she knew it didn't matter to her whether he'd gotten the job teaching. She'd love him anyway. With Bea and Al moving to East Bay and available to baby-sit, maybe she could go visit Nick wherever he ended up. Maybe for long weekends.

Her fingers shook. She tugged one end of the bow loose, until all that was left in the center was a gold silk rosebud. In the middle of it was a sparkling diamond ring.

"Oh, my." She was surprised to hear how breathless she sounded. Her eyes never left his. "Did you bring your dad along to vouch for you?"

Judge Nicholson patted the small Bible he pulled out of his pocket. "No, my son very wisely brought me along to do the honors."

Her eyes were still locked with Nick's, and she was well aware he waited on tenterhooks for her answer.

"Pretty sure of yourself, weren't you?" she teased.

"If you don't hurry up, these roses'll be dead by the time you answer."

Hollie's radiant smile lit up the whole room. "Well, since you brought the judge, I guess the least I can do is supply the witnesses. Mom? Dad?"

To her relief, Bea and Al popped out of their chairs. "I'll get the camera," Bea chirped.

Joey plucked the ribbon off Nick's chest, ring and all. "I'll be the ring bearer."

Hollie replaced the ribbon with her body as she flung herself into Nick's arms. "Just in case you had any doubts, the answer's yes."

"In spite of the fact that I've been let go from fourth grade?"

She hugged him tightly. "Oh, Nick. I'm sorry. We'll work something out."

He held her as if he'd never let go again. His breath was warm and moist and tickled her ear. "If I'm still teaching drama at East Bay High when Joey enrolls there, will you come sit in class with him?"

She leaned back so she could see his warm hazel eyes, but she still couldn't tell if he were teasing her. "You got the job?"

"Well, heck, Hollie, I couldn't ask you to marry an unemployed teacher, could I?"

"When?"

"This morning. Ed called and told me to go clean out my desk, and when I got there, there was a stack of rules and regulations waiting for me—from East Bay High. All tied up with a red ribbon."

The judge cleared his throat. "Shall we?"

A determined chorus of yeses echoed around the room.

SO WHO SAYS there's no Santa Claus?

Joey got everything he wanted—his baby brother in the play with him, a Harley T-shirt, a new dad. Next Christmas he'd ask for another brother and a set of Rollerblades.

And they'd have marshmallows on the Christmas tree.

A HOLIDAY RECIPE FROM THE KITCHEN OF

Jenna McKnight

This makes a wonderful main course on Christmas Day. It's a favorite in my family. Hope you enjoy it, too!

JENNA'S BEEF TENDERLOIN

Beef tenderloin, any size. (Have the butcher remove the side muscle and wrap it up separately for something yummy later—like beef Stroganoff for two.)
Season with garlic salt and pepper. No tenderizer needed.
Roast at 425° F until meat thermometer registers it the way you like it. This should be approximately 45 minutes. Aim for a little on the rare side, as it keeps cooking after you remove it from the oven. Cover with foil and let it sit a few minutes before slicing.

Sauce
Sauté fresh, sliced mushrooms in butter. Add a little red wine. Add beef juices when roast is ready.

Serve over thin slices of beef.

HARLEQUIN®

A M E R I C A N ◆ R O M A N C E®

What's a woman to do when she hasn't got a date for New Year's Eve? *Buy* a man, that's what!

And make sure it's one of the eligible

New Year's Bachelors

That's exactly what friends Dana Shaw and Elise Allen do in the hilarious New Year's Bachelors duet. But the men they get give these women even more than they bargained for!

Don't miss:

#662 DANA & THE CALENDAR MAN
by Lisa Bingham
January 1997

#666 ELISE & THE HOTSHOT LAWYER
by Emily Dalton
February 1997

Ring in the New Year with NEW YEAR'S BACHELORS!

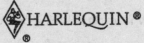

1997
Reader's Engagement Book
A calendar of important dates
and anniversaries for readers to use!

Informative and entertaining—with notable
dates and trivia highlighted throughout the year.

Handy, convenient, pocketbook size to help you
keep track of your own personal important dates.

Added bonus—contains $5.00 worth of coupons
for upcoming Harlequin and Silhouette books.
This calendar more than pays for itself!

Available beginning in November at
your favorite retail outlet.

HARLEQUIN ®   Silhouette®

Look us up on-line at: http://www.romance.net   CAL97

You asked for it...You got it! More MEN!

We're thrilled to bring you another special edition of the popular MORE THAN MEN series.

Like those who have come before him, Adam Walsh is more than tall, dark and handsome. All of those men have extraordinary powers that make them "more than men." But whether they are able to grant you three wishes, or live forever, make no mistake—their greatest, most extraordinary power is of seduction.

So make a date with Adam Walsh in...

#663 ADAM'S KISS
by Mindy Neff
January 1997